Praise for

How to Belong

'A tender story about finding your place in the world, about ordinary lives, belonging and being brave. The kind of book that gives you hope and courage'
Kit de Waal

'In this insightful, thoughtful novel about a farrier and a butcher, Franklin explores the meaning of home and the importance of belonging. It's replete with gorgeous descriptions of forest life'
Carys Bray

'Sarah writes intimately about the forest and the lives it sustains, exploring the human condition with forensic tenderness; we feel every step of Tessa and Jo's journeys. It's a big-hearted novel about how we learn to belong despite ourselves, and I relished every word'
Shelley Harris

How to
Belong

SARAH FRANKLIN grew up in rural Gloucestershire and has lived in Austria, Germany, the USA and Ireland. She lectures in publishing at Oxford Brookes University and has written for the *Guardian*, the *Irish Times*, *Psychologies* magazine and *The Pool*. Her critically acclaimed first novel, *Shelter*, was published in 2017. Sarah lives halfway between Oxford and London with her husband and two children.

How to Belong

SARAH FRANKLIN

Sarah Franklin [signature]

ZAFFRE

First published in Great Britain in 2020
This paperback edition published in 2021 by
ZAFFRE
An imprint of Bonnier Books UK
4th Floor, Victoria House, Bloomsbury Square, London, England, WC1B 4DA
Owned by Bonnier Books
Sveavägen 56, Stockholm, Sweden

Quotes on page vii:

Dennis Potter quote © Professor John Cook

Wallace Stegner quote, from *On Teaching and Writing Fiction*
by Wallace Stegner; reprinted by permission of Don Congdon Associates, Inc.
© 2002 by Page Stegner

Should I Stay Or Should I Go
Words & Music by Mick Jones & Joe Strummer
© Copyright 1982 Nineden Limited.
Universal Music Publishing Limited.
All Rights Reserved. International Copyright Secured.
Used by Permission of Hal Leonard Europe Limited.

A CIP catalogue record for this book is available from the British Library.

ISBN: 978-1-78576-484-4

Also available as an ebook

1 3 5 7 9 10 8 6 4 2

Typeset by Palimpsest Book Production Limited, Falkirk, Stirlingshire
Printed and bound in Great Britain by Clays Ltd, Elcograf S.p.A.

Zaffre is an imprint of Bonnier Books UK
www.bonnierbooks.co.uk

For Caroline Baker, who will always mean home to me wherever we both live

'You have got almost instant access to your emotions and that is dangerous, a dangerous thing to have'
Dennis Potter

'After all, what are any of us ever after but the conviction of belonging?'
Wallace Stegner

'Should I stay or should I go now?
If I go there will be trouble
And if I stay it will be double'
The Clash

Part One

Forging

Chapter One

IT'S ABSOLUTE HEADY BEDLAM IN the butcher's. With just forty-eight hours to go until the day itself, the air is full of the timeless tang of Christmas: meat and gossip, mince pies and anticipation. Tinsel's strung across the fridges, dipping along the bowed curves of the display cabinet in festive smiles. The new Saturday boy has cranked up a Christmas mix; bored kids are ducking and weaving to the front of the till to snake their hands back into the Quality Street. The queue is being constantly splintered by people spotting their neighbours further on up, or remembering they've forgotten the chutney. It's all exactly as it always has been; for the last ten years since Jo Butler moved to London, for the almost two decades beforehand that she grew up here, and probably for at least another four before that when Grandad ran the shop. Jo's life in London – her so-called 'real' life – has no place back here in the Forest of Dean. In the shop, she's the nucleus of herself again, the Jo she was before she became all the other versions. Better not to consider that this is the last Christmas here.

'Jo!' Mum's behind the counter, replenishing the sausage meat and pigs in blankets. They're sludging down the tray; even to look at them is enough to give you the jitters. An unfortunate reaction for a butcher's daughter.

'Time to do the sherries, love.'

'On it!' Jo moves towards the back of the shop, already primed. There's a moment every year where Mum deems the crowd to have reached peak chaos, at which point Jo unleashes trays full of sherry and the shop turns into a full-blown extension of everyone's Christmas party.

Jo yawns as she pushes through the heavy plastic curtains into the back of the shop, nodding at Ron, Dad's right-hand man. It had been a long day in court yesterday, and today hadn't exactly been a lie-in. That had never been an option, though. This'll be the last Christmas they get in the shop, and the realisation gets her in the gut every time it hits home.

Everything's ready on the counter beside the sink where she'd laid it out in the cold black of the small hours. She takes the bottle of sherry and pours toothfuls into the little plastic shot glasses on the tray, then picks it up and turns back to the shop.

'Bugger.'

Dad's parcelling oven-ready turkeys into their posh boxes, the bit that makes the price worth it, apparently.

4

He pushes his hat back with arthritic knuckles and winks. 'Wouldn't be Christmas if you didn't forget about the door.'

He holds open the plastic curtain so that she can negotiate the tray through without spilling anything. It's right that he and Mum are giving up the shop. Forty-odd years of doing the same thing; a blessing or a curse, depending on how you choose to see it. Forty-odd years of getting up at the crack of dawn, rain or shine. Of hands that are constantly red with cold and festooned with plasters. Of the smell of meat as your own personal base note. Of dwindling customers, soaring costs, Veganuary.

But also: of vocation. Of a customer popping their head in to tell you how tasty that bit of beef had been. Of seeing the babes in arms move through the generations into customers in their own right, coming to you for their meat because this is where the family always comes for meat. Of the hustle and bustle of the shop on a Saturday, the slow chats on the slow days with the customers slowed by age. Of belonging.

It's no good thinking like this, every step a memory, every action a reminder that this will all be gone. It's not about her; she doesn't even live here anymore.

But it can't be willed away. There's a sickness in her stomach every time she reaches for a tray, pays a customer, hears the thrum of the machines against the hum of customers waiting, greeting each other. Jo's full of it and it's through her like a skewer, holding her together. Without the shop, without this home to come to, it's impossible to know who she is.

5

The curtain slaps back and Jo's in the throng again.

The crowd seems to have multiplied, the atmosphere buzzing as if they're at a gig. Ron's wife Mo is behind the counter with Mum now, both of them serving at warp speed, smiles as warm as ever.

It's best to start at the back, where the queue is almost out of the door already, but that's easier said than done when there's no obvious straight line through and the tray's wobbling like it's already drunk the sherry itself.

'Back to help your mum and dad, are you, Jo, love?' Phyllis Knight nabs two glasses, the straps of her handbag slung deep over the wrist bones of her left hand.

Phyllis has been queuing here for her Christmas meat since before Mum and Dad took over the shop from Grandad. You could write history from her ever-telescoping orders, Dad says. Phyllis's boys are long since grown and gone, one in Oz and one in America somewhere. She's got a daughter still here in the Forest of Dean, though; she'd been in the year above Jo's brother Gary at school.

'That's right. Can't miss the last time.' Can't trust herself to talk about it either, yet. 'What're you doing for Christmas Day – off over to Sophie's?'

Phyllis swaps her now-empty sherry thimbles for two full ones. At this rate she'll be dancing on the meat counter.

'Oh, they're all coming to me, love!' She beams. 'Chris's home from Perth; he's brought his new girlfriend too, so it must be serious. Then Darren and Claire decided they wanted to meet this Laura, so they're coming too, kids and all – get in tonight, they do.'

'Do you think Darren or Chris will try and persuade you back over with them?'

'Oh no, there's not a chance of me leaving here, love. My life's all here, see? I'm too old for that game.' Phyllis puts a hand on Jo's arm. 'Your mum and dad've got the right idea, moving while they're still young. Gary must be pleased to have them closer, what with the little ones.'

'Yeah. His wife's going back to work in the new year, and with two paramedics in the family it was going to be hard to juggle the kids and their shifts, even with his wife's family nearby. This works out well for everyone.'

'It won't be the same with them gone; fancy Butler's Butcher's without a Butler behind the counter. Do you know who's buying it?'

The deceptive lightness of the question doesn't fool Jo. This is akin to the nuclear codes in terms of town news, but actually she couldn't oblige even if she wanted to. 'There's someone else interested now, after the first buyer fell through, but Mum and Dad are keeping it quiet even with us, to be honest. I think they don't want to tempt fate.'

Phyllis nods stoically, enough of a gossip pro to know when she's beaten. 'How's it going in that smart job of yours?'

The tray judders slightly in Jo's hands.

'It's . . . it's all right, you know. Being a barrister isn't always as glamorous as it sounds, but yeah, it's good.' Phyllis doesn't need the truth: the casual misogyny, the snobbery, the impossibility of getting anywhere near cases that actually matter even though

7

she finished pupillage more than four years ago now. The disillusionment Jo wakes up to every morning. She pulls a smile back over the truth, hoists the tray. 'I'd better keep getting these out. Thirsty work, this queuing.' Not that Phyllis is in any danger of racking up a thirst, the way she went for those sherries.

Phyllis's hand is warm on Jo's forearm, her grip surprisingly tight. 'It's lovely seeing you again. You keep up the good work, all right?'

Good work's overstating it. Jo's halfway to a response when the shop door opens.

'Li! *Liam!*'

Liam hasn't seen her yet; he's steering the kids through the throng. Rosie's shot up again, looks like she'd rather be doing anything than holding Liam's hand. What ages are the girls now, nine and six? Jo and Liam were six when they first met, which means that these two might have also already met their most steadfast friend.

'Li!'

The kids have reached Mum behind the counter; she's bent down and stripped off her gloves, arms open wide for Chloe to come in for a hug. Jo's struck with swift, daft envy. Mum knows Liam's kids so much better than she does. By leaving the Forest Jo washed out of the flow of life here, into a tributary. The waters parted to let her go, then joined back up and the relationships continued as if she'd never been there.

At work, when she's on the last train back to London from, say, Doncaster after a losing case, knackered and unrooted, Jo asks herself: what are Mum and Dad doing now? What's Liam doing now? Just knowing that they're there, that nothing's changed, that with some little effort she could probably name the customers as well as the cuts of meat – this is enough on those evermore-frequent, grey, faceless days for Jo to stop feeling like she's run uphill in a panic and landed in the wrong place. She closes her eyes and lets it play like a tape in front of her: Mum and Dad in the shop; Mum serving up the sausages and the pork pies; Dad with his back to the outside world, working away on the counter behind the curtain, chopping and dicing, his hat pushed back as the shop warmed up with the day.

In her imaginings, Liam's . . . well, presumably Liam would actually be plastering, or doing stuff with Kirsty and the kids, but the details of that are vague. That's Liam's parallel life, the one that really started after she'd left. The Liam in her mind is almost sixteen, sitting on her bed with her, shoes off, backs against the radiator, taking her through their French homework for the fifteenth time until she finally gets how the subjunctive works.

Here, in the shop, Mum reaches up, hugs Liam too, pats him on the cheek in that way she has as she says something to him. Liam's face splits into a beam as he scans the throng, is over in three strides.

'All right, Butler? I thought you were back tomorrow!'

'I was in court in Taunton last minute, couldn't see the point of going back up to London then back down tomorrow, so Dad drove over and met me when I got out last night. I was going to phone you later; thought you'd be at work.'

'I'm on daddy duty. The girls broke up on Tuesday and Kirst's on overtime all week. She says it's mad in the Co-op; half of town's in there every day like the end of the world's coming. But the money's good and nobody wants a plasterer in their house this close to Christmas, anyway.'

Jo wedges the sherry tray on the counter between two mini Christmas puddings. 'In that case, d'you fancy a quick pint? I'll need to get back, but it feels like we should take advantage.'

'What about the girls?'

'Mum's fine with them, look.'

Rosie's behind the counter with Mo, doling out change, and Chloe – well, Chloe's over at the deli counter nicking a wedge of pork pie, but Mum's laughing. She catches Jo's eye, looks at Liam then jerks her head towards the door, still smiling.

'Remember how she used to put up with us "helping" at that age? She's in her element, honest.'

Jo's coat is hung up by the back door, so they push through. The back room's a sea of turkeys in boxes, Dad standing in the middle with a list in one hand and an empty box in another.

'I'm just popping out with Liam for a minute, that OK? We won't be long.'

There are dark shadows under Dad's eyes – he's been up since two this morning getting everything ready, will be here for hours yet tidying up and sorting out. He needs the help, really. But he nods warmly at Liam, smiles at Jo like he always has, and her stomach hoops with love. This man has kept a family and a business running for decades now, and you can see it in the lines etched into those shadows.

'Heard that from you once or twice before, I have. You got your key?' It's a slam-dunk straight into being seventeen again and Jo grins. 'I have, but it's only a half, honest.'

'Yeah, heard that one before an' all.'

Jo laughs. 'See you, Dad.'

There's nothing beats being home for Christmas.

Chapter Two

TESSA DIDN'T THINK THERE WAS anything in town that could remind her of Marnie, but that was without factoring in the holiday. Christmas dusts an extra layer of misery onto everyday existence.

The quickest way from the cottage to the livery yard is three miles into the town and down through the high street, where strings of tinselly lights speckle the drizzle. Tessa learned from Mam to avoid town, and even thirty-odd years on she doesn't come here unless she has to, guarding against the sidelong looks of locals who steal glances as if trying to place her. Sometimes, over the years, the odd person has asked, warmly enough, if they know each other – were they at school together? – but Tessa always shakes her head, keeps conversation to a bare minimum. She's a stranger to everyone here, always has been, and though the spike of loneliness is still sharp, it's buried from long years of practice.

The high street is less welcoming than ever today despite people in Santa hats spilling out of the King's Head and the fairy lights draped everywhere. Inflatable snowmen teeter from pebble-dashed ledges, casting shadows onto the shadows. Even the Aldi car park is in the festive spirit, apparently; mistletoe sellotaped to the 'Two hours' maximum parking' sign, as if this is the obvious place for a festive clinch.

Tessa would laugh, but there's nothing left to laugh at now.

She slows down at the pedestrian crossing beside the butcher's, which is illuminated by fluorescent lights. The huge windows allow a full view of the stream of customers in the shop, which looks more like a pub than somewhere you'd go for meat. A woman in a cosy-looking coat laughs, says something to her neighbour, who laughs too, and Tessa, insulated within the van, nonetheless shrinks from their obvious happiness.

There's a new horse at Susan's livery yard when Tessa arrives there: a thoroughbred stallion, about 16.3 hands, relatively young and quite skittish by the look of things. He's kicking the door of the box, tossing his head as if it were attached to a leading rein still. Horses have always trusted Tessa for her stillness; she stops on her way past and speaks gently to this one, but his ears are back and he's not ready yet to trust anyone. She clucks softly and moves on, knowing the feeling all too well. She'll set the anvil up on the far side of the hardstanding, furthest from his box so that he's not bothered by her.

Tessa goes round to the house and rings the bell. She's

here to shoe the three usual horses, but it's best to let Susan know she's out in the yard. Ern's voice plays in her head, welded there since her years, two decades ago now, learning the trade as his apprentice: 'Good manners never harmed nobody.' Mam would have approved too, not that Mam approved of anything to do with Tessa.

Susan's all right: she's no-nonsense and doesn't scatter words around like horse nuts. But today when she opens the door Susan's eyebrows arch before she can hide it, and belatedly Tessa clocks the row of cars parked up alongside the horse walker.

'Is this a bad time?'

Susan shakes her head vigorously, an attempt to cover the lie demonstrated by the glass in her hand. 'No, no, Tessa, not at all.' She gestures behind her and the wine tips out over the rim. Susan scuffs it into the carpet with her toe. 'I just hadn't expected to see you this side of the new year, I suppose. We've got a few friends over but it's not a problem. Business as usual in the yard.'

Tessa nods and leaves her to the wine and the friends. Her last three Christmases had looked like that: Marnie's friends clustered into the Bristol flat, days joyous and careless with lack of a calendar. It had been cocooning, the belonging. But it's gone now.

She hunches into her jacket as she rounds the corner back into the yard. Truth be told, she'd known that only two days before Christmas was probably too close to the holidays to be showing up for work. But this knowledge made the house colder, emptier. She's come to the yard today, sticking to the usual routine, because something has to give and if she's not careful it'll be her.

The thoroughbred still needs space, so she walks quietly to the other side of the yard and fetches Julie Oldham's old cob, leads him out onto the hardstanding. Susan's yard's great. The tin roof of the stables juts out, so even when it's a bit drizzly like today you can work on a clean, hard surface. Tessa ties the cob up loosely, rubs her knuckles into his flank. He knows what to expect and he knows her, too.

She yawns. Tiredness lies heavy, so that it's hard to know where exhaustion lets off and misery takes over. Focusing on the cob should push it away. She sets to work on the near forehoof, her breath steadying as she accepts its weight into her own body, her back aching in all the usual places as the heft of the horse is transferred to her. Work soothes her, as it always has; the snickering of the horses, the gentle clopping as they shift their weight along their legs, the heat that exudes from them. Horses and Tessa need the same thing for this job: absolute calm. She undoes the clenches with the hitting buffer on the hammer and reaches into her pocketed belt for the clenchers. There are only four nails in this shoe but it's held OK.

She switches to the hoof rasp and starts rasping the sole level. There's a lot of unexfoliated sole here that needs paring off with the hoof knife. Tessa slows her breathing and pares deftly. *Now* it's ready for the rasp again. Her exhalations are smoke signals, puffing out and mingling with the cob's own snorts as he shifts slightly on the hardstanding.

The rasping doesn't take long and the new shoe doesn't look like it will need too many adjustments. Tessa swallows a sense of disappointment. It'll be a quick job today.

It's a short walk across the yard to the mobile forge, a day to be grateful for the fierce red heat of the Swanee in its position in the back of the van. She's just lifting out the horseshoe from the forge with the pritchel, ready to scorch it onto the cob's sole for size, when a car pulls into the yard. Someone else for Susan's party.

But it isn't. A youngish woman in fresh jodhpurs and boots that haven't seen a speck of dirt picks her way through Susan's pristine yard towards the stables. She smiles over at Tessa, peers at the anvil and the clashing orange of the forge, and walks on past to the box with the thoroughbred in it.

That's a turn-up for the books. An animal with so much spirit is going to need careful handling, not someone who looks like she's just watched the *Horse of the Year Show* on telly and been given a horse for an early Christmas present. Tessa bends over the anvil, seemingly concentrated on rasping the shoe, and watches. The girl's pulling at the bolt for the loose box now. It sticks; she tugs again and the bolt shoots open, catching her fingers in it and she yelps in pain, jumps about a foot. Tessa winces in sympathy and turns back to the rasp.

There's another cry from behind and Tessa swings round. The thoroughbred bolts out of the box towards them. The old cob, startled, rears, whinnies and narrowly avoids hitting Tessa's van. The girl races after the horse, screaming, which won't help at all.

It's an instant shock, and as the emotion courses through Tessa, her muscles start to give way. She's going to collapse. She has a split second to decide her movements: risk hitting the anvil with her head on the way down, or get the still-molten horseshoe out of harm's way?

Avoid the anvil; it'll knock her out. Tessa twists and hits the ground. She's cleared the anvil. The horseshoe scorches into her ankle as surely as if she was being branded. The pain is ferocious and the renewed emotion keeps her bolted to the ground.

The girl has recovered the horse. She hurries over, holding him tightly by the halter. Tessa is fully conscious but immobile. The muscle-melting and subsequent falls long since stopped being scary, but being stuck like this in front of a stranger never fails to bring shame, and keeping her eyes closed is protection, however flimsy.

If she can get one muscle moving, sometimes the others will follow. It takes a moment of hard concentration, but then her finger crooks and she breathes out in relief, pushes herself up. That was a bad one.

'Tessa! What happened? Are you OK?'

Susan comes pelting round the side of the barn, all boots and wine glass. The girl hovers at her shoulder. The girl should be sorting out the thoroughbred, by rights. Susan obviously thinks so, too – a none-too-subtle jerk of her head sends the girl back off to the box.

Tessa heaves all the way up, clinging onto the anvil for support. 'I'm fine, thanks.'

'Daisy said you went down like you'd been shot.' Susan cocks her head to the side as if she's assessing the value of a thoroughbred. 'Are you sure you're not hurt?'

People need to see Tessa smile when this happens, however weak the smile. 'No, honest I'm not.'

'Did you trip on something?' Susan considers Tessa, then the yard, shrewd and puzzled. The yard is clear. Tessa's kit bag is beside the van, the anvil a few feet from it.

'No. I just . . .' Can she risk the truth?

I have these funny turns when my muscles become limp, like a ragdoll, and I concertina to the ground. It barely lasts any time and then everything rights itself. It started when I was five and my little sister died, and was harder to control when I was nineteen and my mother finally moved away. I feel like I can get it under control but then something happens, and it swoops back. It's been happening for yonks. It's worse if I let something get under my skin, so I try to avoid feeling anything. It's lonely and it makes me sadder than anyone can know, but it's the way it is. It's all I can do.

Every few years someone well-meaning like you will suggest a doctor, but I know it'll do no good.

I'm scared, and I'm tired, and I'm alone with it.

But there's no point. Susan's exactly the type – confident, rich, concerned – to suggest going to a doctor, and Tessa barely has the strength to keep herself going, let alone cope with that. The doctor couldn't help before, not when she went with Dad as a kid and not when she went on Marnie's urging, so it's a bit late to hope it will help now. If there was a miracle cure, maybe. But there isn't. So she avoids doctors.

'Been a bit tired lately, I have.' She manages a shadow of a smile through the desperate hopelessness clouding everything. 'Christmas, see?'

Susan watches her for a minute.

'You're living back in the cottage again, aren't you?' Susan never met Marnie, never knew about her explicitly, only that Tessa had moved forty minutes away to Bristol a few years ago, and now she's back. The sheer understatement is full of understanding for everything that's been lost and Tessa nods, on guard against the kindness.

'A big change like that can be draining. Could you take some time off over Christmas, rest up a bit?'

'I'll be OK, honest.' If she doesn't work, she doesn't earn, and things are precarious enough as they are.

Susan places a hand tentatively on Tessa's shoulder, as if she's made of porcelain rather than iron. 'Do you want to come in for a minute, warm up, have a drink and make sure you're all right?'

Company. Warmth. People concerned about her. She longs for nothing else, has wanted only this for as long as she can remember. But a collapse among Susan's well-meaning horsey friends could be the end of her livelihood.

'You're all right, ta. It's better if I get on. Thank you, though.'

'Well, if you're sure?' Susan waves and sways off into

19

the gloom towards her guests. The house stands waiting for her, a big white pillared square, bordered either side by fir trees glinting with Christmas lights. Tessa watches her go, then starts loading up the van, slotting everything where it belongs.

If she can't get things under control, this could be the beginning of the end for her working life. She's had bad patches before, but until the last one, she'd always managed to fit her life into a smaller and smaller box, until the threat of a mini-seizure or whatever they are had passed.

She has to keep going or she'll lose the business. Susan's livery clients may not be riding much over Christmas but as soon as the new year's resolutions hit, they'll be out here again, raring to go, and horses with untended hooves just won't wash it. Same with Geoff over at the riding centre, another of her big regular farriery clients. Once the tourists start coming back, he needs those ponies ready for customers who want to go pony trekking in the forest. If Tessa can't do it, they'd have to find another farrier. And then she'll be done for. She's already shoeing fewer horses than she used to; if things get any worse she's going to have to resort to something else to make up the shortfall in income. She's going to have to look beyond farriery for money. But it's not like she has any other skills.

There's the spare room, what used to be the parlour. Things would be a bit easier, money-wise.

But.

A stranger in the house.

It scorches at the very edges of Tessa's thoughts, not permitted any space at the forefront of her brain. Ignore, ignore, and it will go away.

The thought persists, though, expands into even less welcome areas. Someone else in the house might come in handy if these bad spells keep getting worse. Might keep her safe.

Degenerative: the word has bored into Tessa in the weeks since she's been back in the Forest and the symptoms she's had all her life, on and off, have intensified. No doctor has said this out loud but that's only because she's been nowhere near a doctor recently, wanting no confirmation of what she knows has to be true. The word has sharpened itself against her fears, digging into her so that every twist of thought she has ends up in the same unexaminable place. It's a mirrored spear, driving her towards threats, forcing her to look into the dark corners, to see how things only get worse and worse, and there's no getting better, no returning from this.

The brain-zapping she experiences, the melting muscles – this will be only the beginning. Soon they'll be joined by tremors and she'll have to give up work. Or she'll lose more and more movement, becoming increasingly trapped inside an ever-more helpless version of herself before she is unable to move or communicate, being fed through a tube. She doesn't have the Internet – too expensive for something that's spotty at best out here – but her mind spirals around possible causes: motor neurone disease, Parkinson's, or things she doesn't even know to be scared of yet.

Each time, these fears play out to the same bitter truth: there's nobody to take her in. Any tube-feeding will be in a hospice, or out at the old people's home beside the bypass, the youngest there by a couple of decades.

Tessa should probably have spelled things out for Susan. But the truth is this: she's not sure she's up to facing it by herself and there's nobody else. No living siblings. Dad's long dead and Mam . . . Well. And Marnie, the strongest love she'll ever know, is no longer hers. It's piercing, shaming proof that Mam was right all along: she's unlovable.

It's better not to know the specifics. The details never helped anyone. She won't be able to stay alone in the cottage; she'll be at the mercy of the NHS and whichever care home is decided for her. In her forties. If this is the best of her life that's left, she has to do all she can to keep steady and avoid that for as long as possible. Knowledge isn't power when you've got no power to begin with.

Chapter Three

One month later

THEY BUMP DOWN A TRACK into a clearing in the forest, Liam's van groaning behind Mum's Micra – Jo's Micra now – as it hits the unpaved track. Jo feels dizzy and a bit sick, the way you do with carsickness, but this isn't to do with the jolty pathway. It's life whiplash. A month ago she was back for Christmas, mourning her last Christmas in the shop, and now she's given up her place in chambers, persuaded her parents to put off their buyers in order to let her run the shop instead, and rented a room from a complete stranger. It's all gone so scarily fast.

There in front of them are two tiny cottages, the bright grey stone almost a relief against the winter-sodden ranks of late-January oaks. Relief's the opposite of what Jo's feeling right now. Excitement and trepidation leave no room for anything so calming.

The cottage is smaller than the photos made out, but that makes it cuter. Jo scooches out of the car. By the time she's up at the black front door, the cast-iron knocker heavy in her hand, Liam's there beside her. He was at work this morning, doing a cash-in-hand job on a Saturday morning like he often does, and though he's changed out of his work clothes, there's a nick of damp plaster dust in the crescent where his hair doesn't quite meet his ear, the lingering smell of wet sand. It's reassuring, and makes up for the wobble she'd felt at his uncharacteristic reluctance to come with her at all.

Jo's never made any major move without Liam there. When she'd started uni, he'd travelled up with Mum and Dad to settle her in. The two of them had squashed into the back seat like little kids, pillows buffering them and a carrier bag full of pork pies by their feet. (She hadn't been able to eat them, not one. The smell made her so homesick that her throat had closed up in protest.)

And this jump back to her old life: it's about as major a move as she's ever made. Liam's been odd in the few days Jo's been staying with him and Kirsty, though – a bit off. It's something to figure out once things have settled down. Perhaps he's just annoyed at her impulsiveness.

'I left a message to say I'd be here this afternoon.' Her voice judders into the vibrations of the knocker.

Chloe's out of the van now too, bouncing up the flagstones; she'd insisted on coming to see 'Auntie Jo's new house in the woods'. Chloe couldn't care less that Jo's actually only renting a room in the home of a

24

complete stranger; that the house Jo actually called home now belongs to some young family who are just moving down to the Forest. Jo has to not mind this either, but it's hard.

'Careful, poppet! The stones will be slippy from the rain.' But Chloe's a Forester through and through, learned to walk on this kind of uneven camber.

The door creaks open. Jo swallows, takes a hand to her hair to twizzle it, but Liam, hanging back a bit, catches it and gives her a half-strength grin.

Behind Jo, Chloe whispers, 'A witch!' more in awe than in horror. The woman in front of them, regarding them seriously, is in a loose black top and trousers, her hair almost as dark, her eyes piercing blue. She's younger than Jo imagined, though she's easily got a decade or more on her and Liam. Probably in her early forties. So this is her landlady.

'You must be Tessa! Hello! I'm Jo.'

'All right?' Tessa meets Jo's outstretched hand with her own. The palm's calloused, her grip firm and steady, but there's no accompanying smile and Jo's own smile fades.

'You'd better come inside. Is it a lot you have?'

There's a trace of Welsh there among her otherwise-local accent, the whirls and dips forming an imperceptibly different rhythm from a Forest lilt.

'Not much; just a few more boxes in the van.' It was disconcerting, really, how little life there'd been to pack up when leaving London. Ten years since and all she apparently had to show for them were a couple of mugs with ironic catchphrases and a nice throw. And books, of course. There was the usual IKEA clutter, but she'd left that for her housemates. Starting a new life – or, more accurately, restarting an old one – shouldn't be a reason for depriving a London flatshare of its Billy bookcase.

'Your room's here on the left.' Tessa turns without checking that they're following, limps back inside.

They all cram in through the front door. Steep stairs lead off the corridor to the right, and beyond them, light beckons like a promise from an open door at the end of the corridor. Tessa stops almost before they've started, pushes open the door on the left-hand side opposite the stairs.

'Here we are, then. I'll let you get settled, is it?'

'Oh, brilliant, thanks. That's great. The room looks fantastic. I'm sure it won't be too crowded once I've got everything packed away.' Talking to Tessa is like throwing snowballs at a wall, the words melting in the face of indifference, causing Jo to go faster and faster until all that's left is the stain of needless irrelevance. Her stomach curls.

Somewhere further on in the house, the phone rings. Tessa starts, her whole body tensed, but she doesn't move.

It rings again. And again. Tessa doesn't stir an inch. It's as if she's waiting for something. Jo glances at Liam, who shrugs. None of their business.

'Shall I get that, miss?'

Liam puts a restraining hand on Chloe's shoulder. 'It's only in our house you get the phone, love.'

'What's that?' It's as if Tessa's forgotten they're there. She blinks hard, almost as if she's bringing them into focus, and Jo moves closer to Liam.

'The phone.' But Tessa must have heard it. This house is teeny; if you sneezed at one end of the corridor, a person at the other end could offer you a tissue.

'Oh. Yes.' Tessa walks down the corridor towards the noise, one hand pressed against the whitewashed wall as if for support.

'Why didn't she answer it straight away?'

It's an incredibly fair question, but before Jo can even try to reply to Chloe, Tessa's back. Her whole demeanour has altered. She's deflated, bent over as if someone's yanked the string keeping her upright. 'It's for you.'

Jo frowns. 'Already?'

Liam's two steps ahead, as always. Unsmiling, but certain. 'It'll be Brenda. There's no way she'd let you move in without saying hello and you've probably got no signal on your mobile out here.'

The phone's on a little shelf in the corridor just before you get to the main room at the end. Though Tessa could surely have brought the phone over; it's not as if it's corded. Jo bends over the receiver, not wanting to spread herself too fully in this strange, quiet house.

'Hello?'

Liam was right. Of course he was. 'Just me, love. I thought I'd give you a ring to see how you're getting on.' Hearing Mum's voice – Mum being down on the coast in the new house, the new life, and Jo being here

27

– is topsy-turvy. She squeezes her eyes tightly, forces cheer down the line.

'Yeah, all right, thanks. We've just got here.'

'Oh, Liam's with you?'

'Yeah, and Chloe.' Her voice wavers. Stupid. 'Listen, we've only just arrived. Is it OK if I give you a call a bit later?'

Jo hangs up and stands for a minute, staring blankly at the wall. She's done the right thing, hasn't she? She's still come home, even if home isn't where her family lives any longer. She's going to be the keeper of the legacy, the keeper of community. Butler's Butcher's will be hers now, the third generation to run the shop.

OK, so it's a three-month trial, but that's just her parents being cautious, taken aback by the suddenness of her suggestion. They need to sell up as badly as she needed to get out of London, leave the law behind and start doing something that actually puts something back into the community. She hasn't told Liam about the three-month thing; there's the risk it sounds as if her parents don't trust her, don't think it's going to work, and saying it out loud might make that harder to avoid.

Liam and Chloe are still in the bedroom. Liam turns round as Jo enters, gestures with the books he's holding.

'Dunno where you'd want these so we're just piling them onto the floor for the minute. I can take them boxes away in the van that way.'

With the three of them in here, the bedroom shrinks. Jo chucks her bag onto the bed and slumps down beside it. Chloe kneels up beside her, rocking. 'It's a good bed, Auntie Jo; nice and bouncy.'

Tessa's stillness has leached Jo of energy for a bounce. She stares at the alcoves on the opposite wall, where cupboards have been fitted. 'Just as well I haven't got much.'

Liam squeezes round the end of the bed to the window and gazes out at the path they've come up, his elbows on the windowsill. 'You'll be all right.' His tone's flat and Jo's stomach tightens again. Liam's the closest to family she's got left here. He's missing her parents too, probably. They were essentially his second family for decades. It must be as weird for him as it is for her.

Weirder, because he stayed here while she went off to university, even though that hadn't ever been their original plan. They were both going to study in London, quasi-siblings each making the other braver. Leaving the Forest had never felt casual, for all that it was always inevitable. The distance from countryside to city was far greater than the miles on the van, and going together would mean someone there who got it; less guilt at betraying home by leaving it.

But that all changed before A levels, and in the end it was just Jo who went. She had to go. And Liam had to stay.

Now he pushes off the windowsill. 'You wait here a minute with Jo and help her unpack, OK, Chlo?'

'Are you going for a wee, Daddy?' But he's gone.

Jo unzips the bag. It's full of the dark suits and sensible blouses that had made up her last working wardrobe.

God knows why she'd even bothered packing them, to be honest. A vision of her serving behind the butcher's counter in her barrister's wig and gown springs up.

'Where're you going to put all them books? There's no bookshelves in here.'

Chloe's right. And more to the point, no space for bookshelves either. There's a strip of floor either side of the bed, enough for a tiny bedside cabinet. The window-sill's quite deep; maybe she could use that as a sort of shelf if it came to it, but condensation pools in the gummy grouted corners.

There's a whole house out there. This isn't some Edwardian boarding school, even if Tessa doesn't seem the most forthcoming. There must be bookshelves elsewhere.

'Let's go and see where they can live, shall we?' She takes Chloe's hand and they walk down the corridor towards the room at the end. These walls are a subdued whitewash and bare of paintings or photos. There's a white-painted door at the end, with one of those old-fashioned black cast-iron handles that twists like a claw, rough to touch.

The door's stuck slightly ajar so Jo shoves it and stumbles into the room.

Liam's in here, talking to Tessa. Weird. He hadn't mentioned knowing the house, nor its owner. Maybe he'd done some work up here. Liam's plastered half the houses in the Forest; knows them better than their owners, sometimes.

The door slams against the wall and Liam and Tessa

30

step sharply away from each other. The room is lopsided with a pungent bitterness that doesn't speak of idle client-trader chitchat. The earlier strangeness of the empty walls closes in.

Chloe rushes over to Liam and puts her arms around his waist. Jo bites down hard on her cheek. She flicks a glance at Liam – *what was all that about?* – but he won't look at her.

The room they're in spreads across the back of the house, but it's still pretty titchy. To the right, against what must be an outside wall, there's an old fireplace, a sofa barricading it from the rest of the room, its dull brown leather back to them. Chairs crowd at the knee of the sofa and there's a rug tucked onto the flagstones, which looks like it was cheerful once but has long since given up knowing how.

Along the wall there's an old cooking range beside an oven and a drunk-looking fridge, which must be on a wonky bit of flagstone. And in front of her, shoved in beside the kitchen door, is a table and a little bookshelf.

Tessa's shoulders shoot up and then down, pistons bringing her back to herself. She stares past Jo then smiles, her grip on the chair still tight. It's a shadow of a smile, as if she's forgotten how.

Liam turns around from the windowsill. His face is set, the blinds drawn. Jo used to be able to tell what he was thinking at all times; that's what made them invincible as friends. But she can't read this inscrutability. She shivers again, her insides pulling away from her skin. Liam's

31

never one for using twenty words when one would do – 'I leave them up to you, Butler' – but he's deep within himself right now in a way that happens only rarely.

He pulls Chloe away from his legs and takes her hand. 'We'll be off now, then.' He ruffles her hair, but his smile is diminished.

'I'll see you out.' Jo knows it's nuts in a place this tiny – a few strides and they'll be at the front door – but she isn't ready to let Liam go. She steps outside with him and wedges the front door so that it doesn't slam. This doesn't seem like a place for slamming. Chloe lets go of Liam's hand and spins into the fresh air.

'Li. What was all that in there?'

'All what?' Liam watches Chloe wheeling her arms through the air.

'With Tessa.'

'What do you mean?'

'You know. When Chloe and I came in. You leaped back like we'd got you with a cattle prod.'

If Liam looks any harder at Chloe, he'll knock her over. 'Oh, it was nothing. Thought I knew her from somewhere.'

In another mood, Jo'd tease him about Tessa being a crafty shag. It's nonsense, obviously; Liam's devoted to Kirsty and even though they'd met so young he hasn't ever seemed curious about what he might have missed. But Liam's closed down, and in this mood all you can do is tread carefully or he retreats further.

So she nods. 'Fair enough.'

Liam looks at his watch, an old Casio spotted with

plaster. 'Rosie's nearly done at football. I'd better get a move on.'

'Daddy forgot to pick her up in the rain once and Mummy was really, really cross.' Chloe's eyes widen with the delicious memory.

Liam inhales, pushes out the air, looks at Jo and then at Chloe. 'That's right, our Chlo. Don't want to see that again, do we?' He opens the passenger door for Chloe, then comes round the van and slides into his own seat. He's barricaded away into his real life, and nausea rises in Jo's throat at the idea of him being gone.

'Let me know when you're free and we'll do something, go for a pint, yeah? And tell me when you and Kirsty fancy going out and I'll babysit. It's the least I can do after you putting me up last week. And thank Kirst, especially, for finding me the lodger ad on the noticeboard at work.' Her voice catches.

Liam raises his hand on the steering wheel in salute. The exhaust wheezes into life and he twists round over his shoulder, one hand on the seat back, as he wheels the van round. Then they're gone, a shimmy of dust the only proof they were ever here.

Jo goes back into the bedroom and shuts the door. The unfamiliar smell of the room is sharper, more clinical than anywhere she's lived before, at odds with the ramshackleness of the cottage. It's so quiet here after London; even quieter than Jo expects from home. It isn't just the lack of street noise, but the crackling silence of the inside, as though Tessa has simply evanesced. Jo collapses back onto the bed and closes her eyes.

At Christmas, loneliness had been impossible, even with piles of belongings and boxes signalling her parents' imminent move. That house, her childhood home, was dense with the layers of all the versions of herself, her history marked in every room. The kitchen step she tripped and bashed her head on as a toddler, chasing the cat. The marks in the living room ceiling from hurling a paperweight at Gary (and missing). The glow-in-the-dark stars that were so cool when she was fourteen and still hadn't unstuck from the ceiling despite everyone's best efforts. The lumpy spare dining chair that served as her desk chair ever since she started secondary school.

She'd spent hours on that chair, feet hooked around the wooden bars, frowning at her homework, working for the best grades she could reach. Jo's approach to learning had mirrored Gary's love of video games, every achievement unlocking a new level, her parents laughing that they couldn't have raised two more different kids.

Liam loved learning too, but not in the levelling-up, goal-oriented way that she did. It was purer than that with Liam; he just couldn't help absorbing things almost before they'd been explained. When they must have been about fourteen, Jason Bevan in their form had got wind of the idea that Liam was good at schoolwork – Christ knows how, since Jason Bevan seemed hardly ever to show up. He'd briefly stopped mocking Liam for his 'chavvy trainers' and moved on to 'you think you're so clever, don't you?' Liam had just owned it, carried on despite the urge he must have felt to either lamp Jason Bevan or, more dangerously, to dial down the clever.

By the time they'd reached GCSEs, it was clear to everyone around her – and perhaps to Jo last of all – that the educational ladders she scaled so determinedly were leading her upwards and out, away from the Forest, away from the apprenticeships and jobs most of her classmates were starting to consider, towards things that didn't exist within the Forest. It was a bit like climbing Jack's magic beanstalk, striving up and up until you reach a world where the air is different, the opportunities more varied.

Once upon a time, Jo had thought she wanted this. She had stepped off the ladder towards a law degree in London with the keys to the kingdom and the pride at having got there. No – it was more than that, less straightforward. It was pride at how chuffed she'd made everyone else. Not too many people went off to university from here, and nobody she knew well. Now one of their own had done it.

Even though the job quite quickly revealed itself to be not what she'd hoped, the idea of letting people down, coming home and explaining that she couldn't hack it after all, had made Jo feel sick, and this sickness had held her in place for too many years. She owed it to all the people who'd had faith in her to do it.

But at Christmas, with the beanstalk being dismantled beneath her, she'd been overcome with the vertigo of her escape hatch closing. The option to climb back down the ladder whenever she wanted was what had stopped things from falling apart. Home, she knew now, mattered more than a stagnant career in the law; it didn't even come close. So she'd leaped, left behind mindless legal work and came home last week. It had been unflatteringly simple to leave the Bar. Her parents had taken more persuasion that she should assume control of the shop, but that's where years of legal training and an ability to create and present a detailed plan on almost no notice came into its own. They'd already had a buyer lined up, though the deal couldn't have been all that firm because her parents were reasonably unclear about the details, and it seemed to be a straightforward enough process to switch to Jo taking over instead. Perhaps it was one of the other local-area butchers who'd planned on expanding their empire, but understood that if there was still a Butler to run Butler's Butcher's, that's the way it should be. Jo hadn't asked too much, to be honest, not wanting to face the truth that perhaps someone better qualified to take over was waiting in the wings. Someone whose stomach didn't turn at a metal bowl of offcut fat and sinew, maybe. A lifetime of being in the shop had to count for something, and nobody could want this more than she did. The shop was her legacy, held so much purpose beyond just its space on the high street. In understanding this, at least, she was uniquely qualified. And for the rest she could prep and learn.

What Jo hadn't fully considered in the month of planning that preceded the move was the extent to which living elsewhere in the Forest might be strange. The picture of home she would conjure on those deflated

Doncaster train rides has already shifted, as if she's looking at it from an entirely different camera angle. She's five miles away from her old house, back home but not *home* home. Mum and Dad are down on the coast with Gary, and she's not going to see them in the shop. Her room in London is already rented out, and even if she'd wanted to return to chambers, the head clerk will repay her for her betrayal by doling out only awful cases for the rest of her living days. Everything's been so hectic since Christmas that Jo hadn't given any consideration to the fact that her life as she'd known it has effectively imploded.

Jo shuffles up the bed a bit, nudges a pile of clothes to the floor. She's got three months to prove she can turn the shop into a viable business, enough to secure a loan to take over the business, and to convince her parents that this isn't just a reaction to a bad winter in London. Three months to rebuild a social life out here. Three months to work her way into her new old life.

Chapter Four

TESSA DOESN'T BOTHER UNDRESSING. IT'S all she can do to get upstairs and onto the bed before the tiredness fells her. Though 'tiredness' – that's like calling the forest out there 'a little copse'. This is hammering, muscles-to-mush exhaustion. The effort of seeing the lodger in without collapsing had taken everything she had. She's asleep before she's got her other slipper off.

But sleep kicks her out again all too soon, the scab on her ankle itching where the horseshoe scorched it. She lies still in the dark and listens for how deep into the night they are. The old apple tree taps softly against the window but there's no lilt from the blackbird. Downstairs Bamps' old grandfather clock whirrs, catches itself as it gears up to send the time through the house. Three o'clock. Tessa sighs, ferrets her bare foot around on the boards for the other slipper and creeps out for a pee. It still hurts to put weight on her ankle. The floor creaks and the clock metronomes its way through the night, marking off this unshiftable misery.

There's no light on downstairs and everything's quiet. She should probably check in the morning that the lodger's not too disturbed by the noise of the clock.

The lodger. It had been the only way to survive. She's reduced the number of horses she looks after, sticking only with her longest-standing customers, the ones who might cut her some slack without asking too many questions. Truth be told, it can't be too safe to drive like this either, so she's working only with the yards that are closest to home, the radius of her life shrunken again in an attempt to preserve at least some of it.

Fewer clients means less money, though, and there's no space for less money. The tins she buys are the dented ones; meat went a long time ago. But food is non-negotiable, winter bills are higher and things are desperate. And there's the ten pounds that has to go to the savings account, no matter what. It's an unbreakable promise, a show of commitment, that goes right to the very core of what counts. Her pulse quickens at the thought of stopping that, the band around her head tightening.

Two weeks ago she'd had a brainwave, rummaged in the shed for the fork and shovel, and gone out to Dad's old vegetable patch, long since left fallow. She squared the spade into the ground, leaned her weight into it and the earth remembered when it used to be soil, yielded to the familiar bite of the metal. The mud squelched in release, and an earthworm waved in slow motion, its colours gradated like a subterranean rainbow.

A few potatoes, that's all she'd needed. Something to stretch the dented beans a few days longer. But the fork came up empty, time and again, Dad's legacy long gone. No salvation would be forthcoming from the land.

So she'd folded away her pride, put up an ad on the noticeboard in the Co-op. *Lodger wanted*, her first attempt had said, but the phrasing made it sound like she was looking for a Victorian paying guest. *Room to rent*. That's how you phrased this sort of thing.

After that it had all moved quickly – too quickly. And now there was this nervy, smiley woman living in what used to be the parlour, on Tessa's childhood bed dragged down from the box room upstairs, that room too small to charge for (and too close to Tessa and her night terrors, whispers the betraying voice of honesty).

Tessa curls back into bed, tries to focus on the soothing metronome of the pendulum. It's not certain that she can manage this. Living with someone else had been hard enough even when she'd wanted to. Even when it had been Marnie.

When Tessa moved in with Marnie, she left the grandfather clock behind. She left pretty much everything behind, in fairness.

There's no way the furniture from the cottage would have fitted in Marnie's flat; sometimes Tessa wondered how she herself fitted. The flat was like Marnie: open, and floaty, and full of light, built for warmth and friendships.

When Marnie first suggested that Tessa move into her flat in Bristol, Tessa had to turn her face away, certain it was a cruel practical joke. But now she knew it was a miracle. Marnie, who brightened every room just by being in it, whose dimples were pencil-sharp and whose laugh was never far from the surface, had chosen Tessa.

Tessa had been bone-weary ever since she'd moved in, worn out with the constant vigilance required to pretend she belonged in this world, deserved this life.

Marnie seemed to have stayed in touch with everyone she'd gone to school and university with, to say nothing of her management consultant friends from work. The flat filled regularly with a gaggle of bright, laughing women, who waved their hands about as they talked, the stories of their jobs all blending together in Tessa's head as an amorphous collection of emails and bosses and meetings. They'd lounge on Marnie's enormous fuchsia sofa in the vast open space Tessa learned not to call the sitting room, and gesticulate with their wine glasses while Tessa, possessing none of the easy fluency of casual conversation, tucked herself into a corner of the sofa, hyper-vigilant.

'We should stay over at yours sometimes, go out with your friends too,' Marnie suggested once, early on, pulling Tessa close.

Tessa turned round in the circle of the embrace so that she didn't have to look at Marnie while she admitted the next thing.

'The thing is, I don't have any friends.' She closed her eyes tight against Marnie moving away.

But Marnie didn't flinch and, better still, didn't refute it or demand an explanation. She followed Tessa's contour line, burying her face in Tessa's neck, her voice soft. 'Well, you've got me now.'

They were quiet for a moment. Tessa listened to the endless flow of human life outside on the street, the sigh of the buses as they pulled up at the traffic lights, the edges of music from half-opened car windows. She braced, on alert for the tingling feeling to start again in her hands and feet.

This new environment was potholed with dangers. A couple of times, right when she first met Marnie, she'd ragdolled, just for a second.

'Tessa! What the hell just happened?'

Tessa had laughed weakly, brushed it off, clambered upright.

'Don't move, for God's sake – you might be hurt!'

If Marnie knew the extent of this, it might end things between them. Better to minimise it. 'I'm not hurt; just poleaxed by how fabulous you are.' Which, in its own way, was true.

'Oh, come on. People don't go around collapsing for no reason.'

'Honest, bach, it's nothing.' *Don't become a burden.* 'I get a bit faint sometimes, that's all. But it doesn't hurt and I'm right as rain after. You can see that, right?'

'Have you seen a doctor? We could ask Arianne.' Arianne was one of Marnie's shiny friends, from university, maybe; it was hard to keep them all straight. One without a desk job, though she did still seem to have endless emails to fret about. She was a doctor, that was the point.

'We don't want to bother her.'

Marnie was already texting. 'It won't be a bother.'

Arianne, when she replied, suggested making an appointment to see a doctor (Marnie groaned ruefully: 'That's what she always says!'). Did the collapsing happen around the time of Tessa's period? Perhaps it was an iron deficiency, suggested Arianne, who didn't seem to think it peculiar or intrusive to be casually discussing menstrual cycles with her old friend's girlfriend. Marnie was reassured enough for a bit, at least, and Tessa didn't ever go to the doctor, just sidestepped it when it came up. She was learning how to be herself, how to be this new version of herself as she related to Marnie.

Relationships weren't for Tessa. Not in any form, not really. She hadn't had any friends growing up. Mam was too closed in for Tessa to risk bringing a friend home for tea, and at school Tessa often spent playtime on her own by the fence. She spoke funny, that's what the other kids had said when she first arrived in the Forest from the Valleys. That had been enough.

If you didn't have friends as a little kid, it turned out that you didn't have the easy path into relationships that happened in your teenage years when everyone's opinions about their classmates shifted with hormones. She'd been an outsider for so many years now that it had become absorbed into the fabric of her, just part of her like her blue eyes, her pointy nose.

Eventually people had mostly left her to her own, and Tessa had honestly, truly been happy like that. Well, not happy, but getting by. She accepted that this was her life and that had been fine. Until she met Marnie.

But it didn't last. Of course it didn't.

Downstairs, the clock winds up again, prepares for 4 a.m. Tessa stretches, tries to knuckle sleep towards her, but it's out of reach. All she's left with is a weariness that makes her bones ache right through to her soul, her skin rippably thin, and even more of a sense of despair than she has in the daylight. And tomorrow – today, now – she'll have to get up and not wince at the morning habits of a stranger; morning habits that are uncomfortably close to Marnie's in too many ways. The rattle of the coffee grinder, the serious men talking on the radio, the effortless cheerfulness. Through all of this Tessa will need to be vigilant; there's no knowing what might set off the little collapses. They could scare away the tenant before she's even really unpacked and then Tessa would be back to square one. She just has to get used to it.

Part Two
Upsetting

Chapter Five

J o's AGREED WITH RON AND Mo that she'll start properly in the shop tomorrow, wanting time to double-check her plan of action now she's actually here on the ground and not doing things remotely. But having spent two days updating and checking the plans she's put together, she can't resist nipping down at closing time just to see it.

Jo slows down as she reaches the top of town, memory freighting her. She'd brought a university boyfriend back home once. Only one, and only once.

He'd grown up in Singapore, son of lawyers, required to be a lawyer himself, in the UK to study and never before visited the English countryside. He'd stopped dead at the top of the street and gazed at the long, thin strip of shops and businesses running like a seam of ore down one hill and up another, bordered on one side by the ever-widening majesty of the River Severn and on the other by dense overhangs of ancient woodland. As he stared in surprise from one view to the other, Jo had seen the town like an incomer. Empty-eyed stone buildings housed a litter of businesses – the nail salon, the hardware store, the pet shop – brightened only by garish 'to let' signs hanging half off vacant storefronts.

'It's . . .' He swept an arm at the expanse of river, the vastness of the forest, then pointed at the scar of the high street.

'Not all beautiful surroundings come with chocolate-box towns, you know – sometimes there isn't the money for that,' Jo had pointed out, small, messy, ashamed of herself for being embarrassed by this place she loved. Later, in the pub, the same boyfriend asked Liam to repeat himself three times, struggling to make sense of the dialect. They broke up a couple of weeks after they got back to London.

A couple of kids in her old school uniform step back to let her pass and she ages fifteen years in fifteen seconds. This is the route she and Liam took almost every day. And now she's back, with Liam at work a mile away and the rain muzzling down and the mud on her trainers proof that she's home. Happiness surges through her. She's actually done it. She's come home. It doesn't matter what outsiders think.

As for the shop . . . Jo stops outside the front, her eyes prickling. There isn't a day of her life that she hasn't thought about this shop, and now it's hers, actually hers. Not Grandad's, not Mum and Dad's – *she's* the Butler whose name's above the door now. She rubs her eyes with her sleeve, her cheeks hot with excitement. Right up until this morning she thought she'd get the call from her parents to say they'd changed their minds. It's going to be bloody hard work, but right now, out here, what it's mostly going to be is amazing.

There's no sign of Ron through the window, but Mo's in there, setting up the till. The shop's empty of customers, but it's the end of the day. Her new colleagues – her parents' oldest friends. Not quite the head clerk from chambers, but to be treated with similar respect.

Jo straightens, puts her hand on the door as if she's leading troops into battle, and pushes on in.

'Jo, love! Wasn't expecting you 'til the morning!' Mo squeezes out from behind the counter and hugs Jo, surprised and not surprised. Jo was at the shop most nights for years, after all, waiting for a lift home; on some level, the surprise is only that she's been away.

'Yeah, I just thought I'd . . .'

But Mo's barely paying attention, locked into the now-this-then-that of closing down the shop. All the meat has already been heaved back into the cold storage and the blinds pulled on the display fridges. Now Mo's coming through to the shop floor with her brush and bucket.

'Do us a favour, love. Grab the sign in from out the front.'

Mo sweeps the length and breadth of the shop, catching the stray tendrils of sawdust that have mulched into the grit and wet from a day's worth of customers pushing in from the cold. She clatters the broom into the corner out the back, then sets to with the mop, moving methodically across the checked squares as if sussing them out for a game of draughts.

Jo peers through the plastic curtain to where Ron's swabbing down in the back room. He's a giant of a man, almost as tall as the carcasses of the pigs that hang in the cold store, and as ready with a scowl as Dad is with a smile. When she was little, he'd been a central figure in her nightmares, this man-mountain bursting from between the ribs of a hog, overalls bloodied, guts and gore dripping from the cleaver.

Ron sloshes industrial quantities of detergent over knives and boards alike, seemingly not noticing her there at all.

Their movements, so familiar, tug at the thread that's brought Jo home. She watches for a moment, not quite trusting herself to speak. This was what she's come back for. This is what needs saving from developers and Aldi and the whole bunch of them. The shop's always been at the heart of everything, and however truculent Ron can be, he and Mo are part of that, quietly getting on with things, working diligently with her parents all these years and apparently not minding when Mum and Dad decided to close down. When she'd asked Mum about it, Mum had waved an arm and muttered something about, 'Time for a change for all of us,' which seemed a bit heartless. Mo's mum had not long died, though, so perhaps Mo was going to be grateful for a break.

Jo thinks of her project plan, all double-checked and ready for sharing with Ron and Mo tomorrow. She isn't sure how they feel about her taking over from Mum and Dad, especially not when they, too, must have been planning retirement.

'Oh, you know them,' Dad had said vaguely when she broached it, clarifying nothing.

Hopefully they'll be on board with the specifics she's come up with to improve revenues. Or perhaps they'll want to retire anyway, in which case, fair enough, but at least this way they have some choices. A new owner from outside might have wanted to bring in their own people to run the shop with them, force out her parents' oldest friends. This way she's helping even before she's started. They must have been so relieved when they heard she wanted to take it on. Jo allows herself a brief moment of self-satisfaction.

Mo's washing out the mop bucket now, wringing the mop down the sink. Jo doesn't want to get in the way of them getting home, so she waves at Mo and pushes open the shop door. Tomorrow she'll start using the back door, honest, but the novelty hasn't worn off yet.

Just as she's the other side of it, Ron appears in the window. He's waving a sheaf of papers at her; when Jo waves back, he only flourishes them more furiously. Best to go back in and see what's worrying him.

'You all right there, Ron?'

'Thought you might want to get started. This paper-work's all yours now you're the boss.'

'I . . .' He's calling her bluff, and they both know it. Ron's idea of a joke has always been less funny than he thinks.

'Here.' He thrusts the papers at her and there's nothing to do but take them. 'You can do that "working from home" that you lot with your computer jobs love; no need to stay here.' He stalks off through the plastic curtains again before she's got it together enough to point out that she didn't exactly have a 'computer job', and she definitely hadn't had the kind of job that could be done from home.

Jo sighs. Maybe Ron's just had a bad day. It's bound to be weird for him without Dad here; they were always close friends as well as employer and employee. No need to check what the papers are. Hygiene checks, health and safety checks, stock checks; all part and parcel of running a butcher's shop in this day and age. Dad used to mutter about the papers when Jo was still home, and that was ten years ago now. By the looks of it, the government hasn't found a way to streamline things. Anyone would think they had something against people trying to get on, literally minding their own businesses.

The simple euphoria of watching the shop being put to bed for the evening is still with Jo, and there's no need to start things off by antagonising her parents' oldest friends and her soon-to-be employees. She stacks the papers together and tucks them into the crease of an elbow. This is nothing compared with the briefs she'd be ploughing through if she were in chambers right now.

The glow persists. It doesn't matter how many bits of paper Ron flings around. She can go home now, to the little cottage in the woods. It's going to take ten minutes to get home rather than an hour, and that's including slowing down for an errant sheep, because even the sheep don't have to play by the rules out here.

She'll get to know her new housemate, who seemed quiet enough but was probably trying to just give Jo some moving-day space. And she'll spread this out in front of the fire and get it done in a heartbeat, ready for her first proper day tomorrow. Her first day as the third generation of Butlers to own the shop. That's not nothing, not by a long chalk. Her heart tips.

The fire's not lit when she gets back. Tessa's there, though, in one of the chairs either side of the hearth, hands on knees, staring for all the world as if she were staring into a fire.

'Evening!' The room smells cold, not freezing; the range is giving out some heat and Tessa must have just come in herself because she's still in a big coat. 'Do you mind if I light a fire?'

'Eh?' Tessa startles.

'Are you all right? You were miles away!'

Jo plonks Ron's paperwork on the table and comes on through, swallowing down the last of the banana she'd grabbed at the Co-op when she realised she'd forgotten to think about getting food in.

'What's the story with food waste these days? I think my parents had a caddy somewhere.'

Tessa stares again and Jo waggles the banana skin. 'Tell you what, shall I just chuck it out into the woods?'

Still nothing. It's almost as if Tessa can't hear her. Jo frowns, tries again.

'I'll get some wood in at the same time, shall I? Where's the woodshed? Round the corner?'

Tessa nods and it's a relief to finally get any kind of reaction.

Jo pushes open the kitchen door and steps out into the garden. It's easier to breathe out here. There's a patch of hardstanding – calling it a patio would be pushing it a bit – then grass all the way down to a wall. Jo gets out her signal-less phone, puts on the torch function and shines it down the grass. Yeah – ancient apple trees, what looks like the remnants of a vegetable patch, and some kind of wooden and stone structure right down at the end. That can't be the shed, can it? Nobody would have their wood stack that far from the house.

She goes round the corner of the house and bumps more or less straight into the shed. Good guess. There's hardly any wood left in the shed, but she gathers enough for a fire tonight.

Tessa's still sitting in the same position, as if she hasn't moved an inch since. The telly's not on and there's no book in front of her. She's just staring.

Bet she was ace at musical statues as a kid.

'There's not much there so I've only brought in a few bits.'

'OK.' Tessa barely looks up.

Jo bends down in the hearth. It's fine. It's not her. Tessa probably just hasn't had a lodger before. She starts building the fire, but her hands shake and the first twigs she pyramids collapse onto each other.

'So, have you lived here long?' Jo's back is to Tessa.

Sometimes, clients found it easier if they faced away while talking to her. Not that she can spend her whole time here with her back to her landlady. But it's somewhere to start.

'Thirty years, on and off.'

'So you're from here? I wondered if I heard a trace of Welsh.'

'We moved here from the Valleys when I was a kid.'

Jo looks around for kindling. There's a stack of local papers beside the log basket. She scrunches one up a bit. It's old, but it's not too damp.

'Was one of your parents from round here?'

'No.' Tessa's hands rise in the barest flurry of impatience.

Jo gets up. Her knees are sore from the stone floor and her head is sore from drawing conversational blood from a stone. She's dogged, though; anyone who's spent five minutes with her would testify to that. And the only way this will feel like home is if she and Tessa get to know each other a bit.

The matches are nestled beside a neatly rolled ball of string. Jo lights the fire then sits back on her knees, watching the flames find their way.

'So you've lived here all your life then, pretty much? Where did you go to secondary school?' Tessa's a fair bit older than Jo but there are bound to be people they have in common; younger siblings of Tessa's classmates who knew Gary, that sort of thing. Jo turns to Tessa, senses perked. But Tessa sidesteps.

'Nearly all the time. I left for a few years a little while back. Came back a few weeks ago now.'

The effort it's costing her to tell Jo even this is palpable. Jo should stop. But she's beaten to it.

Tessa pushes herself up from the chair. 'I'm off to bed, then. Night.'

Tessa locks up the back door, then moves slowly out of the room, limping as she had before. She does look exhausted, in fairness, but it's – Jo checks the redundant phone again – not even close to 7.30 p.m. Tessa's not tired. She's escaping the interrogation.

Jo sighs, contrite. It's going to take a while to recalibrate, to stop lawyering people. It's all going to take a while.

Or perhaps Tessa just doesn't like her. But she didn't ask a single thing about Jo – she's got no way of knowing whether or not she likes her. She has no idea that tomorrow's going to be a huge day, starting properly to run the business.

It's probably just strange having someone living in her house. Nothing that they can't get past. Nor, unfortunately, is all this admin. Jo pulls Ron's paperwork to her. She just needs to buckle down and do it. Because tomorrow – her heart pulls her up again – tomorrow she runs the shop.

Chapter Six

I N THE FEW DAYS SINCE the lodger arrived, the
weather's shifted from January cold to February wet
and the trees are heavy with it. The old pine at the
near edge of the garden is besieged, the clusters of needles
keening towards Tessa as she opens the kitchen door, as
if to bring her into their confidence. Tessa turns up the
collar on her donkey jacket, pulls her woollen cap right
down and limps as fast as she can from the back door
to the forge at the end of the garden. Her ankle's still
paining her but it's better than it was, more itchy than
sore at night now.

Having the extra person in the house is taking more
getting used to than anticipated. She needs the predict-
ability of metal in fire to bring her back to herself, the
rhythms of the hammer and the rasp to calm that part
of her that persists in reacting to other people despite
the consequences and collapses.

The coals take their time heating up and Tessa blows into cupped hands, stamping from one foot to another on the concrete floor. She could use the Swanee for this job, fire up the propane, save the coals a bit, but though the portable forge is great, and works perfectly when she's out at a client, there's no point using up the gas when she's got the coal forge standing there.

She should show the forge to the lodger, really, let her know what's in here so she knows to stay away. But everything pulls in at the idea of it. Not yet. The lodger – Jo – she doesn't need to know what's in every nook and cranny. The forge is just the other side of the drystone, right down the far end of the garden. If Jo's still here in the spring and asks about it, Tessa can show her then, maybe.

The forge is more of a shed than anything else. Though Dad built it for her in the hut that was already there when they moved, technically it's on land that isn't hers. But there's enough forest to go round out here and nobody's bothered about those scrubby edges where people stop and forest begins. Putting in the coal forge was almost the last thing Dad had done before he died, it was, and Mam had had a right face on her at the idea of 'all that money' going on coal and iron. It was the first reaction Mam had given to any of Tessa's interests in years. Dad had insisted – one of the few times he'd put up resistance.

The shed doesn't take long to warm up once the coals are lit. It's going to be black out here for a couple of hours yet, so she's flicked the main light on for a bit.

Tessa looks back down the garden at the cottages, joined for all time by a shared wall, separated across the years by Mam's policy of shunning all company. Next door's shuttered up for the winter, no holidaymakers fancying a winter weekend break and standing outside to shriek about how quiet everything is.

Even without Tessa having cut down on her customers, there's always less work in the winter. Horses often aren't ridden so much in the depths of winter, so the cycle between shoeing can stretch from six weeks out to eight. The working days are shorter, too; less daylight. You can shoe horses under artificial light if you have to, and occasionally the vet might call you out to a case of laminitis that needs dealing with there and then, but it's work better done outside, in daylight, on good, clean hardstanding. The yards and liveries round here all know that. Everything in the Forest works to the rhythms of daylight and weather. You might occasionally get some new owner who thinks the horse will be more comfortable in their own stable, surrounded by straw, but Tessa's able to put them right.

It's better to make the shoes here in the forge and wait for the daylight to take them out to the next job. She's up to Geoff at the riding centre later this morning. She only has to hope that Susan hasn't mentioned the episode over Christmas.

The forge is full of things she's made recently, whimsical stuff, unlike her normal things. Snails curled up like tiny doorstops, butter knives with oak leaves curled into the handle, a miniature hat stand to go with the sunflower coat stand she made once. She can't stop turning things out; the forge is full of them. She hasn't been able to renew the TV licence, and coming out here, making these, keeps her warm, keeps her mind from wandering too far down bad paths where she might collapse again. She'd thought about selling the things she'd made, before she got the lodger, see if some tourist would buy them. But she hasn't got the foggiest as to how you'd go about something like that, and even the thought of trying to figure it out, having to find shops, then go in, talk to people she didn't know – it's enough to make her a bit wobbly.

The coals are humming deep orange now and look to be almost the right heat. She picks up the tongs from the rack beside the forge and a size five shoe for the first horse on the list today. She'll need to finish it off once she's at the stables, but this will speed things up a bit.

She plunges the edge of the shoe into the coals and waits, standing to the side of the heat. Beyond the fire the little room glistens through starry coal dust and warmed molecules, and the air shimmers in sync with her breath. The rack of tools is all lined up in order, the most-used items nearest the forge (tongs and hammers, mostly, in here, along with the clamps and hammers for the odd bit of smithing), the others neatly waiting their turn. The other tools – the rasps, the picks, the clenchers and that – are all stashed in the back of the van in the specialist toolbox that came with it.

The anvil's right in front of the forge. Tessa flips the shoe among the cartoon-orange of the coals. It's hard

60

not to think of Dad when working in here. He'd been so pleased to get her started.

'If we set things up like this, see, you can look out of the window when you're working on the shoes.' She hadn't had the heart to point out that when she's working on the shoes she needs to concentrate on the fluctuations in the colour and the angle of the ever-changing metal in front of her, that a thirty-second ponder at the apple trees in blossom could result in twenty minutes' extra work. Nor could she tell him that facing out meant facing towards the cottage, where Mam's disapproval glaciated the very calmness Tessa sought from the anvil and the steel.

The shoe's hot now, at the ideal temperature before it becomes bright white and too brittle to be of any use. She grips the tongs and twists round to the anvil, hammer ready. As she raises the hammer, something catches her off-guard and metal greets metal lopsidedly. The shoe bounces out of the tongs and clatters to the floor, pranging off Tessa's boots as she jumps out of the way.

'Bugger!' She bends down and picks it up with the tongs, places the whole lot on the anvil. It's the change in brightness that caught her out. It's not dawn; it's more sudden than that.

The kitchen light. But she'd switched it off when she came out here; she always does. The nearest house is a mile away. Who can it be?

Fear grips Tessa and she drops down, her muscles as much use as a piece of string. It's only a momentary drop, this one, and as she pushes herself back to standing, she's got it.

61

It's the lodger. Jo. Either it's later than Tessa thinks or Jo's more of an early bird than she gives off. Tessa's hands are shaking. It's not a big deal – it's not – but this unpredictability was always the danger of having a stranger in the house. Living with Jo is going to mean being fully on guard.

Tessa brings her attention back to the horseshoe, lying forgotten on the anvil, clamped between the arms of the tongs. It's lost its lustre, the brilliant tangerine promise dulled away. Now it's grey and unremarkable in this room of grey and unremarkable things, waiting for the alchemy of the flame. Waiting for Tessa to bring it to life again, to shape it into its purpose.

But she can't. Not today. The very thing that normally soothes her has deserted her, and until she's certain she can access that calm again, nothing can change.

Chapter Seven

J O THRUSTS FROM DARKEST SLEEP to bright wakefulness with the slick violence of a toreador tossed by a bull, heart pounding as she fumbles for the light switch in this room that still doesn't quite make sense.

It's today.

Today she's taking over the shop.

She squints at the clock. Still an hour before she needs to be getting up. She shuffles back under the bedclothes, but it's half-hearted. Adrenaline courses, clear and true. Today she's taking over the shop.

Jo sits straight up in bed, reaching for her book, but as the cold air hits her, so does a better idea. Her grin sparks out into the solitary blackness.

She pulls on her jeans and a jumper, then tiptoes down the hall, easing her parka off the coat stand. The grandfather clock tocks loudly in the corridor.

The car starts without a hitch and she tilts out of the

driveway. Within fifteen minutes she's up at the edge of the forest, car pointing down across fields. Beyond them, the Severn unfolds on its way to the estuary, a spilled piece of fabric on a brightening carpet, and clouds wisp orange with dawn as the sky lifts into the new day.

Liam had brought her up here to this view to tell her he was going to propose to Kirsty. She'd been a student still, home for the weekend, and he'd let himself in with the key Mum and Dad gave him years ago, rapped on her door at what had felt like the crack of dawn but was in fact even earlier than that. When they'd arrived here, they'd sat in silence and Jo had done her best not to be pissed off at having lost sleep for no discernible gain.

Eventually he'd come out with it, gazing out as the sun filtered rose and amber into the river as it pushed through the tides towards the estuary.

'Li – that's amazing!' Jo had flung herself at him and he'd laughed then, rare unfettered happiness cascading like the light.

'Wanted you to be the first to know, Butler.'

Jo pushes her seat back and sighs at the view in front of her. This is a place for change, for impossible dreams. The day dawns overcast but no less beautiful for it. By the time the sun's fully up, it'll be time for the shop. The cottage will start to feel like home eventually. In the meantime, the Forest will compensate; it feels like home already.

By the time the day's revealed itself fully and Jo's on her way down through the lanes to the shop, overcast has moved into drizzle.

When she reaches town, Jo pulls round the corner and swings right again to park behind the shop, almost coming a cropper before she's begun. There's a silver Ford parked in the space beside the wall. Ron has pinched Mum's old parking spot in the manner of someone not bothering to take the temperature on a grave. She stamps on the brakes and jumps to a halt, practically rubbing noses with the Ford. The Micra bunny-hops and subsides. Jo hacks the car into reverse, stuffs it onto the side of the road, outside the electrical shop. The rain's coming in properly now. The pavements are splashed with stray mulch from the woods, and as she crosses the road to the shop, a four-by-four tilts into the puddle on the corner and zooms on up towards Tesco. It doesn't matter. None of it matters today. Living her best life will have to involve puddle stains from now on. If it weren't for the actual butchering itself, life would be pretty much perfect.

It's disloyal even to admit it privately. She's always loved how the shop, her family, was at the heart of everything, a part of people's everyday lives in a way that was small but meaningful. Jo's time away showed her the value of this, the need for life to be about more than just yourself if it's going to be worthwhile. It stands for so much, this shop; perhaps it's a case of Mum and Dad not being able to see that because they're so close and so knackered. But she could see it.

There's no way she can let all those years of built-up meaning just be sold off to the nearest buyer. But still, at the same time, it would have been great if the family business had been something less . . . flesh-based.

Jo flicks her shoulders, a horse trying to dislodge a fly, and squints at the figures mosaicked in the splodges of rain on the window.

'Morning, Mo!'

'Morning, love.'

Jo follows Mo, jinking past the meat cabinet. The familiar smell hits her, that odd butcher-shop combo of antiseptic and hacked livestock sides. *Home.*

'What time did you get in?'

'Ron left at about four for the market up Gloucester, so I came in around five – thought I may as well make a start on the mince.'

Jo shudders. 'Five! No chance of me getting in before you, then.'

The air's even colder in here than outside, with no redeeming crunch of frozen leaves in it to temper the punch of the wall-to-wall flesh. Her wall-to-wall flesh, now.

'Oh, I shouldn't worry about that. A young thing like you needs her rest.'

The shop's at its new-day best, the tiles sparkling on the floor, the glass cabinets shining with the assurance of meals to come. Mo takes a tray and starts to heap stewing steak and joints into the window. Jo shudders a bit. 'Don't think of it as dead animals,' Dad had said when she was about fifteen and at her most vehement. 'Think of it as Sunday roast, or hot dogs down the rugby.' But it didn't work then and it doesn't work now.

Jo wanders to the back of the shop to find an overall. Mo bustles back.

'Heard anything from your mum and dad since you've been back?'

'Yeah, a bit. Not much, though.'

'Ah.' That tone to Mo's voice again. Jo clutches at the very edges of it but it slides away into the pause that follows.

'Well, I suppose I'd better get started now I'm here.' Jo poppers up her coat and heaves open the door to the cold store. Her hand's cold but the door's from a different frontier and she swears under her breath so that Ron doesn't hear her. Trays hold prepared cuts of meat – people's tea, waiting to be taken home and changed into spag bol or shepherd's pie.

'Do we make meatballs, Mo?'

'You what, love?'

'Meatballs. Do we sell them? We could package them with a sauce, like a ready meal but better for you.'

Mo purses her lips. 'I don't want to be fiddling around with sauces; no room in here for that sort of thing, is there?'

Jo rocks on her heels, tamping down impatience. 'There's bound to be someone local who does them. Or we don't have to worry about the sauce. We could sell the meatballs without it and people could buy the sauce elsewhere. Or make their own. Meatballs just seem like the sort of thing that might sell.'

Before Mo has a chance to reply, there's a clanging behind them at the back door.

'What do we want to be bothering with meatballs for?'

Ron. Jo turns to greet him, facing him square on. The cold air he'd brought in from outside wraps him like a cloak, bedded-in winter meeting the metallic tang of raw meat.

'Hello, Ron.' That'll wind him up. 'How're you?'

Ron looks beyond her rather than at her. Jo's dealt with worse. 'There weren't no lamb so I've got extra beef for stewing steak. Tidy, this time of year.'

'Oh, I—'

But Ron isn't talking to her, he's talking to Mo.

'Cost a pretty penny, it did. Seems half the county's got the same idea.'

The conversation ping-pongs over Jo's head and she twizzles her watch round on its leather strap so that she can see the time on it. Still an hour until the shop's officially open. Plenty of time to try one of the new things she's been thinking about.

'Shall we have a quick team meeting?'

The conversational ping-pong stops with the immediacy of a dropped ball.

'A what, my love?'

'A team meeting. You know, so that we can work out what we're going to do today.'

'Same as we do every day. Chop up meat and sell it to people.' Ron turns away and pulls on his white coat.

Mo shoots Ron a quick, worried glance. 'Your mum and dad didn't ever bother with team meetings, love.'

'No, well. Shall we give it a go anyway, see what we think?'

Ron straightens, gleaming. 'Before you do that, we've

68

got you a welcome back present.' A frown nips the space between Mo and Ron as he hands over a surprisingly heavy bag.

It's chain mail of some sort, threatening to slither to the ground. There are gloves: slippy metal-linked gloves with a purple cloth fastener. Jo holds up the bigger item. An apron. A metallic apron, heavy against her skin. These are the aprons butchers' apprentices are given, so that they don't chop off fingers while they're learning how to wield the cleaver. This isn't a gift. It's an act of aggression.

'Thought you'd be needing this.' Ron's looking straight at her now.

The ten years Jo's been away protect her better than any chain mail. Ron's got nothing on many of her clients, even in the lower courts. Especially in the lower courts.

'I will, you're right. Though I'm going to start out in front on the counter, learn what it is the customers really want. You can't learn much about the shop when you're always out the back, can you?'

Ron pushes past her to the back room, the plastic flaps hissing, and Jo watches the cleaver flash as he bangs it onto the stainless steel counter. She smiles at Mo and slides through the curtain. 'Shall we have the meeting back here?'

Ron's heaving a hunk of cow onto the counter, its skin marbled with fat. Jo swallows down bile.

'This won't take long.'

'You do what you like. I've got this side to break down.'

Jo locks her hands together behind her back, straightens

her shoulders. She looks around. There's a spare quadrant of table, washed down, its scratched surface blurring her reflection.

'Well, let's talk while you get on with that.'

Ron laces his fingers together and flexes them, rolls his shoulders back, a boxer preparing for the first round. He picks up the cleaver as easily as if it were a fallen leaf. Jo flinches as Ron brings down the cleaver, his aim fast and true, ribs splitting under the force and surety of his blade.

Mo grabs Jo by the sleeve and tugs gently, a puppy at the end of a bone. 'Let's do it over here, out of the way, shall we?'

'No, like I said, we'll stay here, then Ron can be part of it.'

Mo edges towards the table, a clear margin between her and the surface. Ron squares his hat onto his forehead, lifts the cleaver again. A seam of revulsion slivers loose. Jo's never, ever been able to manage the violence of butchery, the word itself almost onomatopoeic. Thank God, actually, that Ron's still here.

'OK, so let's quickly review what we need to get done this week.' Ron bangs down the cleaver and the table judders under its force. Motes of flesh flicker out towards Jo and she closes her eyes. When she opens them, Mo's watching her with what is hopefully concern but might equally be the beginnings of a juicy new story for Phyllis to chop down into bite-sized morsels of gossip later.

'Dad said, in terms of new ordering, we should stick to the normal quantities for a bit.' Her voice rises to turn it into a question she hadn't intended, but Ron ignores it and Mo merely nods. Now's the time. She pulls herself as tall as she can, adjusts her stance slightly. Courtroom tricks.

'I won't be a second; just need to get something from my coat.' Not necessarily how it goes in the courtroom.

When they see the paper and the Blu-Tack, Ron rolls his eyes and Mo's brow furrows.

Jo unfolds the chart, laying it on the edge of the table. That's not going to work – blood is pooling, fluid islands on the silver sheen. It's fine. She can just hold it up.

'So, I've been doing some thinking, and some planning. We know we need to change some things to keep ahead of the likes of Lidl.' Ron harrumphs and Jo ignores him.

The chart has the next twelve weeks marked on it, and next to them, a suggestion of what new activity might be introduced each week.

'I'm obviously not expecting us to do all of this at once. I've spaced it out so that we're trying new things every couple of weeks and we have a chance to track them, see what's working and what isn't.' She peers sideways at the plan she knows backwards. If she says so herself, which she obviously won't, it's pretty solid. She spent hours poring over the accounts Mum sent over.

'There doesn't seem to be a problem with the sorts of things people are buying; it's just that fewer people are coming in.'

'Tell us something we don't know.'

Oh, that's exactly what she intends to do. Jo bites her fingers into her palm and smiles sweetly.

'So. We probably can't sell more to the people who're already coming in, but we could try. We can also do a few things to attract more customers into the shop. All these new people in town these days must be crying out for a butcher's; we just need to figure out what they want.'

It's the bridge that's bringing the people to town. After years of rumours, the extortionate tolls had finally been lifted on the Severn Bridge, a few miles down the road. The cost of commuting plummeted. People lured to Bristol from even bigger cities are moving into the Forest now, encroaching like an army of ants. A forty-five-minute drive through the countryside is nothing if you're used to an hour or more on the Tube. But the incomers have been invading the landscape. If you drive the dual carriageway from here to the next town along you can see the destruction in terms of fields turned into new build 'executive estates'. They can't all be vegetarians. She just needs to work out how to entice them in.

Jo shifts her stance, prepares to continue, but is saved by the shop phone ringing.

Ron nods in its direction. 'Go on, then. You're the boss now.'

Oh, bugger off, Ron.

Jo strides through into the shopfront, grabs the phone. 'Butler's Butcher's, can I help you?'

'Oh, don't you sound professional.'

'Mum!'

'Just wanted to give you a ring, see how your first day's going.'

'It's barely started, to be honest.'

'I thought I'd better give you a call now while you still had time to talk. You'll be busy later when things get going.'

'Fingers crossed, eh?' Jo sighs, shifts the phone to the other ear. 'I'm just showing Mo and Ron my ideas for the next few months, the plan I showed you and Dad.'

'Oh, right.' Jo's mother is great, truly she is. Although she's worried about Jo giving up what she sees as the better life, she hasn't once tried to talk her out of it, not seriously. But now she seems to be straying dangerously close to laughing. 'How's that going?'

'About as well as you'd expect.'

'Yes, well. I think it's nice that you've got these little schemes, love.'

Jo grits her teeth. It's not a 'little scheme'. It's the result of evenings spent calculating, weekends spent at other butcher's observing, of talking to her friends in London about what they'd expect from a butcher. It's the result of years of experience sifting through legal research, analysing and cherry-picking, combined with a lifetime within this shop.

Jo rests her forehead briefly against the white tiles of the wall.

'Yeah. Anyway, I'd better get back to it before Ron hacks the spreadsheet in half with that cleaver of his.' No need to mention the chain mail apron and the sniping.

Only after she's hung up does she realise she hasn't asked how the new house is. 'Full of boxes,' Dad had grunted when she'd asked at the weekend, but he'd sounded happy, that note of worry removed.

Jo pushes back through the plastic. Mo's putting sausages in trays for the window and Ron seems to have moved on to lamb, judging by its size. Or perhaps it's the corpse of someone who dared disagree with him.

'Shall we take a quick look at the rest of this plan, then?'

Neither of them stops.

'Need to get these into the window, I do, then get the shop opened. Tell us another time, is it, maybe, love?'

Two can play at that game. 'I know what, I'll stick the plan up here and then you can look at it when you've got a minute.' She flattens it against the wall right beside the chopping bench. The colour codes of the new ideas flash out at her: ready meals, for the new commuters who want to pretend they're eating more healthily than a takeaway and that they're supporting the local community; deliveries to local restaurants and pubs – surely it would be a draw, to be able to say that all their meat is locally sourced?

Out on the shop floor, the bell jangles and Jo snaps out of it.

'Kirsty!'

'All right, Jo?' Kirsty shivers just inside the doorway, her parka still zipped up tight round her face. She's always been Liam's wife rather than Jo's friend, but maybe that'll change now Jo's here permanently. Kirsty's one of those people who's warm to everyone, impossible not to like.

'I'm due on the tills in five minutes, but I thought I'd stick my head in and wish you luck. Liam and the girls told me to say good luck, too.'

Jo hugs her. 'What if I cock it up?' It's the sort of thing she'd usually say to Liam, not Kirsty, but he's not here and she is.

'In what way could you possibly cock this up? Your name's literally on the sign outside the door. I'm surprised it's taken you this long to come back, be honest with you.'

Jo's limbs are limp with relief. 'Really?'

'Yeah, course. God, if my parents owned a shop, I'd be all over it.'

Jo half-laughs, no mirth in it. 'Li doesn't necessarily seem to agree.' She wants to ask Kirsty: 'Did I imagine it or is Liam a bit off with me?' But though she could ask Liam this about Kirsty, the invisible hierarchies of loyalty prevent the question flowing in the other direction.

Kirsty shakes her head. Her own laugh, when it comes, is genuine. 'You know Liam. Not the most obviously excited by things.' She pulls her gloves back on. 'He's got a ton on at the moment – we both have. It's never-ending with the kids' activities, and we're both flat out at work. But we'll see you later, yeah? I've texted round; think a fair few are coming out.' She waves at Jo and is gone, striding up the street.

Kirsty always knew who she was and what life meant for her. She'd started at the Co-op when she finished school, married Liam a few years later, and all her family

75

still live nearby. It can't harm, to be so sure of where you're going to live your life that there's no room for doubt or mistakes. Choice isn't necessarily always helpful.

Mo meanders back over to her. 'You kipping at Liam and Kirsty's at the moment?'

'No.' Jo rubs a finger on the cold surface in front of her, grateful to be released from her thoughts. 'I did for the first few nights but I've moved a bit further out now. I'm renting a room from a woman called Tessa Price.'

'Oh aye, the farrier?' Mo's face sharpens with interest. 'I didn't know she took in lodgers. Proper loner she is, by all accounts. She'll walk past you in the street and you won't even get the time of day. Susan Fowler, she has her horses done by that Miss Price and she says she's just a bit shy, but I think it's more than that. You can be shy without being rude; look at our Ron.'

Jo stares at Mo. But Mo's face is relaxed, unironic. She turns back towards the deli counter as if she's a magician prepping a fake prop before the show starts.

Jo goes through to the back room.

'Where did the jointed beef go? I'll put some of it out front, shall I?'

'Social club finished, then?' Ron doesn't look up.

Oh, for God's sake.

'Not if I can help it. The more people in here, the merrier.'

A childhood memory: leaving the house in the dark

all through winter, sitting quietly with a book in that corner over there while Dad was out at the market and Mum got on with the prep with Mo, before walking Jo to school. Once she was secondary school age, she waited for Liam out on the counter. He cycled from home but always detoured down the high street and always, always stopped by the shop to pick her up – and to pick up the bacon roll Mum insisted he have.

The shop was always buzzing; kids would nip in for a bacon sarnie on the way to school – though the others had to pay for them – and, they suspected, the teachers must have been tipped off because from time to time you'd see one of those in the queue, too. That's what they need again – people stopping off on their way to school and work, a steady stream of bacon sarnies, fading into the Phyllises of this world with their pound of mince, and culminating in the new people in the new houses nipping in for their more-authentic-than-Waitrose ready meals at the end of the day.

Jo had learned a lot about human behaviour during her barrister training and still more in the years since she qualified. What she needs is a community hub again, like the one she remembers from her childhood. And that's where the plan comes in.

'You want to lose that watch in here.' Ron hasn't stopped jointing. Another whack of the cleaver and more detritus flecks across Jo's wrist onto the leather of the strap. Ron raises his eyes and looks at her for the first time. 'It'll get ruined.'

Her shoulders are aching, her back's already sore from all the standing up and her brain is heavy with all the things she's not saying. But the shop is opening under the Butler name, and that's down to her.

As first days go, it was no tougher than being in court, but Ron's going to be a constant needler and it uses up bandwidth she needs for the actual shop.

There are no cooking smells when Jo goes through into the cottage's kitchen, no sign of Tessa. Jo, proving her own point about ready meals, heats up a curry she'd nabbed in the Co-op. She'll do better next time. But tonight's not about fine dining. There's just about time to scarf down the curry and then a quick shower to get rid of the worst flecks of dead animal before it's time to go out again. Tonight's about old friends, about catching up with the people who form the threads of this new future she's weaving from the past.

Chapter Eight

EVERY TIME JO PUSHES OPEN a door here, she's a different age. At the shop, she's a little kid; in Liam and Kirsty's front room she's twenty-two, the year they moved in. As she enters the Star tonight, she's seventeen again. Slightly stale booze and sweat mingle with sharp, fresh notes of aftershave and hope. The pub's packed, rounded vowels dodgem off each other, the urgent joy of it all barrelling out through the door and calling Jo in.

'Butler! Over here!'

She squeezes her way through to Liam and the others over in their usual corner, momentarily shy. Everyone's in the seats they've pretty much always sat in and the evening stretches ahead, every inch of it warm and familiar. Jo wants to hug it. She'll settle for hugging the people.

There are six of them out tonight. Matt Hay's up and

lifting her off her feet before she's all the way there. He swings her like they were still kids, plonks her down at the edge of the table.

'Watch my glass!' Liam's arm curls protectively.

'Don't worry, mate. I'd never do that to a pint.' Matt winks, and the Ready Brek glow surrounding Jo expands in the warm seas of the call-and-answer.

'Anyone need a drink?'

Kirsty scooches up on the bench seat, pats the space she's cleared. 'You all right with red? We've got a bottle in.'

The glass she hands over is full to the brim and Jo slurps it down as if it was the Ribena they were all raised on.

'Perfect – cheers. I'll get the next one.' Pretty much the only correct townie cliché about the countryside is this one: the drinks are so much cheaper, you don't get that panicked feeling when it's time for a round. A memory flashes in, of a morning in chambers just around the time she decided to leave. She'd been making polite conversation with one of the senior counsel, who'd told her keenly how 'smashing' it had been to try a 'rather decent bottle of red from Sainsbury's, of all places' given to him by his daughter's father-in-law. Jo very much got the impression that the father-in-law wouldn't be invited for dinner a second time. The senior counsel would die a death in this pub.

'It's mobbed in here! I thought we'd be all right on a Thursday.'

Matt, perched sideways beside Liam, raises his pint. 'Pay day, ent it?'

Jo sinks into the bench, chinks her glass against Kirsty's. 'Good point.'

80

Matt leans in, elbows on the table, voice slightly raised above the hubbub.

'What brought you back then, Butler? Thought we'd lost you to the bright lights for good.'

They'd had a vague thing years ago, she and Matt. There was never anything proper between them, but she's kept a soft spot for him in that way you do when someone's part of your past. He's a decent bloke, doesn't bother with a question unless he wants the answer, and so she answers instinctively, honestly.

'London, the job – they weren't what I expected, I suppose.'

'What, earning a steady wage without breaking your back for it?' But Matt's face is open, creased with a smile. This is good-natured teasing, proof of belonging, and Jo leans back against the hard wood of the bench.

'It wasn't that steady yet. Fair point, though. I suppose I just thought I'd be making more of a difference than I actually was.'

'I thought you went off to be a lawyer?'

On Jo's other side, Kirsty's chatting to Matt's new girlfriend about the best place to park for shopping in Cheltenham. Jo hasn't met any of Matt's girlfriends since he split up with Shannon a while ago, which to be honest wasn't the biggest loss.

'I did go off to be a lawyer. But it wasn't exactly what I'd hoped for, in the end.'

'What, a lawyer not making a difference? What a shocker.'

When they were at school Jo got teased all the time:

for her endless questions, for bringing a book to the pub, for enjoying homework – well, for seeing a purpose to homework, let's not stretch things. It was all right that she was a bit different, a bit of a bookish weirdo, because she had Liam, and the shop, and those things normalised her, lent her the currency for entry into a group of warm-hearted mates. She wasn't exactly like them, but they didn't care that much, if they ever thought about it. She was the overthinker, not them. They just teased her about it, but she welcomed it. You only teased your friends.

Nothing's changed in the dynamic. Why would it? The teasing is comforting, but at the same time Jo squirms a bit at Matt's casual dismissal of the career she's spent the best part of a decade nurturing, even if she's left it behind. It's like putting on a coat and realising it doesn't fit exactly like it used to because you've grown and the coat hasn't.

'There's *some* making a difference. Right before Christmas, I got to sort out a case for an old lady who lived on her own and had slipped in the supermarket. It turned out the supermarket had mopped up a spillage and forgotten to put a "wet floor" sign out there. It was only a small mistake on their part, but it was affecting everything my client – the woman – could or couldn't do. The money we got from the claim will go towards a cleaner and someone to come in and check she's OK.'

Jo leans forward, eyes glowing.

'I think the thing that actually helped the most was the fact that she'd been listened to, that there was a real problem and she wasn't just getting old, you know? You could tell, even when her daughter first brought her in, that they were beginning to wonder whether this was the start of her not being able to live on her own, whether her quality of life was under threat. It's not fair, is it, that stuff? Some muppet in Morrisons is too hungover to put out the "wet floor" sign, and suddenly you're afraid to call your kids because they might start clearing their throats awkwardly and bringing up nursing homes.'

She leans back and Matt leans back with her.

'Days like that, cases like that – they were great. And during my pupillage – my training, when I was apprenticed to a more senior lawyer – I got to be involved with more cases where you could really see the difference you make. But once I finished training and had to start building my own workload, it was a game of snakes and ladders; back to the bottom, where the best you could hope for was an unsteady old lady.'

'So you thought, stuff that, best come and slum it back down here with the likes of us?' Matt's face is sympathetic but there's a dog-whistle-sharp note of impatience in his tone now, the sense that she didn't know how lucky she had it. 'You haven't given up on it too soon? All jobs are a bit shit sometimes.'

'It's not that it was a bad job. It was a great job in lots of ways. It's just . . . well, look, here's the sort of stuff I mostly had to work on. The last case I was given, it was this bloke up in Nottingham. He'd ordered a pizza and it'd arrived late and cold. So he was suing the pizza company.'

'You're having me on.'

'I wish I was.'

'Who the hell's got money to bother with suing for a pizza?'

'Well, exactly. And there's literally nothing in it for me – no job satisfaction, but no money either. Just the cost of the trip to Nottingham would've wiped out most of my fee.' Jo subsides into her wine, exhausted from trying to explain herself, from being both selves at once.

Matt half-laughs, a pint glass suspended on its way to his lips. 'Don't think work's what any of us expected, tell you the truth, pizza scammers or not. I'm sorry it didn't work out for you, though, mate.'

'D'you know what, though? I'm genuinely so excited to be back in the shop. I'm sort of amazed I didn't think of it sooner.'

Matt chortles, and the warmth of the pub, of the evening, washes over Jo again and rinses out some of the slight off-taste that's starting to curdle.

'*I'm* not blimming surprised you didn't do it sooner. Remember that time in Biology, when we got to dissect the lamb's heart? You went all wobbly and Li here had to get you outside before you chundered. Least likely butcher's kid in the Forest, you were. Not like your Gary, sneaking that pig's eye into school to scare the girls with. Freaked out half the boys too, he did.'

Jo opens her mouth, but there's no point, and she shuts it again. If she starts wanging on about legacies and coming home to save family memories and a community, he'll probably tip that pint over her for her affectations, and nobody'd blame him.

'Where're you actually living now? Your old man sold the house when they packed up, didn't he?'

Jo winces. It's stupid but it's still hard to hear it voiced.

'Yeah – they needed the money to buy somewhere near Gary. I'm out your mum and dad's way, actually – not far from Pillowell – just while I figure things out. It's a room in a cottage owned by Tessa Price – d'you know her?' Jo still hasn't told anyone, not even Liam, about Mum and Dad making this a trial. The countdown clock is only in her head, not anyone else's, and it's better that way. Simpler.

'The farrier? Aye, I know who you mean all right. Keeps herself to herself, don't she?'

'What do you mean?'

Matt leans back and nearly topples over. Liam has been half-listening, half-watching the teenagers at the next table who're trying to hiccup a ten-pence piece into an empty glass using a five-pence piece as leverage. Now he pulls Matt upright, laughing.

'Turn the chair round, you pillock!'

Matt flicks him the casual V-sign, continues. 'She's been out there for years now, built a forge in the back of the garden. D'you remember, Li?'

But Liam snaps shut, looks hard the other way. Jo glances at Kirsty, but she's still chatting to Matt's new woman. They've moved on to the cost of school trips, so presumably this woman has kids too. She's not anyone Jo recognises from school; must be from the other side of the Forest.

'The dad died and the mum moved back to the Valleys

a good while ago now. She stayed on, Miss Price, took over the farrier work from Ern when he retired. Decent enough farrier, I think, but she ent friendly like Ern. Nobody knows her, not really.' Matt tilts back in his seat again and Liam cuffs him.

'Crikey-o, Hay, if you're going to keep doing it at least turn your seat around before you land on your arse.'

'Is that what's in those sheds at the back, behind the garden wall? Her blacksmithing stuff?'

Matt cuffs Liam back and Cossack-squats to spin his chair the right way round.

'Yeah, that'd be it. She went away for a few years – maybe about the same sort of time you did? A bit later, maybe. She hasn't been back long. Keeps herself even more to herself than usual, apparently. Dad was talking to them up at the riding centre and even getting her to come out for the shoeing cycle can be a struggle sometimes.'

In London, Jo would spook herself sometimes by wondering how long it would take for someone to realise she was missing. A good few days, probably. If her flatmates were away for the weekend, if work assumed she was travelling for a case somewhere . . . long enough for things to get pretty dire. Here you'd be hard pushed to go ten minutes, even if you were basically a recluse. People have time and space to observe things. When the heartbeat of a community is steady, reliant on everyone doing what they always do, a skipped beat is noticed sooner. Jo had never been one of those who welcomed the anonymity of London. She'd missed the web of noticers, missed being woven into a life that held her close. It's useful to know she's not the only one who finds Tessa quiet; it ebbs the latent anxiety.

Matt reaches forward and swoops his pint off the table in a practised move. 'What's she like to live with, then?'

The sigh's out before she can stop it.

'That bad, eh?'

'Oh, I don't know. I'm being unfair, probably.'

'Well, you haven't said anything yet, Butler, so we don't know, do we?'

'Fair enough. It's . . . oh, I dunno. Maybe it's weird living with a complete stranger. She's just really hard to make any sort of contact with.'

'You're making her sound like an alien.' Matt crooks his middle finger.

'Not quite that bad, but not far off. It's strange, you know? And we're cramped in on top of each other, so it feels odd not to at least try and talk.'

'Those old cottages ent never going to be massive, are they? Used to be an old sheep badger lived there, according to our dad. Wouldn't have needed much space.' Matt shrugs into his pint, then tips the glass all the way up, peering at Liam through it. 'Oi, Li! This one's empty. Your round, butty.'

Jo waits. He'll be finished with this in a minute and then she can go on. She's having to explain things more than expected, has lost the easy elastic shorthand that existed when she lived here before, the years away having worn the thread thin.

'Yeah, I get that. But she seems to spend tons of time in her room and, I dunno, it seems strange in a grown woman. Teenagers do that, right? Not women in their forties.' Kirsty will back Jo up here. 'I mean, how much time d'you spend alone in your room, Kirst?'

'Chance'd be a fine thing.' Kirsty winks at Liam, holds out the empty wine bottle. 'Get us another of these while you're up there, love.'

Liam swats away Jo's proffered tenner, not quite looking at her. 'You get the next one.'

'What's she like when she *is* there, this Tessa?' Kirsty's interested now, too.

Jo cradles her glass. It feels like failure to admit this next bit in front of her oldest friends. She wants the picture of being home to be glossy, not smeared with her problematic housemate.

'Bit difficult to talk to, if I'm honest. She'll never start a conversation about anything and it's as if there's ice in the room when she talks. She makes me afraid I'm about to say something really stupid.'

'Not everyone finds it easy to talk to strangers.' Kirsty looks as if she knows this to be a theoretical truth but can't actually imagine what's hard about it.

'No, I get that, I totally do. But look. There's this other thing.' Now Jo's started, she can't stop.

'Spit it out.'

'It's hard to describe, really. So, we'll be talking – well, I'll be talking – and she'll sort of disappear.'

88

'What d'you mean? Some sort of magic trick?'

Liam's back. He edges the pint towards Matt, puts the new bottle of red on the table.

'No, nothing that exciting. It's like I'm talking to a blank wall all of a sudden. I mean, she's not the most demonstrative person to start with. But she really does seem to sort of switch off. If you look at her, it's like there's nobody in there. And then thirty seconds later she'll be absolutely fine and back in the conversation.'

It's such a fleeting thing that when it first happened, Jo had assumed Tessa had remembered something else she needed to do and was making a quick mental note. But it happens nearly every time they talk. Sometimes it's as if Tessa will catch herself – she gives a quick start, as if she's surprised herself to be back, and her focus on Jo will intensify, until Jo's almost nervous that she'll crack under the weight of it.

'Huh. That *is* weird.' Kirsty shrugs.

'Right?' But before she can say any more, Matt's telling a raucous story about someone they all seem to know well, and they're laughing, pressing for more details. Jo sits back, sips her wine, the sense of the coat not fitting upon her again. It's great to be back, it is. But it's not going to be as straightforward as she thought.

Chapter Nine

TESSA'S STUCK. SHE'D TAKEN A nap, trying to outrun this unstoppable need for sleep, but she'd been slammed out of it by a noise downstairs. Now she's stuck, proper stuck. She can't drift backwards into sleep, but she can't come all the way out of it, either. Her arms, her legs – they're dead weights, pinning her to the bed.

She's in her bedroom, in her bed. This is certain. But her dream has crept up through sleep with her, is invading her. It's a memory, as her dreams so often are. A haunting. So vivid and lucid that it may as well have happened yesterday.

She's five again. Bamps has come to collect her for her big birthday trip out.

Bethan toddles up behind Tessa with a wooden spoon and a face on her the size of the Sugar Loaf. Having a little sister is a pain and today, just today, Tessa won't have one. She kneels down as if to kiss Bethan. But when Bethan gets close enough ('Me go too!'), Tessa whispers so the grown-ups can't hear, 'You're not coming because I'm the favourite!'

Bethan's little face crumples like an empty chip wrapper and the wailing ramps up so much Mrs Pugh'll be round in a minute to 'see if everything's all right', lips pursed, eyes lit for gossip.

Tessa pulls open the passenger door of the Cortina and hops in. She'll bring Bethan back a jam doughnut, that'll make up for it.

'All the way to Cardiff, Bamps!'

Bamps smiles, pats her knee, but his eyes are on the mirror, wiggling the car backwards and forward where it's parked between two others. That's all right, Tessa can explain the whole day to him.

'Nanna says we'll take the bus from the end of your road and then we'll need a cup of tea and a pick-me-up so I can have the biggest jam doughnut I can ever, ever find in the market, and after that Nanna says we can go shopping for my birthday present and then—'

But Tessa doesn't get to tell Bamps about the stop-off for chips and a pie after they've chosen her present, about how maybe after that they could go to the pound shop and she could find something for Bethan with one of her birthday pounds as being left behind isn't much fun even when it's fair, because there's a thud like he's hit next door's cat. At the same time the front door slams open, which is a thing Tessa didn't even know doors could do, and Mam comes barrelling out, her face all scrunched up and screamy, and Bamps has yanked

91

on the little brake with a squeal that might have been the brake or might have been him, and he's out of the car, not even looking to see what's coming, and through the open door Tessa can hear Mam and she's screaming, 'Get her get her get her' and Tessa's not sure whether she should get out of the car to see what Mam's on about or be a Good Girl and stay put, but then Bamps gets back in and without even shutting his door he's taken off the little brake and he's squeezing the Cortina forward, forward, so gently it's like the car's tiptoeing, and terror rolls in raindrops down his cheeks, and all the time he says nothing, nothing. It's like Tessa isn't even here, or no, like Bamps isn't here even though his body still is, and she can't tell where he's gone because when she looks out of the window again at Mam it's like she's in a Charlie Chaplin movie too, only this one isn't funny, it's all too silent because just like that Mam's stopped screaming.

Tessa's scared now, all thoughts of doughnuts gone, and she curls up on the bouncy plastic seat and puts her thumb in her mouth, which is something she hasn't done since she was a tiny, tiny babby, smaller than even Bethan is now.

Bethan.

Mam's on the phone now, standing in the hallway with the cord pulled long and tight so she's really outside too and her free hand is pointing, waving at Bamps, a desperate movement that says: Save her. Save her now.

*   *   *

Tessa's caught, every muscle, every bone baptised in fear and shame. *Don't make me replay it.* But the memory-dream marches on.

Sirens. Two of them, tripping over each other as they race faster and closer. The noise floods into the car, drowning out the dragon flames of Mam's screams, pushing inside Tessa, banging, clanging, louder, nearer.

They take over the whole house, the whole terrace, and Tessa's breath comes patchy and hard. Putting her hands over her ears doesn't make it go away, doesn't make it change to the moving-past-you music. Instead, it does something she's never heard before. It stops.

The sirens stop right outside the house.

Tessa shudders forward, back into herself, and the room reveals its shapes again. She grabs a corner of the sheet, pushes her face into it with both hands and scrubs off the sweat. Breath comes in jolty gasps, regulating around the remnants of the images.

Tessa killed her sister. Nanna says so to Mam, to Dad, to Mrs Pugh two doors down, to anyone who'd listen, really. 'It wasn't our Gwyn's fault. Nothing he could have done, see. Distracted, he was, by our Tessa. Proper little chatterbox she was, chopsing away even when he told her to hush up a minute so that he could concentrate. Oh, no, not a hope she'd listen. On she went, on and on, and Gwyn didn't have a chance, did he? Caught completely off guard, he was. I'll be honest with you, our Tessa had a lot to do with it, not that you should blame an innocent child.'

But Tessa knows that last bit was tacked on so that the God Nanna prays to every Sunday in chapel isn't cross. It is Tessa's fault, hers alone. If she didn't talk so much, then Bethan would still be alive. Bamps would've seen Bethan dart out behind the car, desperate to go to Cardiff with them, and he'd have stamped on the brakes, stopped in time.

Downstairs the door slams again, and Tessa lies back on the pillows, spent, her breath still not hers. She can't escape it. It's lodged in there, and it will come again. All the bad memories, playing one after another. Nothing will make them stop.

Chapter Ten

ASIDE FROM THAT BRIEF BEWILDERING moment every day when she wakes up and the bed's facing the wrong way in the room, Jo's starting to feel like she lives here. It's nearly her third week back home. The shop seems to be going fine; revenues are consistent with this time last year. But the deadline hovers, hawk-like, and Sundays are an empty, yawning opportunity to fret. She should go for a walk in the forest, get out among the winter-dredged branches. But she needs company, the woods filling otherwise with her own thoughts.

When Jo arrives at Liam's, his van's open and half the kit's laid out like a game of Operation on the driveway, the rest of the space taken up by the skip that has been there since she first got back.

Kirsty opens the door in her supermarket uniform, minus the tabard – black top, black jeans, one hand reaching for the collar of a bounding black lab. Behind her, from the front room, comes the tinny squawk of a kids' TV presenter.

'*Down*, Ennis. All right, Jo? Didn't know you were coming round. Liam's doing Chlo's room.'

'Yeah, I know. I was at a bit of a loose end so Li said I could come over.' It hadn't exactly been a royal invitation, more a grudging agreement that she might as well come if she wanted, and Jo had had to work hard not to let the doubt shrink her. She must be reading things wrong, knackered from standing up all day in the shop and the effort of biting her tongue around Ron.

'Oh, OK.' Kirsty's barely listening, pulling highlighted hair into a ponytail and stepping into trainers. She pulls on her coat and shouts up the stairs, 'Liam! I'm off now. Jo's here. Rosie needs picking up at twelve, OK?'

Jo makes two cups of tea and goes upstairs, following the extension cable and the noise of the radio, which wind from the landing into the room she slept in a few weeks ago.

'Tea's up!'

Liam, in the far corner of the room, nods at the doorway but doesn't come over. He's got what looks like a massive painter's palette in one hand, a huge trowel in the other.

'All right, Butler? I'm about to do the ceiling. Got to keep going before this plaster goes off.'

Jo slides down in the corner nearest the door, tea swaying. The room smells damply sandy. The beach but without the tang of salt.

'You haven't got a dust sheet down.' The ca... sort of scuffed, faded green, which doesn't look like going to be much enhanced by Liam's promised clump, of plaster.

'Don't matter. That old thing's going in the skip when we're done here. Kirsty's auntie – you remember Jean? – she's redoing her spare room, giving us the carpet from there.'

Jo sips her tea. 'God, I remember sitting in a corner of my room like this with you when we were about seventeen. You'd just started going out with Kirst, and I was trying to get it out of you how much you liked her. And look where it's brought you!'

It's weird to feel shy around Liam. But here the evidence of his life swirls around him, a tornado of jobs and kids' activities and DIY, and Liam at the centre of it, his life that doesn't involve her, so she can barely make him out for the blur.

'Well, that's how it goes, you know.' Liam isn't interested in nostalgia.

Jo wiggles further into the corner. 'Am I all right here?'

'Yeah.' Liam doesn't look. He slides the trowel against the palette, hoists it up. He sweeps the trowel across, distributing the plaster onto the ceiling, and the off-white of the surface turns sandy brown, like a beach with the tide coming in. When the board is emptied of its load, he goes over to a huge plastic bin in the corner and scrapes more mixture onto the board. The ceiling turns gradually brown, a coffee stain spreading order from the chaos, and Jo cradles her mug, soothed by the

the actions. Every now and again Liam
edge of the ceiling and take a quick sip
always turned upwards, Michelangelo
eatshirt and splattered cargo trousers,
xt move.

Liam's still recognisably himself, but he's someone else
too. It's like watching a travel show about your home
town and discovering a whole new street you didn't
know existed.

When the ceiling's all brown, the tide of plaster fully
in, Liam scrapes off the trowel onto the board and puts
them both down beside the giant mixer.

'Got the time?'

Jo checks her watch. 'Eleven forty-eight. What time
do you need to go to get Rosie?'

'About now.' He leaves the room and, after a startled
moment, Jo leaves too, her day gaping in front of her
again.

'Can I come along for the ride?' She's fast behind him,
heart racing, but Liam hardly glances her way.

'Yeah, if you want. Better take your car, then – more
room.' He sticks his head into the front room, shrugging
on his coat. 'Chlo, time to go and get your sister.'

Town's pretty quiet on a Sunday, and they're too late
for any church-goers. Liam glances at Jo as they drive
past the shop.

'Feel like it's yours yet?'

She leaps on it, pathetically grateful for the conversation opener.

'Nah, not yet. Still keep waiting for Dad to come in,

tell me to get away from the knives before I do myself damage.'

Liam nods. They drive a while longer, Chloe humming to herself in the back seat.

Liam sits forward. 'You're going the long way round.'

Bugger. He'd noticed.

He knows why, too. 'They moved in yet, the new people?'

'Yeah, a couple of weeks ago. Some young family from Cheltenham, Mum said, nipping in quickly before house prices keep going nuts.'

Liam shifts slightly at the note of bitterness and Jo moves to defend it.

'I know it's silly. I don't know . . . I just feel abandoned or something, like Mum and Dad couldn't wait to get to the coast. And yet at the same time they're on the phone constantly. It feels like they're waiting for me to stuff up the shop so that they can go back to whoever their second buyer was and let them have it after all. I wish they'd stop treating me like a little kid.'

Liam snorts.

'What?'

'Well, you're acting a bit like a little kid, aren't you, all this talk of being abandoned?' His voice is hardened plaster. 'Brenda and Jim don't abandon people. You should know that. I know that.'

Jo's grip tightens on the steering wheel, her cheeks hot.

* * *

They were twelve. It was their second year at the comp, spring time. The new houses hadn't yet encroached on the fields opposite and the lambs were in full frolic. Jo had come down to breakfast, belting down the stairs so she could go and see if any more lambs had been born overnight.

Mum and Dad were murmuring in the hallway, tucked round out of sight of the kitchen. That in itself was weird – Dad was normally up and gone way before Jo came down.

'. . . phone someone, just for a word, like . . .'

'. . . want to keep him here, mind; no knowing what they'll do . . .'

'. . . definitely no other family – no idea who his father is.'

Mum's arms were folded tight across her apron, the frown lines deep on her forehead.

Jo came quietly down the rest of the stairs into the kitchen, where there was a second surprise. Liam was sitting at the kitchen table.

'You're in my seat! You'd better not be eating my muesli.' Jo had just discovered muesli and it was the best thing ever. Gary mocked her, cheerfully sticking with his Crunchy Nut Cornflakes.

'Jo!' Mum's retort came from right behind Jo – they must have followed her into the kitchen – and she jumped.

'I was joking! Liam knows that.' Jo plonked down in Dad's empty place and pulled the muesli and a bowl towards her.

'Yes, well.' Mum sounded dead strange today. 'Liam's going to be staying here for a few days, so be kinder, please.'

'Staying here?' Jo rounded on Liam, spluttering muesli. 'You could have told me! Where's your mum?'

Mum and Dad exchanged glances, and Liam said nothing, his head down, his spoon idle in the bowl (Crunchy Nut Cornflakes, thank goodness).

'She's had to go away for a few days. Liam's going to stay with us until she's back.'

Jo sits upright, peers ahead at the road. It's hard to ask the next question with any pretence at it being casual. 'Speaking of parents, how's your mum doing?'

Debbie continued to be a presence in the town, but a faded one. Mum would mention her from time to time, but only in much the same way she discussed how snarled up the traffic got down by the crossroads, just part of the mosaic of home town life.

'Oh, you know. Up and down.' Liam checks back at Chloe, lowers his voice. Kirsty's on at me to take the kids over, thinks it'll help, but you can never tell how she'll be and she scares 'em sometimes.'

Kirsty's always understood Liam's mum, ever since they were teenagers and Liam and Kirsty had been together only a few months.

Jo was in the shop in her second term of sixth form, avoiding an essay crisis. She was pretending to sort out the display in the shop window but actually indulging in visual gossip, staring out into the street and clocking the people walking past and with whom.

Liam's mum came weaving up the street, muttering to herself. Jo steeled herself to go and call for Mum. Sometimes if you brought Debbie in, gave her a cup of tea and listened to her for five minutes, it calmed her down.

Just as she turned, a peripheral movement had stopped her. Kirsty came out of Woolies and approached Debbie, her head bent towards the older woman's, her hand just at Debbie's elbow but not touching it. Jo stood transfixed as Kirsty, leaning forward to protect Debbie from too many prying eyes (like Jo's own; the irony was not lost), sat Debbie down on the bench beside the war memorial and let Debbie run herself out. Only when the hand gestures subsided and the pace of Debbie's muttering slowed did Kirsty look around. Jo half-ran, half-walked out of the shop, pretended to bump into her.

'Liam's still at work,' she told Kirsty, the answer to a question Kirsty hadn't needed to ask. 'I think Mum and Dad have got a key to her place, though.'

Kirsty nodded, turned to Debbie. 'What do you think, Mrs Harris? Would you like to go home, or are you having a bit of a wander?'

Debbie muttered something unintelligible, but Kirsty nodded again, apparently satisfied. 'She's going to stay out for a bit. I think she'll be OK now.' She smiled at Debbie, who shuffled off in the direction of the news-agents.

Jo rocked back on her heels. 'That was amazing. Did Liam tell you how to deal with her?'

'What?' Kirsty looked almost shocked at the idea and Jo realised, blushing at her own idiocy, that Liam and Kirsty were hardly spending their time talking calming strategies for his erratic mother. 'No, but my nan gets like that sometimes. Just need a bit of company, people do.'

'She still in the flat?'

'Yeah.' He glances in the wing mirror and Jo takes her cue, turns off for the playing field.

Liam twists round. 'Right, Chlo. Time to look for your sister.' Somewhere in the haze of mud and small girls is one that belongs to Liam. There's more to be said, but it's not going to happen now.

Chapter Eleven

T ESSA'S WEARING TWO JUMPERS AT a time these days, but her breath's still frosting the air, as if she had the cash for a smoking habit. If Marnie were here, she'd think it funny. But it isn't. Jo's rent isn't enough to make up the shortfall from not working the full load, and though it should have been obvious, the bills have increased now that there are two of them living there. The electricity's more than double what it had been, and even with Jo paying half, the sums just aren't working.

It's getting hopeless. The coal's all gone and the heating's only on in the evenings when Jo's home.

She sits and stares at the stack of bills tucked under the place mats on the table. There's a crunch of gravel as someone pulls into the driveway and Tessa flinches, steadies herself against the table.

There's a rap on the window. It's that Liam kid. Of

all the people, he has to be friends with her lodger. Tessa pinches her eyes tightly, takes a deep breath and walks over to the back door, her breath pluming out in front. She has nothing to say and the more she says, the riskier things become anyway, so she opens the door, looks at him.

'Jo asked me to bring this over.' Liam is careful, looking nowhere, his gestures small as he opens the van door and pulls out the branch inside. 'It's no good to us; she thought you might be able to use it.'

He's already told her more than he meant to, you can see by the hunch in his shoulders. It's a good, solid piece of beech. Tessa should be grateful. But the old memory is still there.

'Where did it come from?'

Liam knows what she's really asking. He hunches further over, and Tessa wonders whether Jo knows what he used to get up to with that mother of his. 'Our drive. Lopped off from the tree. It belonged to me.'

He's basting in shame; there's no reason not to believe him, and it is freezing. The wood will be proper useful. Tessa wraps her arms around herself, nods.

'Look. I'll put it round here.' Liam's dropped the end of the branch now. 'It's yours if you can use it.'

He's round the corner and delving into the van again, this time for a series of planks.

'I had these for the house but it turns out I don't need 'em all. Jo said something about bookshelves?' He almost smiles. 'Nobody's got enough shelving for all them books she lugs with her.'

Then before Tessa's found the words, he's off again, the gravel crunching beneath the van tyres.

Tessa stares after him. His actions are hard to square with the Liam who has crystallised in her mind over decades. She starts out towards the forge but stops halfway up the garden path. The forge is the worst place for thoughts of Liam as a small kid. It'll bring on another attack, that's for sure.

A drive might help. Driving seems to be OK, for the most part. Sometimes she gets home without remembering any part of the journey, but there's something steadying about the concentration it takes, which should keep her mind off things, keep her safe.

She'll go to Forest Traders, pick up nails to go with the shelves. The brackets she can make, they don't need to cost anything, and the nails shouldn't be too bad.

The best way from here to the traders is through the heart of the Forest. Before long, trees lean forward, swallow up the car along with the persisting light, and soon it's like driving in twilight even though the clock on the dash says 11 a.m. It soothes Tessa. The road is quiet; the odd car passes but it's only locals this time of year, the tourists that litter the soft-cambered lanes deterred by the fine drizzle and the gloom.

Green signs loom to Tessa's right, signalling the car park into the sculpture trail that attracts so many when the summer's at its peak.

She avoids this place during peak season, when the thickets of crowds are too unreliable, every chance interaction a potential threat that might send her to the

106

ground. Truth be told, she hasn't been out in the forest at all since she's moved back from Bristol. It scares her. Not the trees themselves, though their interdependence has always seemed incomprehensible, destined for trouble. But the unpredictability of this dense, unknowable landscape. A deer bounding across her path, a wild boar crashing out of the undergrowth, the hoarse scolding of rooks as she neared a nest – any of these might cause a shock, and a shock might cause a collapse. Though it would last only seconds, usually, the paths are too dippy, the terrain too unreliable for Tessa to be certain she wouldn't inflict worse injury. The forest is closed off.

All the same, she slows down as she passes the turning, allows herself a brief look. Somewhere up there is the stained-glass window that hangs proud and square in an avenue of pines. She took Marnie up to see it once, near the beginning. It had been raining but they were huddled together in the bright, tight first months of their relationship where there was no room for anything bad, when even fat drops of rain were something to be delighted about. Marnie had stood right underneath the huge glass structure, hood down, palms up in supplication to the hard, unfriendly pellets trying out hail for size. Her hair, those crazy dark curls, stuck to her cheeks and rivulets formed, puddling into the crook of her neck. She had thrown her head back and laughed, the noise sending the crows cawing up into the endless treetops, and Tessa had laughed too, fighting the warning fizzing in her brain, unbelieving still that she got to be with this woman who found the joy in every possible moment.

There's no point visiting the stained glass window today. It would be too risky, and there's certainly no joy to be found there now. Tessa keeps driving, collects the nails and turns around to come back, committed against her will. The shelving that Liam dropped off is a splinter, an obligation; a reminder that her life rubs up against that of another person now. Since the split with Marnie, Tessa has kept herself as free of company as she can, and she's withered to fit the space.

It's only shelves.

But it's not. It's thinking about someone else, adapting her space to someone else's needs. Tessa grips the wheel, stares straight ahead, doing her best to keep her breathing regular.

It's letting someone else in, even a lodger. It's risking more collapses and whatever that means for the future.

Up ahead a short, fierce shout breaks into the air, and a car twists round the bend, coming straight towards her on the wrong side of the damn road.

Tessa yelps and for a moment her body won't respond, every muscle limp and useless. It's over in a second and she yanks the wheel round, climbing up onto the verge. The angle's steep and she bites her lip hard. Got to focus. Got to stay level. If the van tips, it won't take much to ignite the propane tank, and then they're all goners.

She bashes into a thick elbow of hawthorn and scrapes along it until she can steer slowly back down the verge, righting the van, her breath ragged. That was close, too close. The shock of the situation melts into her limbs and she folds forward over the steering wheel.

'Oh my goodness! Are you all right?'

The window of the van fills with a concerned face in a riding hat, one hand on a pair of reins. Tessa comes back into herself, pushes back a bit in the seat so that she can see the horse. Not one she looks after, but its breath is soothing nonetheless.

'Yeah. Fine, thanks.' The response is automatic, meaningless. She's very, very far from all right.

Her own breath is ragged and she digs her nails hard into her legs through her jeans. If she loses it here, this woman will cart her off to hospital.

'I'm so sorry. Some idiot came roaring up behind me, scared the horse half to death. She reared, and the stupid driver accelerated and took off just as you came up round the bend. I thought we were all goners.'

The rider is rattled, but she's enjoying the self-righteous indignation too, needing nothing but an audience now everyone's OK.

'But you're all right? You're sure?'

'I am, honest.' All Tessa needs now is to be alone.

(All Tessa really needs now is Marnie. That firm, warm hand in hers. The bubble of levity. Someone who cares. But it's impossible.)

She waits until the rider has clattered off, relief written all over her, then rests her forehead against the steering wheel.

Driving is everything out here, where buses are rarer

than minding your own business, and the entire mobile forge is packed into the van. Without that, even the work she's been able to hang onto will be out of reach.

She's been making life smaller and smaller, folding it away until it's manageable, but the truth is, it's not working. She can pretend all she likes, but that nearly ended in disaster.

Chapter Twelve

RON'S OUT, SO JO CAN finally get into the cold room. There's so much wrong with this. It's her old room. But it's true, the only reason she's able to stock check without Ron sighing dramatically and making un-sotto voce comments to Mo about how 'some of us have done this all our lives' is because he's gone to market again to get the new sides.

Selecting the meat at market is technically her job too: a butcher's shop is only as good as its produce. But the last thing Jo wants to volunteer for is a wander through frigid chandeliers of flesh at dawn surrounded by men with hatchets.

'Need to know how to check meat in this job, you do,' Ron had said self-righteously the night before. 'Your dad ever tell you about the side of beef we got with the abscess in it? Lost the lot, we did, to say nothing of the clean-up job after.'

Jo had had to turn away halfway through the telling, but not before catching the gleam in Ron's eye.

It's a quandary. She can't – won't – let Ron beat her, and she's cracked far tougher nuts than him. But honestly, really, truly honestly, both buying the meat and checking the stockroom are a terrible combination of high-stakes and gross. If there was a way of leaving all the actual butchering to Ron without him being even more unbearably smug, she'd be all over it.

Despite all the prep and the planning, the everyday oxymoron of stressful tedium is changing Jo's long-held assumptions about what her parents did all day. *It'll be fine*, she tells herself each morning as the car winds into the dip caused by the camber. *It'll get better once the plans are working and the shop's less precarious financially. You can be less hands-on, do more planning.*

But that's not true. She realises that now. It's all dull and it's all necessary. And (this is the bit that hurts, because it's truest) it's all super-hard in a way she may never master. Jo lacks the instinct for physical tasks, will never be able to actually joint a side of beef, has taken to dousing a scarf with Marc Jacobs and burying her nose in it whenever she needs to sluice down the counters.

She's a misfit block in one of those shape-sorting toys little kids have. Except it's not even so much that she's a star trying to fit through a circle. It's more like leaving changed things so much that now she belongs to a different shape-sorter altogether and everyone (barring perhaps Ron) is too nice to tell her so.

It's hard on mornings like this, when the cold aroma of dead flesh is everywhere, not to consider calling chambers, reinstating herself. Knowing that's even an option helps, especially when facing down a morning of abscess-hunting.

Jo sighs and heaves open the cold-room door. Just as she does, the plastic curtains into the main shop part.

Saved.

'All right, Butler! Thought it was about time I saw what you were up to.'

'Matt!'

Matt strides over, steps back in mock horror at her bloodstained coat and ruffles her hair instead.

'You're not supposed to be back here – Mo'll kill you!'

'Thought you were in charge now?' Matt's joking but the edge where humour ends and truth lies is painfully close.

There's a pause.

Matt leans against the prep counter, the metal studs of his jeans scraping against the aluminium work surface. He looks beyond Jo, pretends to examine the health and safety list pinned up there.

'You not at work today then?'

'Yeah, later. I'm on two weeks of nights. Bloody nightmare it is an' all, trying to deal with our Brandon. Shannon's on my case about it, says she'll go back to court if I can't keep up my end of the custody deal. But what can I do? I'm picking him up from school every day, hang onto him 'til she's home from work and I have to go in. I can't have him overnight on this shift pattern, she knows that. If I don't go to work there won't be any maintenance, and then she'd have something to complain about.'

Jo's remembering case law. 'You were doing this job when you two split up, weren't you? Similar shift pattern?'

'Too right I was.' Matt's laugh holds no humour at all this time.

'But then it's probably already in the custody arrangements. It's an empty threat.'

'Really?'

Jo goes over to her coat and gets her phone out of the pocket. 'Yeah, I'm pretty sure . . .' No service. 'I'll check it next time I'm near proper broadband and let you know.'

'Cheers, Butler.' Matt laughs, his rangy frame loose as if they were in Jo's parents' old kitchen after the pub, not in a swabbable room breathing in carcasses. 'That fancy job of yours taught you something, then.'

'Yeah, s'pose it did.'

She's just done something she's always consciously avoided before: demonstrated competence in the skill she left here to learn. All the other times she's been back over the years, she either hasn't talked about her job at all or glossed over it as much as she can, especially once the realisation sunk in that it wasn't what she'd hoped. It would have been disloyal. If you get to be the one who left for greener grass, it turns out that your role at home is to agree that the grass really is greener, and to absolutely, never do anything that

114

might look like showing off. But today, stung anew with the knowledge that Ron really is always going to be better than her, that the best she can hope for from herself as a butcher is basic incompetence, it's such a relief to flex the muscle that involves knowledge and ability.

She smiles at Matt and he smiles back, a genuine one this time, and Jo's body remembers the teenage thrill of that full-wattage smile.

'Nights ent all bad, mind. Gave me an extra long stint off the day before the new shift pattern started. Liam and I had a right old time of it.'

'You were out with Liam?'

'Yeah. He got off a bit early and we made a proper session of it.' Matt laughs again at the memory, leaning down on the counter. 'Anyone'd think we were eighteen again, not ten years on that.'

Jo's stomach loops, the emotions mixing and bubbling like a bad Alka-Seltzer ad. She's only just got back; she can't expect Matt – or Liam, for that matter – to remember to invite her to every last little thing.

But Liam can find time to take off with Matt, just not with her. Telling her he's too busy with work, he's got to get the kids – he's been fobbing her off. The bubbling resolves into a hard ball at the bottom of her gut.

Matt unspools to upright. 'Well, time for me to get going.'

'Thanks for coming in. Let's get a pint soon, yeah?'

That easy smile again. 'Sounds good. I'll let you know next time we're all going out.'

Jo is suddenly, ridiculously, on the verge of tears. She's outside the equation, a piece of addition to be factored in once plans are already made.

She wrenches open the stockroom door almost with relief, seeking numbing refuge. It's bloody freezing in here, unsurprisingly, and the huge metal airtight door gives Jo the heebie-jeebies. A butcher in Devon had got trapped in his own cold store not long ago and had to use a black pudding to hack his way through years' worth of built-up ice to get to the emergency release button. 'That'll teach you to read that *Guardian*,' Ron had scoffed when she'd told him and Mo in one of their team meetings.

She props the door open with a chair, then jams another chair sideways across that one, trembling more from imagination than from cold. Health and Safety would be down on her like a ton of bricks if they could see the furniture Meccano she's currently practising, but at least she'd be alive to answer their questions and not trapped in a one-degree room in a long-sleeved T-shirt and an apron.

If Jo's honest, she probably needs Ron in here beside her to tell her what she's looking at and how long it's been there, but they would both rather freeze to death in the cold room than endure that.

Dad always bought things on instinct, years of accrued experience translating into predictions for what people will want for tea. Recently, though, the encroaching supermarket prices had put paid to regular stock expectations and too much has been going to waste. Meat's

116

expensive – a lamb can cost a butcher £150, as Jo always used to like to tell her London friends when they ooh-ed and aaah-ed at pictures of frisky-tailed fluffballs gambolling across social media every spring.

Staring at her spreadsheets late at night, Jo senses that her parents have not so much retired – they're still years off their dotage, after all – as jumped ship while the distance from ship to shore was still doable. She's optimistic, though, at least openly. If they can just tap into the new customer base, things should turn around.

Stock-checking is dull work, even compared with sifting through briefs and caseloads for hours on end. It's a relief when Mo sticks her head through the plastic curtain, white cap pushed slightly back on her head.

'You got a minute, love? I could do with a hand out here; it's got a bit crowded.'

'A bit crowded' is great news. But it turns out to actually mean three women. Mo's doling out mince to a couple of pensioners while a woman Jo's age is browsing the window display in a pair of branded jeans and white trainers that'll last about ten minutes when she gets out into the woods.

'Can I help you with anything?'

'Not really, thanks.' The woman possesses the flat vowels of an out-of-towner and a precise white-blonde haircut that probably cost as much as a side of lamb. 'I'm just having a look.' She smiles. 'We moved in a fortnight ago so I'm still in the excited phase.'

God, it would be so lovely to be properly brand new,

not a weird hybrid. 'Oh, welcome! Where were you before?'

'London, so this is quite a change.' The woman stretches out her hand. 'I'm Poppy.'

'Jo.' She reaches across the counter, remembers the gloves and withdraws her hand. 'Lucky you! I was there for the best part of a decade; came back last month. How are you finding the Forest?'

'So far, so good. We went for it and bought a house in one of the villages just on up into the woods.' Poppy leans forward on the counter. 'Got any suggestions for things we shouldn't miss now we're locals?'

'It depends what you're interested in, really.' Jo catches herself, laughs. 'No. It doesn't. Not in a London sense, anyway. There's tons to do round here, but it's mostly outdoors-related.'

'That figures. Dan – my partner – is a huge mountain biker, so he'll be happy. In London it took forever to reach any kind of outdoor space, and even then it'd be scrappy and overcrowded.'

'Well, there's plenty of nature to go around out here.'

'Yeah, it's fabulous. Though I miss having a bookshop nearby, and if I'm honest, I miss Deliveroo. I know it's ridiculous. I'll get used to it.'

'No, I know exactly what you mean.' Jo hasn't been this in sync with anyone since she's been back. There's a twinge of betrayal, but if she's not going to be automatically included in the old gang, there's nothing stopping her making new friends of her own.

'This might sound a bit mad, but do you fancy meeting

for a coffee one day? I could catch you up on where's good.'

'Fantastic!' Poppy's crimson-lipsticked mouth stretches into a smile. 'When suits?'

'Well, I'm here most days until six, maybe beyond – perils of being the boss. Any time after that would work, though.'

A look crosses Poppy's face that's hard to read.

'This is your shop? I assumed you were just helping out. You don't seem . . .'

You don't seem the type to work at a butcher's, let alone own one.

Jo flinches, deflects. 'Long story. I can do pretty much any evening, so just let me know what works.'

Poppy's expression is quizzical. 'We'll have to make that coffee a drink, then. Unless you know a coffee shop nearby that stays open beyond five thirty? I haven't found one for looking.'

'Bugger – no, you're right!'

Her London expectations are hovering right below the surface and all it takes is someone in the right clothes and the right haircut to tip her straight back into them. Jo closes her eyes for a second.

'Well, a drink, then.'

'Sounds great.'

Poppy buys a couple of chops at Jo's recommendation and leaves. Mo glances at Jo's face. 'These new ones ent all so bad, then?'

'I'm not the one who ever said they were. But no, not all of them.'

119

Jo pulls off the latex gloves, heads back to wash her hands again against cross-contamination and walks into the cold store. She can get this done. Of course she can.

The frying pan lives with the other pans in the bottom of the range, its metal already warm to the touch. The chop starts sizzling as soon as Jo tips it in. It slips off the wrapper, as if desperate to meet the slick of butter, and warms the kitchen with smells of pork chops past.

It's been a weird old day, and nothing roots Jo faster than a chop with cabbage and spuds. She's just pouring on the gravy when the kitchen door squawks open. Tessa follows the trail of steam rising over Jo's plate, her nose slightly lifted like the Bisto kid, and Jo watches Tessa for a moment before standing up and collecting another plate.

'Perfect timing.' She saws the chop in half, forks veg onto the other plate too. It's fine. Half is still loads.

'Have some of this with me?' She thrusts the plate at Tessa and plonks her own down quickly.

Tessa sits down opposite and engages in a staring competition with the chop. A memory shivers through Jo: Liam, years ago, gazing at a plate of sausages like that.

Jo spears away a mouthful, the juice of the chop and gravy bringing her back to herself. Tessa picks up her own knife and fork, finally starts on the chop.

'Oh! I know what I wanted to ask you. When I came in earlier I noticed a dent in the van. Is everything OK?'

'The what?' Tessa comes into herself from miles away. 'The dent? That's from earlier today.'

'What happened?' Jo stuffs in another mouthful of the pork chop.

'I had to get off the road in a bit of a hurry.'

Tessa's so unemotional about it, as if tipping off the road and virtually totalling your van was normal business.

Jo puts down her knife and fork. 'Are you sure you're OK?' She can't possibly be. The side panel looked half bashed in. Even if she's physically OK, it would have been a hell of a shock.

Tessa closes back up again and it's so sudden Jo can virtually watch it happen. 'I'm fine. It's nothing.'

'But what about the van?'

'What about it? Still runs.'

'But—' But the atmosphere has frozen and the words can't break through.

Tessa sits dead still, staring into space. She's put down her knife and fork, a chunk of meat still impaled on its tines.

Jo finishes her share of the chop, cutting as quietly as she can, even her swallowing too loud now. This isn't just new-lodger frostiness. Tessa appears to not react to anything at all. She could have been – could be – really properly hurt, and here she is, refusing to even talk about it. There's something going on, but what it might be is anybody's guess. It's frightening, and hard to get traction on. As soon as she can, Jo sluices her plate under the tap and leaves the room, the door handle cold beneath her fingers.

Chapter Thirteen

T ESSA KNOWS IT WAS A narrow escape; lucky she'd been going steady. She's usually all right driving, sticks to her routes, weighs up the need against the risk. But Jo pressing her for details – that makes it impossible to do what's needed and bury the episode. And what she can't tell Jo is that this wasn't the first time. That was months ago now and while the symptoms were the same as ever, the fact it had happened in the car had been proper terrifying, made her start to reconsider her abilities. Brought about the start of the end of things with Marnie.

When she turned onto the A48 outside Lydney, the sun shining off the Severn caught Tessa. The river was laid out down along the horizon beyond the fields, a bright dream weaving through the land. If she were Marnie, she'd say it filled her soul.

She very much wasn't Marnie, but it was still something to be glad about. Tessa hadn't been able to shake thoughts of their recent visit to the Valleys to see Mam, though she hasn't mentioned this to Marnie, of course. She had focused on keeping busy, finding other things to talk about. She'd be shaping a shoe or getting ready to clench off when the clink of the steel against the anvil, the angle of her own knuckles, would bring Mam back and Tessa would have to pause, catch her breath.

She coughed hard now, lifting one hand from the steering wheel as her body was wracked. She sneezed, her eyes squeezing shut, and when she opened them again the river had twisted out of the light, reverted to its usual slinking.

This coldy fluey thing hadn't helped her mood much, either. It's entirely the wrong weather to be catching something this wintery.

'It's your body's reaction to your mother,' had been Marnie's dark response. It had properly knocked her out, it had.

Tessa was driving on autopilot again, something that was happening more and more recently. She stuck on Radio Glos, concentrated on the road. She was in Chepstow already, through the lights by Tesco and sliding up the hill past the town.

She still hadn't shaken this bug, kept finding herself desperate for a kip at all the wrong times. Today she was literally mid-shoeing, crouched with Ben Turley's colt's front hoof between her hands, when the urge to lie down on the floor and pass out came over her. It was

123

a wave, nothing she could do to stop it. She'd clenched off quickly to make it safe and kept as still as she could. A wisp of straw skittered across the concrete of the barn looking for company. She breathed in, a shallow breath because coughing with a hoof in your hands wasn't so much asking for a kick in the teeth as more or less demanding it, and eventually the wave subsided.

The approach road was empty and she manoeuvred the van round the roundabout and onto the bridge. Her heartbeat steadied as she put her childhood back behind her.

Tessa's been driving to the forest from Bristol for three years and she's used to it now. On a good day she could plan her visits so that she finished the day's work close to the Severn Bridge. Even if she ended up on the far side of the Forest, it's an hour, tops.

Plus, she liked the drive. Tessa would never have said this out loud, but that hour alone in the warmth of the van, surrounded by the smell of horses and molten iron, getting her head straight again before she's plunged back into Marnie's multicoloured cacophony, was worth the world to her.

A glint of late-afternoon sun sharded the windscreen and she blinked towards the new Severn Bridge, away down the estuary towards Mam. The van swerved slightly and she tightened her grip on the steering wheel, set the course again.

A BMW screeched by, so fast she hadn't spotted it in the wing mirror, and screamed on the horn. It came from nowhere and the shock bladed through Tessa, her

124

heart beating so fast she could taste it in her mouth. The Beemer was trying to overtake, but there was an old Ford Fiesta in front of her whose driver looked about ninety and was pootling along oblivious. Tessa needed to slow down, to widen the gap between them so that there was room.

But when she went to move her foot onto the brake, the muscles wouldn't respond, her foot melting into the foot well.

She kicked out, and nothing happened. Nothing at all.

It wasn't just her foot. Her hands wouldn't come off the steering wheel. They were slick with sweat, but useless.

Her head was fixed in place with rigid terror, panic taking over from her collapsed muscles. She couldn't check to the side to see where Beemer Man had gone.

She was hurtling over the Severn Bridge at 66 miles an hour and she'd lost control of the van.

The BMW's driver blasted the horn and it competed with the static in her head and she was going faster and faster and she was going to hit the Fiesta or the crash barrier and at the moment she didn't even know which would be worse except they'd both be worse, of course they would, and the terror built and built and—

The radio, which had been burbling beneath the build-up of noise and horror, quacked at her.

No, not quacked. Ribbited. They were playing the 'Frog Chorus'.

Tessa laughed. Of all the times to play this song, when she was about to meet her death wasn't the most comforting. Sweat dripped into her eyes and she wiped her forehead.

She wiped her forehead. She wasn't frozen anymore. Tessa shifted her foot to the brake and eased the van back, the Beemer slotting into what it apparently considered its rightful place between her and the Fiesta. Everything was back. Everything was moving. She coughed again, a bone-rattling hawking that threatened to mist up the van windows.

Tessa pulled off the motorway after the bridge, steered the car up into the services and pulled into one of the furthermost parking spaces. She turned off the engine and sat there.

Tessa examined her hands. They trembled but otherwise gave away no secrets. She prodded her calf experimentally, lifted her foot. Nothing looked any different. Nothing felt any different, either.

Tessa rested her head back on the headrest and closed her eyes. The hatchback of the Fiesta loomed towards her over and again, and there was a searing pain right behind her eye, as if someone was drilling through from the temple.

Below her, the water lapped soundlessly as the tide pulsed cocoa-brown water out into the Severn estuary, and gulls wheeled on the mud banks. She shouldn't drive herself home now. It wouldn't be safe.

But Marnie hadn't been sleeping recently, not since they visited Mam in the Valleys. She said it was the baby, but the weight of words was different when they were hollow. Pregnancy was supposed to be a happy time; a time when the focus should be on Marnie and their unborn child, not on family dramas from the past. If Tessa phones Marnie now, this becomes all about Tessa and her inability to move on from their visit to Mam, when it should be about Marnie. Tessa hasn't frozen behind the wheel like that before, and if she's ever frozen around Marnie, she's been able to wave it off as part of the occasional fainting thing.

Tessa reached into the glovebox for a Murray Mint. Maybe her blood sugar levels were low or something. She turned the key in the ignition and the van spluttered back, ready for the trip home. Tessa gripped the steering wheel, shook out her feet.

The episodes were increasing again, landing like hayseeds in the least expected moments. The need to sleep all the time, the muscles melting – something was building. Something bad. This was supposed to be the happiest time Tessa had known. But creeping under the miracle of her day-to-day contentment was the disaster she has always deserved. Something was happening to her, something with the power to destroy Tessa, and worse, to take Marnie down with it. She didn't know what it was, or how long it would last. No need to bother Marnie with this right now, not when all the focus needed to be on Marnie and the baby.

All Tessa could do was to keep quiet, keep going, and keep it to herself.

Chapter Fourteen

THE NEXT DAY JO BRINGS home enough sausages for two. Her expensive years of lawyering have trained her to observe. The tins in the cupboard have been dwindling, and there's no sign of them being replaced.

Ron raised an eyebrow as she left, muttered something about eating the profits, but seriously, sod him. Really, he's on one because she's moving ahead with the plans on her chart, and so far they're going all right.

'Nobody's going to want to buy bloody fish from us.'

Jo, leaning against the jamb of the cold-room door, wondered idly whether Ron actually needed to always use the cleaver or whether his vicious slamming of metal through flesh had increased since she'd come back. 'I think they will.'

'Who's going to prepare it? You'd better not be

expecting me to. Whole different way of doing things. I'm a butcher, not a fishmonger.'

You're a bugger is what you are.

He's deliberately trying to splatter her with micro-globs of flesh. She shifts her stance out of the firing line.

'I'm just ordering in things that don't need prepping to start with. Shellfish, that sort of thing. We'll give it a month and if it's not working, we'll stop. But we won't know if we don't try.'

Slam, slam, slam.

She'd picked up the sausages and left for the day. Waving cheerily wasn't grown-up, but it helped.

Living with Tessa is like living with a phantom. The big black coat is on the coat stand, but Tessa's boots aren't there and the house lies silent as usual.

'Hello?' The echo floats down the corridor; if the greeting's heard in the kitchen, it goes unanswered.

Jo's London flatshare – the last one, and all the ones before that over the last ten years – were an onslaught of noise and scent as soon as you opened the door, the output of too many lives being lived too hurriedly. This is the opposite. Jo quells the brief pang that hits her solar plexus. Nostalgia for that shit heap is ridiculous.

She sticks the sausages on, gets the potatoes on to boil and creeps up the stairs as if she's not allowed. Tessa's door's firmly shut. Jo raises her hand, puts it down again by her side, raises it again and knocks firmly.

'Yes?'

Tessa sounds like she's underwater. The door opens a crack and she looks blearily at Jo.

'Sorry – were you asleep?' Teatime's a funny time for a nap, but each to their own. 'I've brought home sausages. Wondered if you fancied some?'

Tessa stares at her as if from the other end of a tunnel, then does that thing and snaps into the present. She frowns, nods. 'I'll be down in a minute.'

The door closes abruptly and Jo's left nose-to-nose with painted wood. She stares at it for a moment, then turns back down the stairs. Tea's going to be an absolute riot. But she's dealt with worse clients.

It strikes Jo just how often she seems to think that now she's home. It was supposed to be easier here.

The sausages are doing their thing, warming the room and making it smell like the past. The fish will sell, she knows it. She just has to not let Ron rile her. And not let Tessa's almost hostile silence freak her out, either.

Tessa snaps back into herself, her focus first on the food in front of her, then the woman frowning on the other side of the table. This is her lodger. For the last few minutes Jo's been asking her yet more things about herself, evidently completely clueless about how it feels to be shot through with questions before you've even had a chance to think about the first one.

Asking questions is almost as painful as answering them, but this way at least she'll get a break from the interrogation.

'What about you, anyway?' Tessa takes a huge bite of food.

'What, the shop? It's fine, I think, thanks. Early days. I hadn't thought about how different it would be to run it rather than to be helping out my parents, you know? I suppose it's like driving a route you've only ever been a passenger for. I'll get there.'

The sausages, like the pork yesterday, are delicious, tender and juicy. Tessa nods, lets Jo run on.

'I was a barrister before. Still am, technically. People in London think it's quaint, moving down to take over the family business, but that's because they've got no idea of the graft involved.' She shrugs. 'And people down here think it's crazy to be a butcher when you could be a barrister. I can't win.'

'What do you think now you're back?' The questions eke out like a rusted bolt, unused to the mechanism, and Tessa's surprised to realise she actually cares about the answer.

'I don't know.' This is a woman who looks like she's always known, before, and the not-knowing is causing pain. 'Half the customers look amazed that I'm not still toddling around in nappies, and the other half seem to think it's a bit rich that I've come swanning back to take over when I don't really belong here anymore.' Jo cradles her mug, hunched over in a way that forces a pang of response from Tessa.

'Don't think you get much more loyal than coming back to run the shop.' There's no way anyone could be more where she came from than Jo. It's in everything

131

she says, her centre of gravity, pulling her back.

'Well. If I'm going to work all hours, I'd rather it was for something I really care about, in a place that means everything to me.' She sighs. 'I've just got to make it work, now. Easier said than done.'

Chapter Fifteen

BEFORE SHE'D TAKEN OVER, JO had no idea that Wednesdays were so busy, but now, almost at the end of the first month, she's prepared. The outgoings are a bit higher this month, but that's to be expected with the outlay for the seafood that they're trying.

By the time Mo comes through the door, coat pulled tight against the wind, the cabinets are already half-filled with what seems to work best for Wednesdays. The Wednesday crowd is a curious one, drawn in by the street market in the town. It's a mixture of things proper locals might actually want to buy (cheap dishcloths, pet bowls) and things people who've moved to the countryside want to be able to buy (butter from the farm down the road, cheese with local place names).

These new locals might also be convinced to eat 'local' produce even if they wouldn't know a doe from a dormouse. So yesterday, she convinced a muttering Ron to prepare extra diced venison and wild boar. Jo fetches it now from the cold store, the cling film peeling off like a plaster as the maroon cubes dollop out into the storefront trays. There's a satisfaction to a job done well, even if she can't feel her fingers.

Liam had shrugged when she'd asked how long the market had been there. 'Five, six years? Around the same time the house prices all started shooting up.'

Once business at the shop itself has picked up a bit, and there's time to diversify, it would be great to have a stand at the market as well. For now, Jo optimistically puts her locally sourced venison and boar front and centre, and hopes they sell enough to cover the slacker days too.

Phyllis is first in this morning, as usual. Jo leaves Mo in the back, sorting out more mince, and comes through. Phyllis is at the till, examining one of Jo's new flyers.

'"Forest Stew", eh? Can't say as I've ever heard of that before.' She waves the leaflet.

'Mm, I might have taken a bit of poetic licence there, Phyllis.'

Phyllis peers at the recipe. 'Venison and wild boar in the same meal? That won't be cheap.'

'But you won't be able to get it at Tesco, will you?'

'Ah, there's sense in that all right.' Phyllis puts the leaflet carefully back on the pile by the till, smooths it down. 'Best thing to do with a bit of venison is pop it in the slow cooker, love. It's a bit chewy otherwise.'

'I'll have to figure out a slow cooker recipe too, then; good idea.'

'I'm old enough to remember when, if you wanted venison, you waited 'til the right bugger shot one, love. Weren't no boar around pretending to be a delicacy then, neither.' She points into the display cabinets. 'Just a half of mince, please, love; lamb, if you've got it. Our Kyle's coming over after rugby today so I'm making him a shepherd's pie.'

'Is this Sophie's eldest? I still can't believe he's a teenager.'

'Well, that's what kids do, love. They keep growing up. Look at you, running the shop, full of these new ideas your parents managed without for years.'

Jo takes Phyllis's proffered fiver and looks down for slightly longer than necessary to find the change.

The bell rings and there's a new face to focus on, thank God. A smart-looking woman in her fifties smiles vaguely in Jo's direction, then moves over to peer into the cabinet. She, at least, won't think it's strange Jo's in charge of a business while also a fully-grown woman. It would have been better still if it was Poppy again. They'd had a drink earlier in the week and it had been fine, but those first few chats with anyone are always awkward, a bit first-date-y, so it's good to get them under your belt quickly. Home will start to feel more like home when Jo's made a few more friends. She hadn't bargained on needing new friends here, but then she hadn't bargained on a lot of things.

The woman outside walking past the shop isn't an old friend, but she definitely isn't a stranger. Before there's time to think, Jo's dipped six links of the pork sausage into a plastic bag and legged it to the doorway.

135

'Debbie!'

The passerby stops and looks up at Jo with milky eyes. She's shockingly thin these days, and the long hair that straggles between her shoulder blades is fully grey now. This is a good day, though. She's not shuffling, and as Jo gets nearer, there's no muttering.

'Joanne Butler. You were in school uniform last time I clapped eyes on you.'

'It's been a while. I was living away, but now I'm back.' Jo shifts from one foot to the other. 'You're looking well. Liam said you're still in the flat.'

Debbie stands ever so slightly taller. Jo thrusts the sausages at her. 'Thought you might like these. Sausages.'

'Sausages! Thank you.' Debbie inclines her head. 'Your mother and father never used to do that sort of thing.'

Clearly the multiple cups of tea and the years being in loco parentis for her son don't count. Jo bites back a retort. Not helpful, and not fair.

The bag hangs limply from Debbie's hand, bulging pinkly.

'Well, I'd better get on. It was nice to see you again.'

Liam's mother doesn't reply, walks on past the shop. Jo stands in the doorway and watches her go. Now that she's back she can keep an eye out for Debbie, pass on the odd bit of mince. No, not mince. Mince needs other things with it. Sausages are best.

The new customer's still browsing, unaffected by Jo's dash. Phyllis, of course, has watched the transaction through the window and leans forward when Jo comes back in. 'Seemed all right today, did she?'

Jo's head's locked in the past and it takes a minute.

'Sorry, Phyllis. Yeah, I think so.' There have been plenty of days, though, when Debbie has seemed fine, until she wasn't.

'Let's hope it lasts this time.'

The new customer approaches the counter and Phyllis mouths: 'See you again' as she dings her way out.

'Two venison steaks, please. And four of the wild boar sausages to try.' She picks up the Forest Stew recipe, tucks it into her tote bag.

'Of course. And will there be anything else?'

There won't be. People are buying less, not more. But she has to try.

Chapter Sixteen

TESSA'S MORE TIRED THAN EVER at the moment and can barely keep her eyes open at times; only the worry spikes her awake into the late-February chill. She's working less than ever but that merely seems to make this sleepiness prey on her more, eating into her like fire, scorching any hope of normality. Today she'd only just got the van up and out of the drive when the need to kip hammered her and she pulled over into the verge, then turned round to come home, heavy with misery and defeat. If she can't go to work, she can at least make the tea this time – make up for the meat Jo brings home.

She still had a couple of tins of tomatoes left. She delved into the veg bag Jo had brought home a week or more ago, quashing guilt. There were no herbs or the like, but it wasn't the work of a minute to brown off the carrots and the turnip while she scrubbed the potatoes. The parsnip sputtered slowly in a knob of butter (Jo's again; more guilt to suppress), until it was almost caramelised, sugary brown on the outside, ready for the pot.

You couldn't cook like this, not for yourself. She'd made stews and the like occasionally for Marnie, but Marnie was more of a sushi and salad person. And when Marnie said salad, she meant a *recipe*, from some celebrity chef who wanted to use ingredients you'd have to send off for, not a head of lettuce with a couple of tomatoes and a cucumber from the garden. They used to laugh about how differently two people could envisage the one meal. That was the thing about Marnie (one of the many, many things about Marnie). She never once looked down on Tessa, never once got superior, despite her fancy flat and fancy car and the job that she wriggled into a suit for every morning. She loved Tessa because she was Tessa, and it was as simple and as unfathomable as that.

By the time the clattering door announces Jo's arrival in the evening, darkness is already cloaking the cottage, and inside the aroma is rich and red.

'Wow – something smells amazing!'

Tessa's bent down at the range, lifting the pot out to hide sudden nerves at the assumptions she's made about pinching Jo's things. 'Thought I'd make the tea tonight. Used some of your veg – that all right, is it?'

'It's more than all right; it's fantastic. Thanks so much.'

Tessa's already laid the table and now she ladles the stew into two bowls, finding two that aren't chipped, and brings those over.

'God, this is brilliant.' Jo's halfway through before Tessa starts on her own dinner. The parsnips have done their thing and it's good; rich and satisfying.

'I was wondering how I was going to fit tea in tonight, too.' Jo slurps down another mouthful.

'Oh?'

'I'm meeting a few old friends down the pub, back in town.' Jo's smile has a wariness round the edges.

'Oh, right.' Tessa's spoon slows in her bowl at the thought of a night out with friends. It's too late for her now to have long-standing friendships with people who'd known you forever and forgave you anything. The best she ever managed was being folded into Marnie's friendship group, but now that's gone too.

Tessa had trained herself so well to manage without friends that she's rerouted the part of her who would know how to make them. It wasn't until Marnie arrived in technicolour and blew Tessa's life up in the best ways imaginable that she understood how friendships – relationships – could be so magical. Without Marnie, she has no idea how to conjure that magic back.

'Look – why don't you come with me?'

But the thinness in Jo's offer is clear in the lack of eye contact, and anyway, Tessa can't possibly go. There's no money for a pint, let alone a round. And drinking isn't a good idea. It'll let down her boundaries and she'll feel things more keenly, and that might provoke an attack. Groups are the worst; there's no knowing what might happen to start something off. Even among Marnie's almost parodically welcoming friends, Tessa's guard stayed up, her glass stayed empty, and the attacks were minimal.

Jo can't know any of this or it'll scare her away, when her rent's the only thing keeping it all together.

'I can't tonight. But ta. Another time, maybe?'

It will never, ever happen.

Jo rinses off her plate and leaves to get ready. The brusque emptiness is filled with a memory of another, different night out. One when Tessa kept everything under control, even though what she saw was impossible to process.

When Tessa was twelve, one of the teachers had brought in a pair of binoculars. She can't remember what the lesson was about now, but the whole class trooped out into the playground and trained them on things for forty minutes. It was like entering a different world. Car number plates became readable even from a distance, and the leaves on the apple tree were latticed with tiny veins she'd only been able to feel before.

Life with Marnie was like that. Everything was in sharper focus. Things became apparent that had been hiding in plain sight. Like the huge gay disco at Cheltenham racecourse.

'But babe! That's been there for years.' Marnie was spectacular that day, in a sparkly jumper with a low dip at the back, jeans so tight that getting them back off looked impossible (in the end it wasn't, Tessa discovered to her delight) and leopard-skin boots with heels as pointy and sharp as any hoofing tool. She sat on the kitchen counter, legs swinging gently, humming lightly as Tessa scrubbed the pans after tea. *Supper*.

Marnie had cooked, so Tessa was washing up. That seemed fair enough, though Marnie appeared to have taken the approach to cookery that if half the food stayed stuck to the bottom of the pan, so be it.

Tessa looked up from a particularly stubborn patch of rice. Late evening sun spotlit Marnie, and her dark curls glinted.

'Cheltenham's miles away from the Forest.'

'It's a damn sight closer to the Forest than Bristol is, and I've been loads of times. And there's a whole crew that come down from Birmingham, and that's probably twice the distance.'

'Yes, but those are cities. Cheltenham and the Forest aren't the same. Look at the horses. Cheltenham's got glossy racehorses and we've got stumpy Welsh cobs.' It was more true than funny, and Tessa's laugh petered out.

'It's different in the Forest. I didn't know anyone like me until I met you.'

Marnie's feet stopped swinging as she leaned forward, elbows on her thighs. The look she gave Tessa was half-sympathy, half-sadness, and Tessa clenched her fists under cover of the washing-up bubbles. She couldn't collapse here, doing the dishes.

'But babe – you can't actually have been the only gay in the village, surely?' Marnie was trying to understand, and Tessa's heart, which already pretty firmly belonged to Marnie, lurched with the extra jolt of love for this

142

effort. Marnie couldn't help not understanding. She was a product of her upbringing, just like Tessa; she tried her best to empathise, but their starting points were light years apart.

It was impossible for Marnie to feel the meld of fear and loneliness that had coated Tessa's every mood. Marnie had come of age in a city, with bookshops and gay pubs, and, more crucially, with parents who cared for her no matter what. It was up to Tessa to try to explain, to meet her halfway.

'When we were at school there was a woman worked in Woolies, back when there still was Woolies. People said she was gay. I used to go in sometimes, pretend to be looking at the music and study her. She didn't look anything like me, so I figured if that's what it looked like to be gay, I obviously wasn't.' She shrugged. 'She was a Goth, and we didn't have many of them either, so I didn't realise that was separate. I just thought that's how you dressed if you were gay. And you remember what school was like?' Though Marnie's liberal private school had probably been a different species from the Forest comp.

'Teachers never brought it up, pretended being gay wasn't a thing that happened. I know it sounds daft, like, but I wouldn't have known to name it.' There'd never been any question that she was different from the majority of her classmates, that the complete lack of interest in the urgent search for a boyfriend that preoccupied apparently all the girls in her class wasn't just down to reservedness, but even if she'd had a friend to talk to, there'd have been no way on earth of talking about that sort of stuff, of using words she wasn't even able to use in her own head.

By the time she'd started work, she'd known for sure that boys – men – were never going to be her thing, but there was absolutely bugger all to do with this information, living as and where she did. One of the blokes on the farriery course in Hereford, where she was virtually the only woman, had asked her once if she fancied getting a drink after class. His offer was a sudden life raft buoying her out of the sea of isolation she'd been adrift on for years now, and she'd said yes without thinking, pathetically grateful for the company. But it had become clear that the drink and chat weren't the point, and next time he'd suggested a drink she'd said no, terrified he'd guess why.

'Oh, *Tess*.' Marnie was close to tears.

Tessa wiped the suds onto her jeans, pushed her soaking fingers into the tangle of Marnie's curls. 'It wasn't so bad, honest.'

The lie was necessary. Nobody, not even someone as incredible as Marnie, could love her if they knew how unlovable she really was.

'I didn't know what I was missing, see?'

Nowadays she would know what she was missing, though. If anything were to happen to part her from Marnie . . .

A wave of nausea threatened. Tessa pushed her hands deeper into the warmth of Marnie's hair, grounding herself. Then she shifted her weight and kissed Marnie's forehead. They'd only been together for three months and already her life had changed beyond measure. She spent every free moment of the weekend in Marnie's flat in Bristol, surrounded by people who lived life out loud in a way that was equal parts compelling and terrifying. Tessa's life was a silent movie, black and white. Marnie's was technicolour, a musical.

Yesterday, Geoff at the checking yard had commented that he'd never heard Tessa sing before, and she had smiled at him, kept up the tune. The horses had all picked up her mood and were happier for it as well, greeting her with snuffles and pushing into her pockets for horse nuts and Polos.

Marnie disentangled herself from Tessa, kept her arms on Tessa's waist. Her eyes were bright with unshed tears. 'Well, you're not on your own now. Tonight I'll show you just how unalone you are.'

Tessa took a nap before they went out, starfished in Marnie's crisp white bed, safe enough to forego the hedgehog position she'd slept in for so long in the cottage. Long, unlined drapes fluttered against the open windows, sashes pulled up as high as they dared. She didn't know how long she'd slept for; it was still light when she woke up and she curled into herself, yawned, then stretched again.

Marnie was there, staring down at her with a look of such tenderness that Tessa's brain shot a warning fizz. This is how Marnie looked at her when she thought Tessa didn't know. It was almost too much to bear.

'You're awake!' She leaned in and kissed Tessa – not an amorous kiss, more a meeting of certainties. And in that moment Tessa realised, with hot contentment, a truth she wouldn't have dared to imagine. *Marnie loved her.* This woman, this too-good-to-be-true woman who had changed Tessa's life forever: she felt the same way.

The thrill of recognition stayed with Tessa all through into the sweaty August night. They were somewhere in the town centre, not far from the big Primark. Marnie strode ahead, her top outstretched behind her like a falcon's wingspan, and it took Tessa a minute to catch her up. She wanted desperately to hold Marnie's hand, to hold on and never let go. But she mustn't.

Abruptly, they stopped at a nondescript strip mall.

'Ta da!' Marnie grinned at Tessa, delighted with herself. She was gorgeous: all long limbs and long hair, another pair of impossibly skinny jeans below a sequined top.

There was a sign hanging above a door. 'The She Club.' Ah. OK. That must be it. Not the disco at Cheltenham racecourse but a bar for women.

Tessa didn't want to go in.

'You need to start coming out on the gay scene, see how ordinary it all is,' Marnie had said a few weeks ago, but Tessa didn't want it to be ordinary. Marnie had turned her life upside down, made it extraordinary, and Tessa wanted to stay in this feeling for as long as possible.

Still, it was something Marnie wanted, for her, and

the simple act of kindness blew Tessa's mind. She would follow Marnie anywhere.

She headed over towards the sign, which was flashing neon.

'Tess! No!' Marnie looked like she didn't know whether to laugh or cry. 'That's a strip club!'

She took Tessa's shoulders, steered her down a flight of steps that had been concealed by the corner of the building. There was another sign above the window, but this one wasn't neon and wasn't flashing. It was small and painted: 'The Scarlet Coat'.

Marnie grabbed Tessa's hand and pulled her past the bouncer, a tall woman in a long leather coat with a stick. The building was as teeny inside as it looked outside, the perfume and sweat of scores of women undercut by vinegar and steak.

'What is this place?'

'It's our bar. Well, not mine, not really, though it may as well be.' Marnie's teeth flashed white against the glittering dark, the light pulsing off them with the music. 'I started sneaking in here when I was about fifteen. I'm sure Mum and Dad knew where I was coming, in retrospect.'

'So it's been going a long time?'

'Years. Jane and Bernie, the women that own it, they run it as a restaurant during the day. It's there for people who've finished shopping and can't be arsed to get home to make supper. Apparently the food's not bad.'

'You don't eat here, then?'

Marnie laughed, her eyes sparkling with the disco

lights. 'God, no. I come here to dance. Twice a week, Thursdays and Saturdays, they turn it into a club. Newer places have opened up around it, but this is still one of the best.'

Tessa looked around, her eyes adjusting to the light. She'd never been anywhere that was just full of women before and it was another adjustment, a flooding of her brain. The music was thumping, and tables had been shoved back towards the walls to form a makeshift dance floor, where a mass of bodies heaved along with the music.

Marnie rested her chin on Tessa's shoulder and Tessa shifted away automatically.

Marnie grabbed her hand, pulled her down so that she could yell in her ear, a caress of a shout. 'Nobody cares, babe. That's the point of this place.'

Nobody cares. Tessa didn't have to try and explain anything, not to any of these women here, and not even to herself. Her shoulders dropped, and if it weren't risking it, she would have cried. It was noisy and crowded, and the high notes of vinegar made her want chips something bad. But she was with Marnie, and she was happy. Anything else could wait.

Chapter Seventeen

I T SHOULD BE GETTING WARMER by now, but they're
at the beginning of March and still the rain slants
endlessly through the trees, whipping out onto the
road and glancing back off. The potholes along the
lane from the shop are increasing by the week as the
rain freezes overnight and cracks its way back out
in the morning. When Jo finally makes it back to
the house, she sits in the car for a minute, gathering
herself after driving those bends in the scudding fog.
Sometimes it's hard to remember that this is better
than the Tube.

The windscreen wipers freeze as if in their own private
game of musical statues. The rain drums down onto the
car, the gaps between beats barely perceptible. It pulls
the darkness from the clouds down into the sky, the last
of the light washed away in the early evening downpour,
maroon leaves beached in hedgerows like slick shoals

of fish. She's been here six weeks. Halfway along her parents' timeline. The fish is working, despite Ron, and the five pubs that trialled the meat enjoyed it and have placed small orders, with the promise of more to come. It's not yet enough to make up for the lack of footfall in the shop, but it's a start.

Jo had phoned her parents yesterday to chat about the accounts she'd emailed across. But her dad was oddly stilted, kept changing the topic back to how the soil in their new garden was different, clayier, and things weren't going in as he'd expect them to. In the end, Jo had given up trying to talk business. Maybe it was hard to imagine someone else doing what you loved for all those years. *Maybe*, her treacherous inner voice whispered, *maybe he isn't proud of you now you're not a barrister. Maybe you've let him down by turning your back on everything he worked so hard to afford for you.*

Mum was round at Gary's, minding the children, so Jo didn't get to speak to her. She'd hung up and put her face in her hands.

The house is cocoon-warm after the rain. Jo slings her parka on the coat stand beside the front door and walks up the corridor. The cottage isn't going to feel like home if she stays stuck in her tiny room all the time. There's no getting around that. But when Tessa's there, everything's still a bit freighted, every blank space holding invisible traps that gum up Jo's words before she can get them out.

The new shelves, though – they're gorgeous. She'd come home one night just as Tessa was slotting the last of the planks into place. Black metal handmade brackets beckon like speech marks the length of the corridor.

'Thought these might help.'

'Help? They're beautiful!'

'I haven't put any books on them – didn't know what you'd want to do, see?' Tessa turned away, almost as if she was embarrassed to be caught in the act of kindness.

Now Jo reaches up and touches the twisted black spiral brackets carrying her books at head height. She's had many a landlord over the years and none of them has ever done anything as effortfully thoughtful as this. Walking down here now is almost ceremonial; it makes it easier to come further into the cottage, clearer that perhaps Tessa doesn't resent her presence as much as it sometimes seems.

Jo pushes open the door into the main room. It grumbles a bit, sticking on the bottom, so she pushes hard and stumbles through, almost tripping into Tessa. Think of the devil . . .

'Sorry!' Jo puts out a hand and Tessa flinches, so she hurries on. 'Have you eaten? I was going to put some pasta on, use up the last of that veg.'

'Yeah. Pasta and veg sounds nice.' Soft and carefully articulated, like clients who want to maintain plausible deniability.

It's good to sit and eat with someone again, even if it's someone as wary as Tessa. The rain timpanis down outside the kitchen window, the most tenacious droplets mosaicking the black dark of the evening outside.

'That was good. Ta.' Tessa lays down her knife and fork, as relaxed as Jo's seen her.

'There's a ton left – would you like some more?'

'You sure?'

'God, yeah. If we don't eat it tonight, I'll be forced to eat it all week.'

'Go on, then. Thanks.' Tessa pushes her chair back to go to the hob, but Jo's up before her. She twists and pain shoots up.

'Shit!'

'You all right?'

'I'm fine, really, my hip's just a bit sore. I keep whacking into the same bit of the counter at work every day. It's right beside the door, so all the little old ladies coming in with their sticks have to sort of shimmy round.'

Tessa doesn't answer, but she never answers straight away. There's always a pause to weigh up every sentence, as if it's an undetonated bomb, before deciding how to respond.

'It gets you every day?'

'Most days, yes.'

'And it's tricky for the customers, too?'

'Some of them, yeah.'

Tessa turns her fork round and round, as if she's looking for a hidden trick. 'Why don't you change it then, like? Is it fixed to the wall?'

'No, not at all. It needs to be plugged in, but it would move OK, I think.'

'You look like I've suggested murdering your mother.'

152

'It's just . . . well, it's always been like that, all my life.'

Tessa forks in another mouthful of pasta, swallows. 'Is there anywhere else it could go?'

'Yeah, I suppose so. There's more blank space on the other side of the door.' Jo sits up straight. 'If I move it across, I'll be able to get the ready meals cabinets in, too. I can call the bloke, see if he'll deliver them on a Sunday, then it could all be set up for Monday.' Ready meals are going to make such a difference, keep pushing things in the right direction. 'Why didn't I think of this myself? It's genius!'

'Well, I wouldn't go that far, like.' But Tessa's smiling, and Jo beams back.

It's early; earlier than Jo's used to being up on a Sunday, and the rain's still sheeting it down.

'Here.' Tessa proffers a parcel wrapped in a tea towel. She's as still as ever, perfectly ready to go. Tessa doesn't seem to sleep.

'Toast.' And butter, leaking warm grease into the nip of the day.

Jo slams the protesting windscreen wipers into action and stuffs the toast into her mouth. The road's pretty empty, the only cars they pass crowned with mountain bikes.

'Where've all these outdoor warriors come from?' she'd asked Liam the last time they'd taken the girls out, twisting past the stream of Lycra on the forest track.

Liam had laughed. 'It's not new, you know. Plenty of

153

people were biking up here when we were at school. You had your head in a book, is all.'

Liam. Jo's stomach swoops with unease as she steers into the bend down into town. She'd thought he might come and give them a hand today. But Liam said he was 'busy', not even bothering with an excuse.

Jo knows why he won't come, though. On Friday he'd appeared in the shop at lunchtime, through the front, as if he was a proper customer. Friday lunchtimes were one of their busiest times. Even Ron was at the front of the shop serving people, transformed, Stars-in-Your-Eyes style, as he came through the plastic curtains, his usual gruffness replaced with a more customer-friendly bonhomie whose unlikeliness always gave Jo the willies.

Jo looked up from slicing ham to see Liam standing in the doorway in his work clothes. He didn't make any motion to come into the shop, didn't smile, just jerked his head towards the entrance in an unmistakable sign of emergency. Jo rushed through her customer's pound-of-king-prawns-pound-of-mince without heed to any of the niceties, virtually throwing the bags across the counter.

'Li! What's happened? Is it one of the kids?'

'No, no. They're OK.'

Her heart stopped hammering and her breathing came more easily. 'Oh, thank God.'

'Look, can we have a word? Outside, like?'

'Could we do it once we're closed, if everything's OK?' There was a queue forming at the till. There was never a queue, not a proper one, and it brought as much anxiety as it did satisfaction. 'Are you around later?'

'Got the girls to sort later. It'll only take a minute.'

They stepped just outside and stood huddled under the awning against the rain.

Liam looked beyond her, his fists balled.

'It's just . . . It's about the sausages you gave our mum.'

'Oh, yeah – I meant to tell you!' But she hadn't seen him to tell him, though it hadn't been for want of trying. Liam hadn't been in touch once in the weeks she'd been home. Kirsty had invited her round for tea with the kids a couple of times, and Jo had texted Liam, but he hadn't made any sign of caring whether she was there or not. It was starting to be hard not to take it personally. And now he'd shown up at one of the busiest times for the shop, wanting to talk about Debbie's sausages as if it was an enormous problem rather than an easy favour.

'She didn't pay for them, you know.'

Liam rounded on her, the closest to fury he'd ever been. 'You saying she nicked them?'

'What? No, of course not! I gave them to her!'

He'd got an expression on his face that hadn't been there since he was about eight or nine, belligerent and afraid all at once.

'I don't expect you to pay, either. It was a gift.' Was that what this was about?

The silence stretched, thinning the air between them.

'She was looking well, Li. It was so good to see.'

Still nothing.

This was stupid. Whatever Liam's problem was, they were getting nowhere.

She stood up straighter. 'Look, I'd better get on; that queue'll be like Christmas soon.'

'No.'

'*Liam!* What is it?'

Liam ran his hand through his hair, and it stuck up with plaster dust.

'It's Mum. She's not well. You saw her on a good day. But it's all day-by-day. And a thing like them sausages, it can throw her right off. She ate the lot of them, Jo. All at once.'

'Well, that's what you want, surely? It's good that she's feeding herself.'

Jo was watching the counters. At least two people were pointing at the prawns. She really needed to get back to that queue before Ron started talking about shellfish poisoning.

'Feeding herself's one thing. But you've got to be careful how much you give her when she's like this. She got proper gut-ache from eating so much so quick, convinced herself she was at death's door. The neighbours got worried, called me because they could hear her wailing. She's sure now that you're part of a plot to try and poison her, and hasn't left the house since.'

'Oh, God. I was just trying to do my bit for her. I'm so sorry.' Shame knotted in Jo's intestine as realisation seeped in.

'I know you didn't mean nothing by it. But you've been gone a long time and things change. She's got worse in lots of ways, even when she's in a good patch. She doesn't always react to things the way you'd expect.'

Liam's mum was the bruise at the centre of his being. He'd spent much of his life trying to conceal it from view, and when that hadn't been possible, protecting it. Anything that touched upon his home life seared right to his core, and Jo, of all people, should know that. She'd stuffed up hugely.

'I'm really sorry. I should have found out more how she was.'

Liam still didn't respond. Through the window, Ron was shaking his head at yet another customer who pointed towards the shellfish. His mask of good cheer would slip any moment in the face of Jo's plan working, and with margins so tight, the loss of even a single one of these customers could be a problem.

'Look, Li, I've got to go. I'm really sorry. Next time I'll talk to her about not eating them all at once.'

'Don't worry about giving her no more. Kirst and I get her food in when we get ours. It's harder if we don't know what she's had. I was on a job with a new builder, plaster going off that needed skimming, and Kirst had to miss a shift to sort this lot out. Let us worry about her ourselves.' Liam crossed the road to his van. 'You'd better get back to your customers.'

Cold, wet drops splodged down her neck from the awning as she watched him drive off. They hadn't spoken since.

* * *

Now Jo slides into the parking space and switches off the ignition, glad again for the oblivion of the endless rain.

'Here we are then!'

Tessa stands silently beside Jo at the back door to the shop while the rain drips down from the gutter and Jo jiggles the key in the lock.

Please let this be something that goes right for once.

Chapter Eighteen

MOVING THE CABINETS IS A fiddlier business than Tessa has imagined. The two main units are straightforward enough – they're empty, waiting to be refilled in the morning – but there are two big upright display freezers against the other wall.

Jo's a solid worker. She's also like the radio. A constant stream of conversation pours out, like it or not. This should be companionable, but it's terrifying, not knowing what reactions might be triggered by Jo's endless chatter.

'So, tell me more about the sorts of things you could make with cast iron?'

'All sorts, really.'

'But what sort of all sorts?' Jo tugs two packs of chicken pieces from the freezer, balancing them between pinched fingers with the delicacy of a brain surgeon, then plonking them down in the path of the freezer. It's as if she sees half the solution.

'Well, you know . . . Wine bottle racks out of soldered horse shoes. Did tiny reindeer shoes once, round Christmastime.' Another memory bumps up, like it or not. 'I made a coat stand for someone once, twisted into the shape of a sunflower.'

She still doesn't know what Marnie was doing there, not really.

Some friend of a friend had been looking to buy a horse and Tessa was at the dealers' yard doing her usual rounds. The friends went off riding, trying out the horse. It was mid-June, everything at its greenest, except for the rapeseed fields, which were in competition with the sun for the brightest yellow.

'This view's incredible!'

Tessa, shifting horseshoes around in the Swanee, glanced up and her hand shook violently, the shoe dropping from the tongs. A woman stood just off from the heat of the forge beside the van, as if she'd dropped from the sky. There was nobody else around but still Tessa checked furtively in case anyone had seen her reaction. Her cheeks burned and every inch of her body moved to high alert.

The woman looked a bit younger than Tessa and was like nobody Tessa had ever seen in the Forest, before or since. It was ridiculous but she was just like a warrior goddess, legs akimbo, one hand shielding her eyes as she gazed over the hedge, out towards the river. Her clothes were more suited to the telly than a dealers' yard in the Forest. Tessa, who never paid any attention to this kind of thing, was transfixed by the floaty skirt catching the breeze and the bright white top straight from a Persil ad. The woman's hair wasn't floating, though. It was bouncing, tight curls picking up the light and refracting it.

The woman smiled, clearly awaiting a response.

'Yeah. Good day for it.' Emotion thickened Tessa's tongue. She lifted the top shoe out of the Swanee with the pritchel and banged it down onto the anvil with more force than was strictly necessary, bashing away the feelings before they could do harm. The shoe's glow faded through the oranges and ambers, like turning down a dimmer switch.

The woman wandered closer, squatted down and Tessa tensed. The woman's face was dangerously close to the edge of the shoe, now the colour of a maple leaf in summer, but Tessa didn't dare risk her voice to warn her away.

'Bit hot for that today, I'd think.'

Tessa tried to wipe away sweat, nodded. This was pathetic. In a minute she'd be panting, and not because of the heat.

The woman observed her with open curiosity, moving closer to the Swanee.

'Watch yourself.' It was a croak. But if the horse sale didn't go through because one of the guests set fire to herself on a horseshoe, Tessa'd be in for it. She was doing well these days, Mam gone years now, the work long since established and the working day suiting her down to the ground. She was keeping herself to herself as much as possible. It was lonely, but the ragdolling was under control. She was still dog-tired at the end of the day and prone to falling asleep in the oddest of places, but by and large she was on the most even keel she'd known.

The woman smiled again and it was like sunburst. Helpless against it, Tessa's hand slipped slightly and the hammer clanged on the anvil.

'What are you making?'

'Horseshoes.' This woman smelled like sunburst too, bright and hopeful, and she was so close that Tessa could reach out and lightly touch her calf, just to see if it felt like the woman looked. Silky soft with a core as steely as any shoe Tessa could forge. Tessa bent down over her tools again, keeping herself as far out of reach as she could.

'Can you make anything you set your mind to?'

'Not quite.' To look the woman in the eye would be too much, but Tessa straightened up, sucked in her gut. 'A fair few bits, though. Metal bends any which way you like once you know what you're doing.'

The woman squatted back on her heels and watched. Her dress sense might be all floaty, but the set of her eyes betrayed a sharp mind.

Later, much later, Tessa would learn that Marnie was calculating what to request, working out something of enough complexity so as not to patronise Tessa but not so complicated that she'd just issue a flat 'no'. 'This expensively trained mind is good at figuring out how to work with people so they think it's their idea, you know,' she teased Tessa later.

162

Marnie had felt the same way about her, right from the start. That was the thing that blew Tessa's mind. It wasn't just her own brain, her own body, that had come to a complete standstill in the face of Marnie. Marnie, too, had fallen for Tessa in that first minute. Marnie, who rode horses like a dream, had persuaded her friends she had a headache so that she could stay behind in the stables with Tessa. Marnie had spent ten minutes thinking of good opening lines and discarding them all in favour of a platitude about the view.

But Tessa didn't know any of this yet, didn't know what was to come, didn't know that she'd make the requested sunflower coat stand, spend hours on it, her mind fizzing, trying not to feel things. She didn't know that she'd think of Marnie as soon as she woke up and as she fell asleep. She didn't know that within six months she'd have moved over to Bristol, moved in with Marnie, be driving back over this bridge and loving the views in all directions. She didn't know that the ragdolling would rush back with a vengeance when she fell in love, or that Marnie, against all the odds, would fall in love with her too. She didn't know a thing. She only knew that her breath was struggling to come steady, that swallowing had become hard, that she needed to put down the horseshoe and follow this woman, understand this feeling that dared her so.

'Will you make something for me? I'll pay you, of course.'

And that was it.

She wishes, with all her heart, that she could have made it last.

Chapter Nineteen

SLEEP WON'T COME TONIGHT. JO'S body is spent and aching after all the shunting around at the shop, but her mind won't shut up, circling her conversation with Liam, nagging and nagging for an explanation she just can't find. Just after two o'clock, she pushes off the duvet and pads down the corridor. The flagstones are cold and she pulls her pyjamas tighter around her, as if that will help.

There's enough water swishing in the kettle. She drops a mint teabag into a mug and leans against the iron bar of the range. The garden has switched modes in the inky light; it's rustling and crackling, full of sound rather than sights, but no less comforting.

The kettle purrs and she lifts it off the boil before it can start to roar and wake Tessa. The shop will be so much more manageable like this. Phyllis will be a good test case; if she doesn't like it, she won't be shy to say so. Jo pokes at the teabag with her finger, withdrawing it too fast and splashing hot tea everywhere. If only sorting out what's gone wrong between her and Liam could be as straightforward as swapping over a couple of freezers.

Jo takes her mug over to the sofa, tucks her feet up for warmth. They've been through odd patches before. Right after their GCSEs he went a bit distant for a while, but that . . . well, that was understandable. This is a mystery, though. It can't just be about his mum, though the idea that Jo's not allowed to even try to help makes her feel sick with its underlying message of: You're not part of this now.

He's been off with her since she got back, asking the bare minimum and volunteering even less. Whenever she'd been home for weekends and holidays over the last ten years it had always been great; compressed, and no time to really do much beyond go to the pub one evening or out for a walk with the kids, but easy, same as it had ever been. They aren't eighteen now, of course, but their friendship has grown with the years like it always had, lack of time being the only reason – or so she'd assumed – why they didn't hang out more. Except now she's back, she seems gone from being Liam's automatic partner in crime (after Kirsty, obviously) to someone that at best is an add-on and at worst – well, at worst she's told to back off and leave him to it, as if she'd never met his mum before, didn't know exactly what was involved. Jo curls up tighter, but still the amorphous discomfort gnaws, eroding the excitement and enjoyment of being home, and leaving her exposed.

Jo frowns into her tea. There has to be a way to fix things. Liam's more of a brother to her than Gary; he's been around almost as long, too. And with Liam it was different. He chose them. She doesn't get to abandon him.

'Jo, come away from that window. Tea's on the table.'

'But Mummy, he's still out there again today. It's raining. Why isn't it teatime at his house too?' Jo backed away from the window, still watching, and collided with Mum.

'Careful there! This fat's still hot and you don't want it all over you.' Mum poured water into the grill pan and it sizzled from its sideways position in the sink, sausage-scented steam fluting up. The kitchen window fogged over and even when Jo kneeled up in her seat at the table, Liam was invisible, washed out into the gloom.

'But he's been out there all afternoon.'

Mum sat down beside her, opposite Gary and facing the window like always. Dad had stayed on at the shop today to break down a side of beef that he'd picked up at Gloucester, so his sausages and mash were being kept warm on a plate inside the oven.

'Is he still out there now?' Now Mum was peering through the fog too. 'What did you say his name was?'

'Liam.'

'Liam what?'

'Dunno. He started in our class this week.'

'Huh.' Mum speared a sausage, but it got lost in the thought that was round her like a duvet and didn't make it as far as her mouth. 'Where's he moved from?'

'Dunno that either.'

'Don't know anything, do you?' Gary sneered. Jo swiped at him under the table and missed. Gary stuck out his tongue.

Mum had cut up Jo's sausages and they were just big enough to fill her mouth but leave room for the words to come out round the edges. 'He's nice. Liam.' Not Gary, obviously. He was a horrible brother. 'Mrs Henderson sent me to talk to him at break on Monday because he didn't have any friends and she said I talked to anyone.' Gary snorted and Jo slid down in her seat to kick him. 'Shut *up*.'

'Jo, I've told you before—'

'Sorry, Mum. Anyway, I went over and I thought I could ask him where his last school had been but he was scratching in the dirt with a stick and he didn't answer. So then I asked him what he was drawing and he said he wasn't *drawing*, he was *writing*. And I said that was stupid because—'

'Nice way to treat the new kid.'

'Shut *up, Gary. Sorry*, Mum. Anyway, it *is* stupid because he only joined Mrs Henderson's class this week and not even Jonty can write yet, except his name, and he's already *five*. He's the biggest in the class, but not the cleverest – that's Samantha Jones and sometimes me. But now it might be Liam because he moved his stick and it was true, he'd done actual words. I didn't know some of them but I could see all the letters and they were all proper letters like we've been taught, and with the spaces between them for the words, and it was a big sentence, Mum, a really big sentence—' The sausage flew off Jo's fork and splashed the gravy all over her shirt.

'Oh, Jo! Pay a bit more attention!' But Mum was still gazing out of the window. It was less steamy in the kitchen now and Mum was taller than Jo.

'Is he still there?'

'What, love? Oh, yes. Yes, he's still there.' Mum hadn't started her sausages yet and her eyes were half-closed, like she was doing a really hard sum. 'So you played together?'

'Yes. And now we're friends. Every lunchtime we make words in the dirt.'

'And he's going to follow you home every night like a weirdo?'

'I didn't know he'd do that, did I?' Jo stretched to kick Gary again, but he copped on to it.

Now Mum pushed her chair back, pulled at the strings of her apron. 'Gary, get the plate out of the oven. Careful, mind.'

Jo and Gary stared, united for once.

'But that's Dad's,' Gary said.

Mum was halfway out of the door. 'Don't you worry about that. Jo, get the cutlery out.'

Jo and Gary, astounded, did as they were told. They ate in silence, the sausages warm and juicy.

A couple of minutes later Mum was back inside, Liam beside her. 'Here we are then, love, you eat that and

168

then I'll phone your mummy and get you home. Do you know her number?' She set down a glass of orange squash beside Liam.

He stared at the plate of food. 'No.' He hadn't picked up his knife and fork yet.

Mum paced from the window to the table and back, her hard-sum face on. 'OK, don't worry. I'll see if someone else knows it.'

'No number. She ent got no phone.' Liam's eyes were firmly on his plate.

This time they all stared, even Mum.

'None at all?'

Liam shook his head. He had his fork in his hands, but was juggling it from side to side, not eating. Maybe Jo could have his sausage if he didn't want it.

'OK. Well, Liam, love, do you know where you live? Would you be able to find it if we walked over?'

'It's up on the estate,' Jo added helpfully. Maybe an actual fact would help Mum's face lose the hard-sums look. It didn't.

'Right. Well, in that case maybe we'll take the car rather than walking all the way there.'

Perhaps Mum had muddled Liam's house with somewhere else. It wasn't that far to walk at all, not if you used the cut-through and missed out the high street. Jo opened her mouth to explain but then shut it again.

Liam stared at his sausage and Jo joined him, leaning over it. 'Aren't you hungry?' Greedy hope rose.

Mum shooed her away from the table. 'It'd be hard for anyone to eat with you two gawping at them. Come over here and help me put things in the dishwasher, can you? And Gary, haven't you got homework to do?'

After Liam had eaten up the sausage, and all the mash, and even the carrots, and said thank you to Mum in a way that made Mum ruffle his hair, Gary roll his eyes and Liam blush, Mum left a note for Dad on the kitchen table and the four of them piled into her car, Gary as curious as anybody. Mum had been right to bring the car. All the houses looked the same with their brown and grey pebbles on the front and even the same sorts of curtains on the windows – those lacy ones like Nan's curtains but sagging off a wire, and greyer, to match the pebbles. Jo sat on her hands, made herself as small as she could.

'This is it,' Liam said, and Mum pulled on the handbrake in the middle of a row. Liam's house didn't have the grey curtains. In fact, it didn't seem to have any curtains at all.

Liam pulled at the car door handle.

'You'll have to wait for Mum to open the door; it's got the child locks on.'

For someone who could write so many words, there was a lot Liam didn't know.

'You two stay in the car.'

Jo pouted, but she knew better than to try to convince Mum to change her mind.

'Come on, Liam, love; I'll take you to the door and explain to your mum where you've been.'

Jo leaned over Gary to see what Liam's mum looked like, but the door hadn't opened yet. It was black, with wavy paint that came out like curls at the bottom of the door.

Mum knocked on the window. Maybe they didn't have a doorbell or maybe Liam's mum was in the kitchen making tea with the telly on and couldn't hear them. She might be cross that Liam had already had tea. Mum cupped her hands to the window and peered in, and Jo peered at Mum, a whole domino-row of peering.

'Stop leaning like that – you're squashing me!' Gary complained, but she paid no notice.

The door cracked open. Mum stood upright and inside the car Jo straightened up too. But the lady who came to the door wasn't playing the same game because she was all stooped over. That couldn't be Liam's mum, could it? She looked too sharp-edged to be a mummy, and she was still wearing her nightie. There was a little cloud in between her and Mum, like she had her own fog-maker. It was impossible to hear what Mum said but the lady sort of grabbed Liam by his hair and yanked him through the door. It shut really quickly and the curls of paint on the bottom of the door waved.

'Was that really Liam's mum? Was she angry he'd already had his tea? Why did she grab him in like that? Can he come and play again?' Jo needed to know all the answers right now so that her tummy would feel right again, but Mum looked like she had a tummy ache of her own.

'I've said he can come whenever he likes.' Mum turned and looked right at Jo, her eyes shiny. 'Do you understand, Jo? If Liam wants to come to tea, then you say yes.'

Why wouldn't she say yes? But Mum was wiping her nose on her arm now and Mum went *mad* when anyone did that, so Jo buttoned it and they rode home in what passed for silence in their family.

The tea's almost all gone. Jo yawns and stretches; sometimes faking it will bring on proper sleepiness. She doesn't know anyone better than Liam; she should have thought properly about his mum. But she hadn't meant any harm by it.

Jo sighs again, a half-yawn this time. Sleep is starting to creep back in at the edges. She's going to be knackered in the morning. Best to try and get as much kip as she can.

Chapter Twenty

TESSA NORMALLY WAITS UNTIL SHE'S heard Jo's car in the driveway before coming down for breakfast, but she's been awake since dawn, her ankle itching where the horseshoe burn is healing.

Jo's there at the table, book in one hand, slice of toast in another. When she sees Tessa, she jumps up. 'I can leave if you need breakfast in silence. Running a bit late this morning.'

Tessa shakes her head. 'You're all right.'

'There's coffee in the pot – d'you want some?'

Jo pours the coffee with the earnestness of a papal blessing. She's using smaller movements, is pulled closer into herself. The coffee, though, when she hands it over, is delicious. Tessa smiles her thanks and yawns, and Jo follows suit.

'Sorry. I didn't sleep so well last night.'

'Is something on your mind?' Taking over that

173

butcher's can't be the easiest thing, especially not solo. Jo seems to Tessa to be the sort of person who makes all decisions in a crowd.

Jo looks nervous. Perhaps she can't make the rent. Tessa takes a breath.

'The shop's OK, I think, thanks. A lot going on, but that's all to the good. It's just . . . I know you two don't seem to have hit it off, but I was worrying about Liam. He's been acting so odd since I've been back, and he's basically family.'

Tessa's shoulders tense. 'Oh?' She sips the coffee carefully.

'I mean, we're not related or anything, but he more or less lived at my house when we were growing up. I'm not saying anything that isn't already out there, really. You'd probably know his mum if you saw her. She's always struggled a bit, and Mum and Dad were worried about Liam, not that I figured that out until I was much older. So he was at ours as much as he was at his own place, except when Debbie was in one of her good phases. It sounds pathetic, I know, but when something's off between us, it completely throws me.'

Tessa doesn't know anyone in the Forest, not really. Just Ern, and her clients. But she met Liam's mum once, and that was enough. To say he needed protecting didn't come close.

She'd been a lot younger then; they all had. It wasn't long after Dad had died and Mam went back to the

Valleys, so she had the place to herself, but she was careful. Tessa had definitely locked the door to the garden forge. Probably definitely. She twisted her wrist, veins showing in the soft underbelly, to see if that would awaken a memory of twisting the key in the lock. Nothing.

Well, it wasn't locked now. A crack of darkness pierced the light and drew Tessa in. As she stepped from shade into obscurity, the forest whispered.

'You're plenty old enough to take care of yourself, Theresa.' Her mother approached through the trees. Tessa dropped the keys to the ground, their jangle discordant against the crackle of the leaves. She couldn't be back. Tessa's head pounded and her heart joined in. It's as if she'd put herself on the anvil. The pressure built and built, her body tipping itself inside out. Mam was getting closer and closer and she couldn't stand it. It was too late now, too late.

'Stop, please stop.' She didn't know if she was pleading with Mam or herself, but it whispered out into the wind and she scrunched her eyes shut against having to go through all that again. When she opened them, Mam was gone.

Mam was gone.

Mam went a month ago. She wasn't coming back.

It wasn't real.

Tessa was nineteen, and all alone in the cottage, free to do what she wanted. But still the forge acted as a repository for all she couldn't think out loud in the house. She stood outside its door, one hand on the lock, waiting for her heartbeat to subside. She couldn't go in like this, however much she craved the soothing heat of the forge to bring her back into herself. Mam may have gone but the headache was real, needling like an unbreakable promise into the space behind her eye. She inhaled. The air wasn't sure of itself either; a lingering damp from the earlier rain mingled with the very last of the leaves falling through it on their way to become mulch.

Tessa eased open the forge door, welcoming the darkness. Her eyes had always adjusted quickly to the gloom, the glow of the fire drawing her forward. She was happiest in the shadows. To stand quietly is what Tessa learned as a child; to stand quietly and avoid other people's fallout.

Over towards the fire, something moved. Tessa turned her head a fraction, her breath catching in her throat.

The movement was followed by a clatter from the far shelf and Tessa plummeted with shock, pushed herself back up before there was a chance to think. Two figures moved out of the shadow towards the glow of the fire. The larger one was female, ill-defined and unshapen in the gloom. She prodded a smaller figure, a boy; reluctant, stooped over. He kinked to avoid the woman's prodding, and a bag she was gripping in the other hand dropped with a clank.

No haunting this time. No mind tricks. Simply Tessa's belongings, about to be stolen from her forge.

Tessa started forward, but before she made any distance, the woman gripped the child by the tender underside of his arm. The boy bent back, legs planted, torso contorted, and Tessa shuddered, the headache storming back.

That kid's in danger.

The woman cuffed the boy and he tilted back again. Tessa tilted in sympathy, unable to help herself. She couldn't move, couldn't stop watching.

She had to act.

She had to be careful, too, or she might collapse again. And then the woman would do God knows what.

The woman was delving around, oblivious to Tessa approaching her. The boy tracked her movements with huge eyes but said nothing; didn't budge an inch.

'Those are my things – can I help you?'

Quicker than Tessa would have credited, the woman grabbed the poker from the fire and waved it in Tessa's general direction. Tessa wasn't scared. She'd caught herself with red-hot horseshoes enough times.

The boy was about eight or nine. He didn't move, showed no surprise. She looked at the boy and tried to tell him silently: *You'll be all right.* But it wasn't true. Her head was a tight band of pain.

The woman shuffled over. Her hair hung lank over her shoulders, grease mingling with stale booze.

'You want to drop that bag, right now.'

The woman looked Tessa up and down, hostility in every line. 'Why'd I want to do that?'

Tessa took a pace forward, her fingers starting to tingle.

'Put it down, please.'

The woman stopped sneering and eyed her up. Then

she dropped her arm and braced for battle, legs apart, daring Tessa. This wasn't going to end easily.

But if Tessa confronted her further, the tingling would get worse and there was no knowing what might happen.

Tessa backed slowly towards the bench, sat down.

'If you get out and never, ever come back, I'll say nothing.' It would get this awful woman out of her space; it would keep her safe and protected. But Tessa knew it wasn't enough, not really.

She glanced again at the kid. He'd separated himself from his mother, was holding himself in the sagged manner of someone who expects defeat. He wasn't looking at Tessa.

He was too young for this. And she was old enough to do something about it, to talk to people, try and find help for him. But she couldn't, she simply couldn't. Tessa's pulse quickened; her fingers tingled again. If she were to interfere with this, it would bring on a whole heap of emotional reactions that would leave her destined for collapse.

Self-preservation threatened to choke her. She couldn't possibly help this kid. It had to remain none of her business. She had to stay out of it, even if that made her the sort of person she'd never want to be.

Now Tessa pointed at the door, risked a glare at the woman. 'Out. And if I see you here again, I'll be going straight to the police.'

'All right, all right.' The woman shuffled off, turned round halfway as if remembering something. 'Come on, Liam.'

Afterwards, Tessa sat, stared. She should have been furious that someone was here, trying to nick her stuff. But shame swept up her, in from her fingers and toes, out from her heart.

She stayed there, fixed with it, until the sun shifted from the windows and the fire in the forge had burned right down. She only had herself to protect. And in this moment, she protected nothing. Nothing at all.

Tessa sits now, allows the relief to flood in. She'd wondered about the boy for decades since, had even asked Geoff up at the riding centre once if he knew him, though it seemed unlikely that he'd be up there for weekly lessons. But she'd left out most of the detail for fear of sounding like a monster for her inaction, and the question was blanched, useless. Tessa would look out for him when she was in town, but she was there so rarely and Tessa wasn't the sort of person who bumped into people.

The shock when Liam had shown up with Jo had nearly sent her to the ground. He'd recognised her before she'd had a chance to take it in, had come out to the kitchen to find her. He'd just started speaking when Jo barged in with the little girl, and Tessa's spent the past weeks wondering whether he'd been gearing up to an apology or, more likely, to lay into her for not helping. What kind of person leaves a child with someone like that? The next time she saw him, when he brought round the wood, he was silent on the matter and she didn't dare raise the subject.

Now the guilt recedes. Not entirely; she was still a coward, a selfish one at that. But Jo's parents were not such cowards. She slumps with relief.

Chapter Twenty-One

'WHAT THE BLOODY HELL'S SHE gone and done now?'

Ron doesn't even entertain the notion that this layout might be better. He fills the middle of the shop like a particularly outraged Miss Trunchbull.

'No need to ask Mo when you can ask me yourself. I'm here, you know. We can all get around now without banging into each other and that counter. Look!' Jo swishes from the front door to the new counter, describing large arcs with her arms for good measure. She pirouettes to a stop in front of Ron and fixes him with a saccharine beam. 'See?'

Ron is unmoved, quite literally. He scowls down at her. 'Stop acting like a bloody kid. That nonsense might have been all right when you were seven, but we've all aged since then. And some of us could do with growing up.'

All those years in the lower courts have equipped her for this kind of hollow intimidation. Remain unruffled and stand your ground, that's what you have to do.

Mo looks from one of them to the other. 'I hope you didn't go hurting your back, lugging that counter across the shop.'

'It doesn't weigh as much as you'd think, not when it's empty.'

'Are you telling me you took out all that meat?'

'Yes, of course I did. But only for a few minutes. It won't have done it any harm.'

'No harm!' Ron harrumphs, actually harrumphs. 'What the hell would you know about whether or not something's causing any harm? Marching in here, changing things around. You could've given the whole town salmonella.'

Most of the town is shopping in sodding Aldi these days; that's why her parents quit and why she's busting a gut trying to diversify the business. But pointing that out isn't going to help with anything.

'Well, the counter's moved now.' Ron and Jo both start at the sound of Mo's voice. 'Why don't we leave it there for the week, at least, see if anyone minds—'

'Minds! Of course they'll damn well mind! They've always known which way to expect the meat to be served and now that's all been messed about with. There'll be letters to the Parish Council before you know it.' Ron's absolute confidence in his own opinion is as awe-inspiring as it's wrong. He's simply never prepared to accept Jo might actually be on to something.

Mo's aiming her remarks at Ron but looking at Jo. 'Like I was saying, let's leave the counter where it is now, and then decide at the end of next week if we want to keep it there?'

It takes more effort than it should not to just say: 'No! This is my shop and I can do what I want.'

Jo turns to Mo, bright smile plastered on. 'Sounds like a plan. Let's try that.'

Ron mutters and stalks away into the back room. The clink of metal reverberates as he yanks the cleaver down from the wall. Jo rolls her eyes. She'll buy him a new bloody one for his birthday; at the rate he's going he'll have worn this one out.

Liam would be proud of how calm she'd stayed. Except Liam doesn't seem to be proud of her for anything at all at the moment. Jo pings the till open, starts pulling the float out of its bags ready for the morning's customers.

Yesterday's apron is lying behind the till where she must have chucked it when shifting around the counter. Ron needs no more reasons to have a go at her. Jo bundles up the apron, squirming at the bloodstains, and backs out from behind the counter into the prep room. Maybe tonight she'll try and get hold of Liam, in between his ferrying duties, and sit down properly, ask what the best way to help with Debbie would be.

What happens next isn't clear. One of the apron strings must have got loose and Jo trips on it as she's edging through the plastic curtain towards the laundry bin at the edge of the prep room. As she trips, she bodges the side of the counter and jolts Ron mid-slice.

'Owwww!' Ron collapses to the ground, his hand clutched between his knees, nose almost touching the floor. The cleaver lies on the floor beside him. On the prep counter just above is a heaped pile of some kind of meat. It's impossible to tell if the blood belongs to Ron or to the bloodied cubes of flesh above him.

Jo can't move. Jesus wept. Has he chopped off his hand?

'Mo! Mo!'

Ron's doubled over. She tiptoes over to him, voice scared down to a whisper. 'Where does it hurt, Ron? Can you show me?'

Ron lifts his hand up towards her, pain pulling his face taut. 'My finger.'

There's a huge gash through the meat of his thumb and into his palm. It's so deep that flesh forms a gorge, heading down towards the bone. There's blood everywhere and her mouth waters as if she'll be sick.

'First aid kit . . . I'll just . . .' She bolts, bumping into Mo.

'Oh, thank God! Where do we keep the first aid kit? Or maybe we need an ambulance? Can you go and see, Mo?' She's babbling, fear pouring from her mouth in these bubbles of words, nausea lurking beneath them.

There's got to be a first aid kit here somewhere. Mum and Dad used to keep it under the till. Jo rummages around in the cupboard, her fingers hitting the sharp edge, as if in sympathy with Ron's finger.

She's never been able to cope with sick humans; they upset her so viscerally that she doesn't know where to put herself. It's as if her limbs, her voice, all stop co-ordinating and leave her flailing and panicked. There's a ringing sensation from somewhere, as if her ears are resonating with the trauma.

The ringing doesn't stop; it's only adding to the stress of the situation. There's no time to answer it, though.

Back in the cold storage room, Ron's sitting on a stool against the wall, his hand up above his head. Mo's holding it up there, only now his thumb isn't visible – thank God – because Mo's wrapped it in what must be her butcher's coat. Something thick and white, anyway. And – Jo can't unsee it – there's blood seeping through. Even though the hand is basically the size of a baseball mitt, there is still blood escaping.

Jo hands over the first aid kit, forces out the words past rising nausea. 'How are you feeling?' She can't look at Ron.

'Got any more stupid questions?'

Not on death's door, then.

Mo turns round from replacing her makeshift bandage with an actual one. Jo has never learned any of this stuff, somehow feeling exempt from it all due to Gary's unquestioned professional paramedic expertise. As if that would help her when he's hundreds of miles away.

Mo finishes off the bandage with something suspiciously like a flourish.

'I'll run him up the hospital, see if they can sew it back together. Probably needs some Steri-Strips at the very least, it does. You'll be all right for a minute, won't you?'

185

'Yeah, that should be fine.'

They've barely left the shop when Jo's phone rings again.

'What?' She breathes heavily, the nausea still threatening.

'Jo?'

The voice is tentative, and it takes her a second.

'Tessa! You all right?' Stupid question. There's no way Tessa would voluntarily call her if she were all right.

'I think so.'

'Are you sure?'

There's no answer from the other end of the phone.

'Tessa?'

'Sorry. I'm still here.'

'Are you sure there's nothing wrong? Only I'm—'

Tessa's words rush down the line like ketchup after you've whacked the bottle. 'Could you meet me at home? Locked myself out, I have, no spare key, and I really don't want to have to change the locks again.'

Again?

'OK, I'll be there in about ten minutes. See you then.'

Jo flips the shop sign to 'closed', goes out to the car and heads up the hill. It's like playing hooky.

Ron. The sheen of his wound looms before her, the flesh gaping and deep red against the scrubbed whiteness of the prep room. Jo puts her foot to the floor and hurtles for the safety of the forest.

Chapter Twenty-Two

TESSA'S SAFE DOWN HERE, HER back pressed against the front wall, hands tucked up inside her jacket. March is doing what March always does, weather-wise; there's no telling if any given day will be a lion or a lamb. Working alongside molten metal has its advantages; Tessa never really needs to care what the weather's doing, just puts on the same jeans and sweatshirt and thick leather apron regardless. But it makes a difference, all the same; the horses are tetchier when it's colder, especially if they're lame, and don't want her cold hands on their forelegs, even if she's there to help them. They don't know that, not to begin with, at least.

There's a car slowing down, the engine puttering softly. Tessa stands up carefully, the walls of the cottage firm and cold under her palms. She'd only popped up to Susan's to take care of the old cobs. She'd been feeling fine all morning but must have blanked out at some point. Her keys are absolutely nowhere to be found.

Jo looks none too clever herself, to be honest, handing herself out of the car with care.

'You sure you're OK?'

Tessa takes a minute to answer, lets Jo get the door open and follows her in.

When Jo gets to the stairs, she stops. 'Shall I make you a cup of tea?'

'Ta.'

Tessa sits at the kitchen table and watches as Jo pauses in front of the cupboard.

'The cups are in the next one along.'

'Sorry?' Jo's attention snaps towards Tessa. 'Oh, yeah.'

She makes the tea and brings it over to the table, lowering herself down gently. Tessa recognises the steady movements of someone using all her energy to merely stay upright in life.

'Is something wrong?'

She's startled by her own sheer nosiness.

'What? No. Well, maybe. Oh, it's just . . . I don't know.' Jo waves a hand and knocks over her mug. 'Oh God! I'm sorry! Did I get you?' She jumps up and there's another waterfall of tea.

Tessa rises too. 'Don't worry about it. I'm waterproof.'

'But you're covered in tea. It'll burn you.' Jo's close to tears; a bit of an overreaction for a spilled drink.

Tessa splays her hands so that Jo can see the weals and scars. 'Par for the course in my line of work.'

Jo gets a cloth, dabs at the floor. Tessa sits and waits. She's good at sitting and waiting.

The dabbing stops. Here it comes. Tessa tenses, readies herself against anything that might cause a collapse.

'Ron was getting at me about moving the meat counter and next thing I knew I'd accidentally made him cut halfway through his hand.'

Accidentally? 'But he's OK, is he?'

Jo nods, wobbly. 'I'm such an idiot.'

For a second, Tessa's overcome with biting envy for the sheer ease of Jo's life, which has given her no serious cause to develop any coping mechanisms. Imagine so little happening to you that a slip of the knife feels like a disaster. Imagine, come to that, knowing where your next meal's coming from, to being so certain of your friends and family that coming home seems the obvious thing to do.

There's a warning tingling in Tessa's fingers and she cops on before it can reach further, moves away from this line of thinking.

'It won't be the first accident in a butcher's shop, that's for sure.' She reaches out, gently, gently, and puts a hand on Jo's shoulder. 'It'll be all right, honest it will.'

Jo shudders. 'I hope so. Mo was going to take him to the hospital and I scarpered. I should get going, really, open the shop back up.'

This muted, reversed Jo is unsettling, like waking up thinking it's daytime and finding life still shrouded by night – something that's been happening all too often

189

recently, as well. Jo casting shadows throws everything into relief, sharpens Tessa's own grief. She's so sad, so very, very bone-deep sad, and more than that, she's bringing down Jo with her, smart, happy Jo, who upon contact with Tessa has lost all ability to be her natural, joyful self.

It's too much.

The kettle clamours to a standstill and she pours the water onto a teabag she can't remember putting in the mug, then picks it up to take over to Jo. She's living too much on autopilot these days, lost in her own world of pain and recrimination.

And now it's spreading to others. Tessa stares at the top of Jo's head bent into her hands, at her shoulders shaking.

The tingling rushes in and in that split second before she hits the ground, Tessa knows what's happening. She looks around for somewhere to put the tea but the table's still too far away. The mug hits the ground with her, boiling liquid flying everywhere. Tessa struggles to push up to her knees, but nothing's moving.

She's paralysed.

She's terrified.

Try as she might, she can't find any movement. She has to focus, to will her little finger to move, then the rest will follow, but the tea has puddled beside her, is seeping into her overalls, and she can't escape it, can't even roll out of its way.

'Tessa!' Jo's hair tickles Tessa's face and Tessa forces herself to open her eyes. Jo's kneeling beside her, fear coursing so strongly it's a current, pinning Tessa further.

Jo's voice is high, trembling. 'What's happened? Are you all right?'

But Tessa can't nod, can't move. Jo lifts Tessa's head in a manner that's not as gentle as she obviously intends, stares into her eyes again, her own dark with lack of understanding.

'Tessa! Can you hear me?'

Yes, Tessa wants to say. *Yes, I can hear you. I need you to be calm then I can explain.*

But that's not happening. Jo drops Tessa's head back to the ground as if she's forgotten it's attached to Tessa's actual body. 'Tessa!' She's shouting now, pushes Tessa's body at the side in an attempt to get some kind of reaction, and all it's doing is freezing Tessa further still, giving her no spare moment in which to breathe, focus, come back into herself.

That's what she must do: breathe. Focus. This will end. It always does.

Jo stands up abruptly, almost runs from the room. She's gone to phone an ambulance. She mustn't do that. It won't help. Tessa pushes up with one hand to better see where Jo is.

Wait a minute. She's pushed up with one hand.

She wiggles the fingers of the hand experimentally. She's working again.

'Jo!' she croaks. There's no way Jo's going to hear that. She has to get there before Jo sends the ambulance sprinting round. A fuss is the one thing guaranteed to make matters worse.

Tessa heaves off the floor and goes down the corridor.

Jo's in the doorway to the parlour. When she sees Tessa she says something into the phone and springs forward, almost shrieking.

'Lie down! You're injured! Lie back down! I'm just getting help.'

'I'm fine.' But Jo's listening intently to someone on the other end of the phone, doesn't hear.

Louder this time. 'I'm fine.' More firmly than Tessa had necessarily intended, but it's the truth. She feels perfectly all right now. This is how it usually is, though people can never believe it. She reaches over, presses one finger on the phone to end the call.

'Tessa!' But Jo makes no attempt to redial. She stares at Tessa. 'But you're upright, and talking. I don't get it.'

'I told you, I'm fine.' Tessa forces a smile. 'Come on. Let's go through and try for that tea again.'

The tea steams its reassurance into them both and Jo's colour returns.

'Do you mind if I ask you something?' The high panic of earlier has gone, replaced with trepidation.

'No, of course not.' Tessa's toes clench.

'Tell me if I'm out of line. But . . . you didn't seem freaked out by that at all. Has it happened before?' Jo swallows her tea, won't look at Tessa. 'Not to be rude, but I've noticed a few other things. The van in the hedge, and the keys; and you seem to act as if it's all perfectly normal. Is something up?' She darts a glance, stares back at the tea. 'Don't say if you don't want to, obviously.'

Perhaps it's because the exhaustion is through Tessa

192

like rust. Perhaps it's because this concern of Jo's is warm, sincere, and it's been months and months since Tessa's been near any kind of warmth. Perhaps it's because it's just all too much to carry alone for any longer.

'To be honest with you, there has been the odd thing recently.' She sighs. In for a penny, in for a pound. 'No, not just recently. It's happened most of my life. But it's getting worse.'

'Have you seen a doctor?'

If she goes steady, she might not collapse in the telling. 'A couple of times when I was little. They couldn't find anything.'

'But surely you've been since? Someone would have followed this up!'

The differences between their two experiences of living in the same place is there again, chasm-wide. If something like this had happened to Jo, no doubt the entire town would have got involved in sorting it out as they passed through the butcher's shop. But Tessa's life wasn't like that, not at all. At least, not until she got to Bristol.

'I just went back the once, a few years ago.' Because Marnie had asked her to, and it isn't – wasn't – in Tessa's gift to deny Marnie anything. It had been impossible, though, to articulate anything of how she felt to the earnest, harried city doctor in the five-minute slot, so instead she'd mumbled something about not sleeping well and the doctor told her to try a bath and 'soothing music'. It wasn't the doctor's fault. At least she'd been able to go back to Marnie with some sort of response.

'And they found nothing?' Jo frowns. 'Look, don't take this the wrong way, but how would you feel about trying again? You can't live like this!'

Dare Tessa tell her the whole of it? The vein in her head throbs and her toes clench again.

'Be honest with you, I've been putting it down to sadness, really. The recent stuff, anyway.' It echoes in the room, catching the light and hanging there. It can't be unsaid now.

'I . . . well, I was in a relationship, and it had to end not long ago. Knocked me for six, it has.'

Jo nods, waits.

'I didn't know . . . I mean, I've had other things happen and I thought I knew grief.' Jo's gaze is locked on, but Tessa finds she doesn't mind it so much. 'But this . . . It's like a living thing, you know?' Jo nods again and Tessa tips forward into her feelings, can't stop.

'So I thought, well, that's what's going on: I'm miserable, that's all it is. I've had times like this before and it's come under control eventually. But . . .' Her temple is hammering. 'It's not the whole fact of it, not really. Some of this – the losing things, the collapsing – some of this was already happening before. So I don't know if it has to do with the split, or whether it's worse because of it, or what's going on. It's how I live.'

'But you can't keep living like this, surely.'

Tessa had been right: Jo hasn't known grief, not really.

'I'll have to. Working's a bit tricky at the moment, and driving, but it should pass.'

'But there must be something a doctor can do.

Probably not a GP, but a specialist, perhaps over in Bristol? I suppose it's a matter of figuring out what all the symptoms mean.' Jo sits forward, elbows on knees. 'Would you mind if I had a look, see what I can come up with? I'm good at this sort of thing.'

Exhaustion nips hungrily. Tessa has to get upstairs before she passes out again. 'OK. Don't tell me too much, though.'

She's receding. Jo stares, puzzled. But Tessa has faded out and can't finish the sentence properly: *Not hope. Don't give me hope. I can't bear it if it breaks again.*

Chapter Twenty-Three

'THAT'S IT, CHLO!' LIAM LEANS in behind Chloe and swings the rod backwards, and Jo, arriving unannounced at the fishing lake, steps aside in a hurry before she's whacked in the head with a trout. Rosie, watching, giggles, and Jo giggles too, despite the thick rope of nerves coiled in the pit of her stomach.

She'd spent the morning researching – or trying to research – solutions for Tessa. Nobody could walk round with the worry of collapse hanging over them; no wonder she kept herself to herself. It's no way to live. Ordinarily, this is just the sort of challenge Jo loves and she's been relishing getting stuck in. But each time she sits down to clear her mind, get stuck in, she remembers. Liam. Perhaps if she clears things with him, tries to explain properly, she'll get back the bandwidth she needs to do a proper job trying to help Tessa. Easier said than done, apparently.

Liam snaps round at the sound, his expression fully blank, and Jo's gut twists. That's the expression he always used when Jason Bevan started on about his trainers, or if someone dared to bring up his mum (although for the most part, however cruel things got, Debbie was kept out of it, the town too small and everyone too interrelated to risk the throwing of the sharpest stones). Not giving someone the satisfaction of a reaction. The blanker the look, the stronger the emotion being repressed.

'Morning, gang!'

'Auntie Jo!' Chloe hugs her, the line with its dangling fish threatening to tangle them together. Jo pulls her in tightly, exhaling her worries into Chloe's bobble hat. 'How did you know we'd be here?'

'Well, I went to your house but nobody was there. So I popped in to see Mummy at the Co-op, and she told me that Daddy brings you here before football sometimes.' The smile goes over Chloe's head to Rosie, who smiles back in acknowledgement of the football comment, but the explanation is all directed at Liam, who's standing a couple of feet away, unpicking the fishing line. He swears, brings his finger up to his mouth, studiously making no response.

'I used to come up here with your daddy when we were about your age, you know.' She crouches down, pulls Chloe's hat over her eyes and the little girl laughs, pushes it back up and sticks out her tongue.

'I loved it because I was always better than Gary, my big brother. But your daddy was better than all of us, even my own daddy.'

'Better than Uncle Jim?' Rosie's eyes are wide as she looks towards Liam.

'Better than everyone. You've got a good teacher, you two.'

Jo pulls her hood tight against the drizzle. She's always loved it up here, loved the enforced patience of fishing. She'd never got the hang of figuring out which fly is best for the conditions, but the rest of it is weirdly relaxing, and if she doesn't catch a fish it doesn't matter too much. You're compelled to stand still, to pay attention. And you get to stand outside, on the lee of a hill with views down across the fields to the Severn. Not that there's much to see today; the river's a slither of brown velvet amid grey murk.

'Here you go, our Chlo.' Liam hands Chloe the dehooked fish. It slips through her fingers and flaps, vacant-eyed, on the wet grass. Jo's stomach twists again but it's impossible to tell the cause at this point. She rifles through Liam's kit bag and hands an item to Chloe.

'You'll need the bishop for the gory bit.'

Liam puts his hands over Chloe's and positions her properly. His words fling over his shoulder in the breeze. 'Priest, not bishop, you amateur.'

'Really?'

Liam grins, and for the merest of moments they're fifteen again. 'Yeah. Bashing the bishop's definitely not something you want to be talking about to our girls.'

'Oh, good grief!' The laughter spins through her and she leans forward to inspect the solid lump of wood.

'It's an honest mistake, though, when you look at the shape of the thing.'

Liam shakes his head and turns to Chloe, but something's lifted between them, ever so slightly.

'Whack him as hard as you can, right?'

This was the part, even as a kid, that had Jo squirming worse than the trout. She turns away, unable to watch, and peers through the mists at the fields that patchwork their way down to the Severn, their green shouting through the weft and heft of the grey, copses sidelining her view.

Chloe's making good headway, no such squeamishness in her. Jo can hear the poor trout's head slurping as the priest's brought down on it. Her stomach lurches. Better to focus on the river shifting the horizon, the Severn bright with clay. There's no way of telling which direction it's travelling in unless you already know the landscape, know it's being pulled inexorably towards the estuary and out to sea.

The breeze is just right, not over-cold against her cheeks, and she can risk saying out loud the thing she's driven halfway around the Forest to find him for.

'Sorry about your mum. I really am. I wasn't thinking.'

Liam half-turns to look at her, jumps as Chloe barely misses his fingers with the priest. 'Steady there, love.' He frowns, just barely. 'Don't worry about it.' He doesn't look across again.

All the time Jo lived in London, the Liam in her mind was soft-focused, always cheerful, hanging out with the kids and Kirsty, going for walks in the woods and basic-ally smiling a lot. That was it. He was the Liam of her teens. That Liam had been . . . well, he wasn't ever the life and soul of the party, he was more reflective than that, and the situation with his mum had always lingered, adding weight. But he was great company, gently calling her on any nonsense, refusing to do her homework for her but happy to spend hours debating the finer points of *Macbeth* if that's what it took to get Jo through it. And they were always in sync, always knew what the other meant.

'You two going to end up together then, or what?' Matt Hay had asked once when they were about sixteen, lying out by the brook, bike abandoned beside him. She and Liam had both recoiled, not a murmur of consideration from either of them. They were twins, almost. But somewhere along the line the telepathy has faded, even though they've stayed in touch as much as two people in different cities with their own lives ever can.

The Liam she sees now she's home again is clearer and less happy, and they're so far off sync they're in different time zones. Jo's been in her own little bubble for years, flitting back occasionally for visits and just assuming everyone's exactly as they always were. And now she doesn't have to imagine what he's doing; she knows. When he's not scraping sand onto people's walls and waiting for it to dry before doing it all over again, he's driving Chloe through the lanes in the rain to go and get Rosie from football. Half the time, Rosie's tired and cross and filthy, and Liam goes all funny around muck, has always needed to be scrupulously clean.

He'll get them home, and Chloe'll be grouchy from an evening in the van, and knackered because she's supposed to have been in bed half an hour ago, and Rosie will demand a snack, and the first three Liam'll offer her will be wrong. When he's got them both off to bed there'll be sandwiches to make for the four of them for the morning, and a wash to put on, and then Kirsty will get home, worn out from the extra shifts she's doing to pay for Rosie's football and Chloe's school trips, and they'll bicker about the endless damp of a half-plastered house, the mess of bags in the hallway and the hedge that needs trimming.

Standing here beside Liam, watching him bend his head to hear Rosie's question, Jo's homesick all over again. She's homesick for happy Liam, who doesn't exist anymore; perhaps never did outside her own naïve bubble. She's properly, actively homesick for current Liam, who she's apparently hacking off without even trying to.

Most of all, she's homesick for her old self. She'd been so desperate to come back that she hadn't paid even a second's attention to what it might actually be like to be back. Jo's not living a real life. She's playing at real life, and she's doing it really, really badly. She needs to cop on, to work out how to be a decent friend to this version of Liam, to Kirsty and Matt and the rest of them, not expect everything to revolve around her now she's bounced back into their lives. She needs to make an effort with new friends like Poppy and Tessa (who, against all the odds, is becoming a friend) so that she's not so fragile when the old ones don't immediately have room for her. And she needs to figure out where she's going to live long-term and how the hell she'll handle Ron.

The ground down here right at the edge of the lake is almost bouncy where it's so waterlogged. Jo pokes at it with her boot and it fills back up with water. *You and me both*, she thinks, so bogged down with everything she feels that she barely knows where to start.

'But I do worry about it. You know I wouldn't ever try to hurt your mum. I just wanted to help. I know you said it's better to leave it alone, but perhaps I could try something else – a pie or something, that wouldn't need cooking? Or smaller portions so that she can't eat it all at once again.'

Liam's indifference shrinks Jo's words into the ground. He leans back again towards Chloe. Rosie comes over and peers at her sister's spoils.

'That fish'll have enough of a headache now, mind.' He removes the priest from Chloe's fist and pivots so that he's side by side with Jo, looking out over the view.

'Things have never been easy for Mum, you don't need me to tell you that. But it's all more precarious now she's older. Everything moves on, even the stuff we don't want to.'

'I know that! Honest I do.' Though what's only now emerging is which things move on and how far, in what directions. None of it's straightforward. None of this is learned by going away. Only by coming back.

'Aye. Well.'

They stand and watch the river as it drifts slowly away from them.

Chapter Twenty-Four

J O'S AT THE KITCHEN TABLE when Tessa comes in from the forge, the paper spread out in front of her and a spoon sticking out from a bowl.

'There's probably some soup left if you fancy it? It'd only need warming up a bit.' Jo's quietish, for her; things must not be sorted out yet with Liam. But it's none of Tessa's business.

'You're all right. I'll grab something later.' She can't keep taking Jo's food.

Jo straightens in her chair and in that small movement the wannabe butcher evanesces and the lawyer appears. The change is so sudden it's almost jarring.

'Do you have a minute?'

Tessa nods mutely, lowers into her seat. People wanting a minute is never good news, and the Jo sitting opposite her now isn't doing anything to change her opinion. The usual smiles are gone and she's square to the table, businesslike. As she opens up the lid on her laptop, Tessa sees that it's been there all along, underneath the papers. This is an ambush. Tessa's head throbs.

Jo must spot some tiny movement because in an instant her expression breaks. 'Don't worry! It's good news.'

She leans forward, one arm snaking round the side of the computer. 'I know you didn't want to know anything until I'd found something. The thing is, I think I have.'

The last few nights, every time Tessa fled her room after another horrific haunting, Jo was through here with the computer, tapping away as if in a dream world of her own. They didn't speak, each acknowledging the liminal space they found the other in, not wanting to disturb the fragility of that.

'It took some digging.' Jo's eyes are bright.

Tessa stares straight ahead, can't react to this. She needs Jo to hurry up before another collapse happens, but Jo's done all this work. She can't appear rude, even though the odds of Jo having turned up anything useful are so slim. Her breath catches.

'Have you heard of something called narcolepsy?'

Tessa shakes her head. Her breath is shallow and her head's banging. She could really do with a cup of tea, but the dangers of hot fluids are too high with where Jo's going with this chat. It's not at all clear right now that having an answer would be a better thing than the way she's managed for the past thirty-odd years.

'I hadn't either, really. Basically, it means your brain doesn't always know when you're awake or when you're asleep.' Jo peers at her screen, taps something and sits back against the chair. 'Here's an official description: "a rare neurological condition that affects the brain's ability to regulate the normal sleep–wake cycle."' She looks up. 'It can mean your sleep is really disturbed at night, you're dead sleepy during the day, and you can end up with daytime hallucinations and tiny naps – micro-sleeps, they call them. It's different for everyone but most people with narcolepsy have one or more of these symptoms.'

Jo ticks them off on her fingers, the barrister fully in the room now. 'Disturbed night-time sleep – well, you were up at two a.m. last night, same as me, so I'd say that was a yes. Hallucinations – do you see people when they aren't actually there?' Tessa nods, and Jo pushes back another finger. 'Then there's automatic behaviour, where you might respond to someone, or do something, and have absolutely no recollection of it later.'

Tessa feels things slipping. All these things that she thought were just her. The hauntings. The naps. All these things, spelled out like that. All of it.

Jo's still talking. 'Hang on a minute, though; here's the bit that made me certain. Part of narcolepsy is this thing called cataplexy.'

Tessa's still grappling with the list of things that describe her life, and her brain hiccups over the new word. 'What?'

'Cataplexy. Well, narcolepsy with cataplexy is probably what you've got. You can't have cataplexy without narcolepsy. Basically, your brain thinks you're asleep when you're awake, so if you experience an emotion, it protects you the way it does when you're dreaming. You lose all muscle tone – that's what makes you collapse, even though you're still awake. And you're completely aware of everything that's going on around you, even though people think you've fainted.'

'That's . . . but that's exactly me.' It's too much all at once. Distraction is needed, fast, or cataplexy-in-action might hit. Tessa gets up to make that cup of tea.

Jo follows her to the counter, laptop wedged at her hip like a baby.

'It's confusing, isn't it? I had to dig around for hours to understand it a bit more. They aren't really seizures when you collapse. It's muscle paralysis, like it would be if you were dreaming, so that you don't do yourself any harm.'

She puts down the laptop and moves towards Tessa. Tessa flinches. 'Oh! And some people get those tingles like you get. They're a symptom too.'

'So none of it's seizures?' The kettle's already half full, as usual. Tessa plonks it in the middle of the burner on the range. The list of names and conditions swirl like snowflakes.

'Nope – not at all.' Jo's back in lawyer mode, delivering the news calmly and factually, but there's a trembling of excitement under the veneer. Tessa wants to believe her, wants to believe this could be something as harmless as sleep. The pain in her head increases.

'You've pulled all this from the Internet, like? In your spare time?'

'The Internet's not all bad, you know!'

They take the tea over to the table. Jo sits back in

her chair, lets her arms fall loose against the table, palms up. The light angling in through the window above the table casts everything in an unthreatening sepia glow.

'It's not as if I've just randomly stuck stuff in and let Dr Google diagnose you. I've gone through all sorts: medical journals, forums. It's all out there if you know where to find it.'

Ridiculously, Tessa's struck by guilt here. Jo must have paid for an Internet booster; there's no way she got all of that from the data on her phone's spotty 4G. And she's worried enough about the business without taking time out to scour old journals on Tessa's behalf.

Jo leans forward again. 'I could be wrong. But it might at least be worth a go, going to the doctor and seeing if they can take it any further. Diagnosis sounds relatively unintrusive. Just a night sleeping somewhere under observation.'

Tessa sips the tea. It's too hot.

'How does it work then, this sleep clinic thing? Did the Internet tell you that an' all?'

Jo smiles. 'It did, as a matter of fact. You need an appointment with your GP, then they refer you. I called in to the surgery yesterday – Lisa on the desk was in Geography with me all the way through school, so we looked up the next available appointments. There's one at ten a.m. tomorrow, if that would work?'

Tessa shakes her head. 'I can't.'

Jo takes her mug and walks towards the kitchen window. She stares out at the garden. The oaks are dancing, glad of the change of season.

'How about if I came with you, explained all this research?'

'But I don't understand. Marnie . . . my . . . she looked on the Internet a few years back.'

'Well, things come to prominence all the time. And this is my job; I don't stop until I've found the evidence I need.' Jo didn't even break stride when Tessa mentioned Marnie, is utterly focused on this narcolepsy.

Tessa's head pounds. 'But the shop . . .'

'Oh, Ron'll be delighted if I'm not there for a couple of hours.'

When Jo approaches Tessa again, the lawyer has disappeared. Now she's Tessa's tenant, everything in her body poised for adventure. 'What do you reckon?'

Tessa's on the verge of collapse but Jo's enthusiasm is pulling her back. What if there really is something to be done? What if it took meeting someone as persistent as Jo to figure it out? At the very least, Jo's being kinder than anyone has any need to be. Tessa owes it to her to at least try it out.

'OK. Let's see.'

Part Three

Welding

Chapter Twenty-Five

EVERYTHING'S GATHERED PACE OVER THE last few weeks. That initial trip to the GP led to a referral to a neurologist, which they were warned might take months to come through. But then a cancellation had cropped up and within a fortnight Tessa was meeting with a specialist. Tessa, panicked by the speed, asked Jo to attend the meeting, and it was great to have the excuse to put on the old London-lawyer clothes, to go in to the appointment and present Tessa's case. The specialist listened carefully to Jo's notes and made a further referral, this time to a sleep clinic, where apparently they can monitor Tessa's responses to things and find out what's going on.

This isn't something to admit to Tessa, but Jo's loved grappling with all this. It's the combination of using her brain again and knowing that she's actively helping someone. From time to time, there's been a bit of reluctance from Tessa, largely due to the speed at which things finally moved, but that's something that came up occasionally in barrister work too. Not in the cold-pizza cases, but the more worthwhile ones she sporadically had a fingerhold on.

Tessa's at the sleep clinic right now and it's hard not to be hyperbolic, but it could well be that she'll come out with a diagnosis and a treatment plan after thirty-odd years of not knowing. Jo's supposed to be focusing again on the shop, but it's hard and, to be honest, it's not as interesting as the standing up and advocating has been. The told-you-so flames lick at her heels.

It's not like there isn't plenty to be getting on with in the shop. There are only four weeks left until Jo hands over her three-month report to her parents' accountant and she's going to have to make them count. The margins are still perilously tight; keeping the shop afloat is going to rely on all the new ideas coming through. She understands now – viscerally understands – why her parents had been ready to retire. There was no guarantee the business would last the year on the numbers she'd inherited. In fact, if she had to guess now about her parents' mystery buyer – about the reason they'd been keeping the mystery, in fact – she'd change her mind from the original assumption that it was another local butcher. It seems far more likely that a supermarket was coming in, maybe one of those small-sized convenience ones.

But her parents turned down the other buyer so that she could indulge her need to come back. It's bad enough that she hasn't stuck to being a barrister when everyone was so pleased for her; now she's disrupted their retirement plans. The least she can do is prove that it's been worth it.

Still, though, it had been glorious just to spend some hours being the closest to her barrister self she might ever get to be down here. It was the same sense of satisfaction she'd got when she'd been able to sort out the custody thing for Matt, the same exercising of a muscle she no longer used. It was a good call back to what had been attractive about the law in the first place: the digging through details, connecting the dots and coming to a conclusion that was really, solidly, able to provide an outcome.

There hasn't been much contact with chambers since she left in January. To begin with, this was deliberate. The head clerk would call with this or that 'unmissable' case, but after Jo turned down the fifth one, he seemed to understand that she was quite happy missing them.

It's getting harder and harder to convince herself of that, though. This past month, since helping Tessa, really, it's not been uncommon to wake up with a pang of – not regret, exactly, but more a realisation that another world is cracking on perfectly comfortably without her while this one is more of a struggle every day.

Right now, the most pressing thing to do is to regain control after the Great Hand-Slicing Incident. Ron's fine. Dad had laughed when she'd told him. 'Not the first time; he's tougher than stewing steak, our Ron.' But some of the balance has shifted. Jo's nervy in the mornings now, can hear her greetings unnecessarily deferential. She can't let Ron be right about her. But increasingly she wonders whether he is.

Improbable as it sounds, sausage is the answer. Jo is up at five thirty, in the shop at six, the displays all out by six thirty.

Despite its customer-readiness, the shop's 'open' sign remains firmly turned inward right now. Jo can't be distracted this morning; any early risers desperate for a lamb chop will have to wait for Mo. Jo needs this win. Sausages are the mainstay of any butcher, and they don't involve the kind of action that might get her fingers cut off. Mo's been doing them these last few weeks, but they were Mum's domain, and it's about time Jo got to grips with it.

She'll do them out the back, in the side room that was the kitchen in Grandad's day. Mum used to do them in the little prep room, but that room's the wrong side of the plastic curtain, still visible to customers. The last thing she needs is Phyllis meandering in to observe that Jo's getting it wrong, and why isn't she doing it in her wig and gown?

There's a lot to gather for sausages, but it's all written down. She tips odourless rusk, nearly indistinguishable from sawdust sweepings, into the huge plastic bucket that sits below the grinder. *How much rusk?* she'd texted Mum last night, unable to sleep for thinking about Tessa at the clinic, and had received the desperately helpful response: *Whatever looks like enough*. Strangely, though, this does look like enough.

A few herbs should help the thing along. They lie, grey like ash, on top of the rusk, and now there's nothing to do but start loading the meat into the grinder. *Make sure it's fatty enough* had been Mum's other caution. Jo peers at the hunks of pork shoulder, as if the squares of white will communicate whether or not they're fatty enough. She fills the jug with a litre of water, tips that in too.

The meat pushes out through the grinder like coffee grounds going through a filter. Jo plunges her hands into the bowl to mix in the rusk. Thank God this is a job she actually can do with her eyes closed, though the smell shoots frigidly up her nostrils and lodges as an unswallowable flavour at the back of her throat.

Duly mixed, the meat has to go through the grinder again now according to Mum.

Twice through the grinder.

Really?

It had seemed excessive, or perhaps she was just trying to avoid it.

YES. Mum's text had exuded horror. *This isn't Wall's. People want to taste the sausage in their sausage.*

Plenty of people like Wall's sausages, Jo didn't text back. Just as well Mum didn't know of her plan for wild boar and scrumpy apple sausage – and, closer to Easter, Scotch eggs with Creme Eggs in the middle.

She loads the sausage meat into the machine, tamps it down until no more will fit in. These are chipolatas, so it'll be the smaller nozzle – though not the cocktail nozzle. They've still got plenty of cocktail sausages out in the cold store, left over from Christmas. The baby Jesus must have had a real thing for sausages; the people of this town, at least, celebrate with cocktail sausages, chipolatas, bangers, pigs in blankets and, of course, sausage meat for turkey-stuffing and for those who for some unfathomable reason haven't spotted the sausage product of their choice and need to make their own at home. Dad always reckoned they got through a ton of pork for sausages at Christmas. A literal ton, not a metaphorical one.

Now for the bit that turns Jo's stomach. She wrenches open the door to the cold store. The fans are blasting, keeping the meat at the requisite temperature, and the air bashes against her wet fingers, freezes them further.

Jo swallows hard as she picks up the bucket she'd prepped last night and takes it over to the sausage filler. The skins stare up at her, huge tapeworms floating in the water.

Tessa. She has to think of Tessa. She has to think of anything but this. By the time she's done with the first batch of sausages, Tessa should be finished at the sleep clinic and Jo can go over and collect her, see what they say. A sleep condition had seemed a pretty plausible assumption, but what if it's something else – something worse – and she's sent Tessa merrily off on a wild goose chase?

Jo delves her hand into the bucket of skins. The water's freezing and the salt that's leeched out of the skins stings the cuts on her. She shoves the skin onto the nozzle as if she's in some terrible Sex Education video from the 1980s, eyes closed against the slime. People never think of slime when they think of meat, but Jo's fingers carry the memory of the parts between the flesh: tiny bendy tubes like old strips of Tippex, bits of cartilage, clingfilmy connective layers that linger like a clammy handshake when you try to shake them off.

The skin is in place and it's time to think positively. Tessa's probably right now receiving a diagnosis that will help her to live her life better. Jo's here, in her home town, where she's wanted to be ever since she left. It's a Thursday morning and she's her own boss. Jo puts all this hope into pressing the paddle beside her knee, standing up slightly on tiptoe to get full leverage.

The sausage meat whizzes up from the guts of the machine, shoots through the nozzle and bangs into the skins with the clap of a balloon bursting. Meat splatters the sides of the receiving pan, keeps looping from the machine until Jo jumps back in delayed horror and removes the pressure from the paddle. The paddle stops with the release of her knee, and the spooling sausage sputters to a merciful halt.

Bugger. Still, it isn't the first time someone burst a sausage skin, and it won't be the last, that's for sure. Jo rolls another skin onto the nozzle and twists the dial on the side of the machine to tamp it all back down. She pushes the lid firmly back on, brings her knee back up towards the paddle. Easy does it. The sausage meat cracks like gunshot into the new skin, a length of almost-chipolata following the pressure from Jo's knee, a pipeline of glistening pink in desalinated skins, curling into the pan like a coiled snake. It's hard to know whether to laugh or cry.

Chapter Twenty-Six

THERE'S NO DENYING IT; GOING into the sleep clinic is terrifying. More than once on the drive over Tessa wants to tell Jo to stop the car, turn around. There's no way this is going to end positively.

But she can't. She and Jo don't know each other well enough for that.

The doctor and nurse she meets are kind but it's disconcerting all the same. A technician shows her to a bedroom and fits her up with electrodes on her head, her limbs and her torso. The room is sparse: a bed and a chair, and presumably a camera somewhere so that they can watch her behaviour. Better not to think about that.

After that, all she really has to do is sleep while the electrodes monitor her sleep patterns. To begin with, the very idea of sleep is an impossibility in these circumstances, but sleep always knows where to find Tessa.

And tonight, during sleep, Mam comes to visit, as

Mam always does at times when her mind is at its most vulnerable. Tessa is stuck in her dream, unable to move, replaying only bad memories.

Or, more accurately, one particularly bad memory. That last visit to Mam. With Marnie. The point where everything started to go so horribly wrong.

As she turned off the Heads of the Valleys Road and wound down the streets that lead to Pen-y-Pandy, Tessa muted the radio. Marnie glanced across but for once didn't say anything. The rain drilled onto the windscreen, insistent.

Tessa hadn't been down by here for years. Row upon row of terraces zippered their way up and down invisible ridges in the valley. A rollercoaster town, where all the highs and lows happened behind the curtain nets and people would stretch out their arms if they think you're in danger of falling but cross them and turn away if you've wronged them.

'Why's it all so steep?' Marnie had rubbed a porthole in the condensation on the van. She'd suggested taking her car, but the bright blue Fiat 500 would have made them visible from the Heads of the Valleys Road and the van was safer in all respects.

'Well, we're in the Valleys, see? That's what you get with a valley – hills.'

Marnie poked her gently in the arm, dimple deepening. 'Very funny. What I mean is, why didn't they build the town on the flat?'

The answer was so obvious that to begin with Tessa

assumed Marnie was joking. But Marnie was staring out with the same intensity she'd once looked at the Forest, her knuckles taut with concentration on the edge of the seat.

'They can't build the houses on the hilltops; that's where the pit heads are. Were.' The past tense tasted metallic. 'We're nearly there.'

Marnie nodded and frowned out of the window. There were smaller, steeper streets than this in Bristol – Marnie saw them every blessed day – and for a fleeting second Marnie's affectation was irritating; the exaggerated concern because they were in a Welsh mining town, as if she was expecting Arthur Scargill to come rushing at her with a megaphone.

But it vanished as soon as it arrived. Marnie was fourteen weeks' pregnant, the first scan safely behind them, and she'd never met Mam before. Nerves made sense. Every time Tessa had turned over in bed in the last few weeks, ever since Marnie had persuaded Tessa they needed to make this trip, Marnie's reading light had been on too. This morning she'd spent twenty minutes in front of the mirror, trying and discarding a rainbow of floaty scarves to wear with her 'best' black maternity dress (she had embraced maternity wear straight away, her many friends dropping off what seemed to be an entire new wardrobe of loaned belongings), before settling on a canary yellow one. The canary coming to the coal mine. Better to leave the logical conclusion of this thought unuttered.

They pulled up outside the house, so familiar and so

unknowable. Tessa stared forward. The next step seemed impossible.

'I don't think it'll make any difference, you know.'

Marnie rested a hand on Tessa's knee and squeezed. 'It's worth a try.' They'd been having a version of this conversation for weeks now. 'You can't become a parent without your own mother knowing. Maybe your mum will like being a granny.'

Marnie was a sunflower in Tessa's world of iron and fire, not that she'd ever be so soppy out loud. Tessa remembers the flash of joy she felt when the first pregnancy test declared its news, the starburst of happiness at seeing the baby – their baby – on the scan. She glances involuntarily sideways, her gaze seeking the reassurance of the tiny neat bump that she can only see because she knows it's there. She's going to be a mother. Marnie's right. This changes everything.

The house hadn't changed, not a jot. Same black door with the brass knocker.

Marnie popped off her seat belt and stretched as it zithered back into place. 'I'm knackered! D'you think your mum will have a cup of tea and a biscuit, or are we planning on going out?'

For a moment Tessa let herself imagine what it might be like to have a mother with whom you'd casually have a cup of tea.

Marnie's family was easy, welcoming. Whenever Tessa and Marnie popped in – Marnie was always finding some reason for them to pop in – Tessa braced for the silent treatment that must surely be around the next corner, but it never, ever came. Even after years of knowing them, she couldn't quite trust herself, and she would never be able to bring herself to obey Marnie's mam's command to call her Jennifer.

Oblivious, Marnie snapped down the passenger side mirror and reapplied shocking pink lipstick, lips pulled taut over her gums. Tessa half-raised her hand to stop her – it'd only make things worse if Mam saw Marnie as the type to care about worthless fripperies.

The door was highly polished, and the nets looked new, but other than that it was like it had always been when Nanna and Bamps lived here. Mam would be the other side of the nets right now, watching the unfamiliar van parked outside and wondering who was in it that had got business with the likes of them.

Tessa snapped off her own seat belt, glanced across at Marnie. 'Ready?'

Marnie clicked the lipstick shut and slid it into her bag. 'As I'll ever be. How do I look?'

'Gorgeous.' She always did. But here, her dark eyes bright with anticipation, her orange cardigan flaming against the yellow of the scarf, she looked amazing.

Marnie stepped out of the van and yawned, stretching again, the bump already prominent in silhouette. The baby was virtually shouting at them to be seen.

'I'm quite looking forward to meeting your mum. I wonder if I'll see any of you in her?' This was another thing Marnie had transplanted from her own life. She and Jennifer were forever finding things they had in common. Whereas Mam . . . well.

Marnie put an arm around Tessa and hugged her, here where anyone might see, and Tessa stiffened. It was barely a movement, as minute as a twitch of the net curtains, but Marnie dropped her arm in a flash, took a tiny step away. Tessa longed to take her hand, but that wasn't behaviour for a small place like this. She'd been at the riding centre once back in the Forest when two men – tourists – had come in wanting to rent a pony for their daughter. Nobody had said anything but the sidelong looks, the over-politeness had clogged her with filaments of prejudice and fear.

'Let's get this over and done with, shall we?' She rang the doorbell, her finger shaking on the buzzer.

There was no dust in the air, not like when the mines were running, but there was that same hilly damp, as if the rain was lingering in the sky, waiting for the return of the coal dust so that it could douse it.

It would have been possible, even now, to run away. Leg it round the corner, pretend it's a game of knock down ginger. Her hands trembled and she was livid with herself at how much this mattered.

The door opened on the chain. 'Yes? Can I help you?'

Mam hadn't even recognised her. Tessa's palms tingled with shame that Marnie was here to see this.

'Mam.' It was a croak, loaded with years of learning not to say it.

The chain rattled off the door.

'That you, Theresa?' No surprise in Mam's tone. It would cost too much to betray real emotion, even after all these decades.

'Hello, Mam.'

Mam swiped a head-to-toe glance at Marnie. The door didn't open any wider.

'This is Marnie.'

'I see.'

Did she? Was this going to be easy after all? There was no knowing with Mam. Her emotions were buried deep, a seam as impenetrable as the mines had now become.

'You'd better come in.' Mam hesitated, flicked a dagger-sharp look at Marnie. 'Both of you.'

The door opened and Mam flattened herself against it so that they could get in. 'Go through to the parlour, Theresa.'

To the best room; she was being treated like a guest. Tessa squeezed by, concentrated on the clacking of her feet on the red quarry tile, the clicking of the clock as it marked her passage back into her childhood. They had lived in a house just like this for Tessa's first few years of life. Until they didn't anymore. Until they moved to the cottage.

'Tea?' It wasn't really a question.

'Do you want a hand?'

'No need, is it? It's only a cup of tea.' Mam left, the straightness of her back bringing to mind a cat, tail up, stalking out in disgust.

'Have we offended her?' Marnie was whispering. It was the effect of this room, more of a mausoleum than anything else, its walls framed with dead people.

'No. This is just her.'

Marnie's eyes widened a fraction in disbelief, but she let it drop, stared around at all the photos, pointing at one in the alcove above the bureau.

'Is that you?'

It was the picture of her and Bethan. They were dressed up for the eisteddfod in hats and capes, all but posed in front of a spinning wheel.

'Yeah, that's us. Five and two we must have been then.'

The headache was already present, knuckling the back of Tessa's eyes, and she could barely dare look. In the picture, Bethan's hair was a beacon, flashing from beneath her tall black hat and clashing with the red of her cape, which dragged down onto the ground. The cape had belonged to Tessa, who had been making do for the picture with a shawl and a scowl. In the photo they were outside the house (doorknob especially shiny for 1st March), Bethan beaming at her pretty national costume, and Tessa trying not to mind her costume relegation. She had, though, terribly, and in those days she had still let it show.

'Here we are, then.' Mam was back in the room and Tessa, caught in the act of examining the unexaminable past, hurried over to help with the tray. They bent down together to lift the cups onto the bureau and Mam's scent hit right in the back of Tessa's throat, knocked her back thirty-odd years so that she was barely older than she had been in the photo. She gulps the emotion back down. When they'd passed in the hall there had been no tripping of memories, no scent in the air. Mam must have nipped

228

upstairs to put on scent because she had visitors. Tessa hadn't lived with Mam for years, but to have outsider status confirmed like this was still a violation.

'Tea?'

'Oh yes, please,' Marnie started again with a burst of effusiveness, but the room shuttered it and she took the proffered china cup with a silent smile.

If it didn't all matter so much, it'd be comical, really. But it mattered terribly.

Tessa balanced her saucer with one hand and waited for Mam to pour her own tea, the hollow tinkle as the milk met the bottom of the cup providing a melody to the bass rhythm of the clock.

They were all bolt upright like horses who've scented danger.

'Shall we sit down?' Tessa asked into the widening silence.

Mam's lips pursed a tiny smidge, a wordless reminder that this wasn't Tessa's home, she had no right to be suggesting what people should or shouldn't be doing.

Mam took her usual chair, sitting stiffly forward, knees clamped together, tea balanced on them.

'You're keeping well, Theresa?'

Tessa nodded. 'And yourself?'

Mam placed the teacup on the crocheted mat on the side table. They all silently followed its progress.

'Can't complain.'

Beside her on the settee Marnie shifted.

'I know this is a bit out of the blue, like, Mam, and I'm sorry we didn't give you more notice.'

'Oh.'

Tessa, vertiginous with fear, plummeted on. 'Marnie and I – we're having a baby.'

After a moment she risked a glance at Mam, who was staring into her cup, a pose that was as familiar to Tessa as her scent, her censure.

'What do you mean, you and Marnie?' Now she stared pointedly at Tessa.

She was being deliberately obtuse, she must be. They had never sat down and talked about it, but Mam must have known.

'Marnie and me together, Mam. We live together. I wrote and told you that.'

That Christmas, though, and the one that followed, the usual card came to the cottage, addressed to Tessa alone.

'I don't see what your living arrangements have to do with a baby.'

The childhood despair surged, and Tessa was five again, desperate for Mam to notice she was still there. Her muscles started to soften, and she used every bit of willpower not to collapse, pushing hard against the couch cushions.

'The thing is . . . I know we haven't seen each other since you moved back here. But now there's a grandchild on the way, more family . . .'

Mam made a muffled sound that might have been a snort. 'I don't see what a baby's going to change.'

Marnie stiffened, ready for battle. But she'd only make it worse. This is the bit Tessa had practised, over and over again. But she couldn't say it. She couldn't undo what she did all those years ago. But perhaps a baby would be a peace offering. It was too late for herself, she knew that now, but perhaps with this baby Mam could find her way back to caring about some part of Tessa's life. Of her family.

'I'm surprised at you, Theresa, to be honest. I thought I made it clear when I came back here that my obligations to you were over.' Mam stood up and the teacup rattled a full stop. 'Was that all? I'll be getting on now, then.'

It hurt every much as bit as it always had.

Marnie tensed and Tessa's muscles tightened too. But Marnie was simply pushing up off the weathered arm of the couch.

She stretched out a hand. 'Very nice to meet you, Mrs Price. Thank you for taking the time to see us.' She was sleek, all feelings polished away, and Tessa followed behind, brain zapping in warning, determined not to let Mam see.

Marnie wept for the ninety minutes home, staring sightless out of the fogged-up window as if that had been her own mother.

'I'm sorry,' she kept repeating. 'So sorry. We never should have come.'

Tessa sat silent beside her, Marnie's own tears doing the work for them both. She couldn't move the headache, couldn't stop Mam's words hissing down her capillaries, flooding her body. It wasn't Marnie's fault. Marnie was the only good thing to ever happen to Tessa – Marnie and the baby – and she would never, ever let anything like this happen to them.

She couldn't ever see Mam again. It wasn't situational; it wasn't circumstance. It wasn't even because she and Marnie were together, though Marnie, understandably, saw it like that. There had never been any kindness shown to Tessa since Bethan died, and she'd been boastful, stupid, to think that might have changed. Mam simply didn't want her, would never want her, not after what happened.

What Tessa had always believed – through self-preservation – to be temporary, had always, always been permanent as far as Mam was concerned. Mam had no daughters now.

Chapter Twenty-Seven

WAKING UP IS ONLY A relief.
Later, after the techs have removed the wires from Tessa's scalp, the doctor comes in and confirms the diagnosis. Narcolepsy with cataplexy; symptomatic hypnogogic hallucinations.

'Pretty much textbook', he says with a smile, as if to have an illness that made it into a textbook is reassuring. The condition can be managed with the right medicines, if she takes care not to overdo it and to set regular sleep patterns. Driving is OK, given how critical it is to her livelihood, but she has to report her condition to the DVLA and to take care. The narcolepsy will never go away, but it wasn't going away before, and – crucially – it shouldn't get worse now they can manage it. *She isn't dying.*

To leave with a name for her symptoms, a list of medications to try until they have the right combination – to know that Jo was right, this is an actual thing and not just her being mad and bad – it's hard to take in. It's a weight off, but it's also a spotlight on all the lives she hadn't been able to live, and the anger that brings is jolting.

To know that things with Marnie might have gone differently if the right doctor had found the answer, started her on medication. Further back than that – that she might have had friends at school. Might have been able to laugh at playground jokes without fear of collapse and ridicule. Might have had all the tortured teenage joy of first kisses with all the wrong people. Might have found a way to break through Mam's grief and make her own life, a bigger life.

This isn't a safe line of thought. Not yet.

She nods her goodbyes and walks out through the automatic doors to find Jo. The kind consultant has given her protective clothing from these emotions that betray her. Armour and a sword, in the form of a diagnosis and a medication routine. Once she can find the money for the medicine, or for the bits she has to pay for.

Jo's waiting at the bottom of the steps, desperate for every last detail of the sleep clinic. The car's parked nearby and it doesn't take long to leave Bristol. The landscape opens up as they reach the Severn Bridge and ribbon over the flowing estuary, the land dividing below them, the sky opening up, stretching itself flat along the horizon. The silvery struts of the second bridge, two miles away to the west, twist and hide in the sparkling mist, and Tessa breathes more deeply, comforted by the emptiness, wanting to think about something else.

'How's the shop?'

'Yeah, all right, I think.' But Jo looks away. There's something she's not saying, but that means it's none of Tessa's business to speculate. Jo will be all right. She's very earnest about the butcher's, really seems to want to make it work. But even if it doesn't, Jo has her family, her friends, her legal training.

When they reach town, Jo pulls into the car park behind her shop, tucks the car into a corner.

'I need to just pop in for a minute. D'you want to come in?'

But there's no space for anything else, the need to sleep is overwhelming after the events of the last twenty-four hours, and Tessa shakes her head, mute with exhaustion. The adrenaline that came with the potential of a diagnosis has dropped and all that's left is despair at the life she couldn't live, along with bone weariness, the armour weighing her down moment by moment.

'All right, then. I'll be back soon, OK?' Jo disappears round the corner.

Unconsciousness closes in, fast and dense. Marnie's there, so vivid that she might almost be real. She's waiting for Tessa, reproachful.

Why didn't you tell me it was this bad? I thought you just fainted a bit; I had no idea.

I didn't want to worry you.

But that's what I'm there for. We share things.

I tried. I told you, and I went to the doctor like you said. But the doctor didn't find anything, remember?

We could have tried another doctor.

I was scared. I thought you wouldn't want me. Then when you were pregnant and the episodes got worse, I thought you'd end up with no choice but to kick me out in case I harmed you or the baby.

Haunting-Marnie isn't mollified. One hand is on her hip, those heartbreaking curls dangerously still.

That time when I was worried the baby wasn't moving and you ignored me . . .

It closes in like it's happening again . . .

Marnie's waiting for Tessa when she gets home from work, the door open before she's even made it up the last flight of stairs. Down the corridor into the living space, the fan's whirring gently; the bedroom one must be on too because the fronds of the hallway ferns are waving at her in the breeze.

Tessa's so tired all she can think is: thank goodness, *she won't have to muster the energy to wrestle her key into the door. She smiles gratefully, silently at Marnie and walks through, dropping her bag in the hallway so that she doesn't traipse dust all over the white walls, wooden floors.*

It must be this late-summer heat that has got her so knackered; anyone would think she's the one carrying the baby. She can feel tiredness pushing forward like the countdown on a clock.

Tessa sits down on the bright blue throw at the end of the bed and pulls off her work socks. The fan's on in the bedroom, so it's cool in here, the white cotton sheets Marnie's so fond of crumpled in the manner that suggests a nap. Tessa needs to go through, start on tea so that Marnie isn't having to do everything as well as carry their child, the child that Tessa had persuaded her to carry. The child she is going to love, and care for, and protect. To make up for Bethan. To make up for her own younger self, who had none of this.

But first she needs to nap.

She's half-asleep, drifting into dreams, when the bed jounces and Marnie curls up beside her.

'I can't feel anything from the baby. I haven't felt anything all day.'

'I'm sure it's . . .' But the end of the sentence is slurred. She's answering on auto-pilot, unable to untangle herself from unconsciousness and pay proper attention.

Marnie shifts on the bed. 'Should I call the doctor, do you think? It says online that I should be feeling movement daily by this stage.'

'Yes,' Tessa manages. She needs to stay with this. It's important. 'Why don't you phone the midwife?'

'Could you do it?' Marnie is fretting with worry, her wide features pinched in. Tessa needs to do this. But she's more asleep than not, and her nod tails off further into sleep. There's a long sigh and the bed jounces again as Marnie leaves it.

From the front room she can hear Marnie's voice on the phone, calm and measured, the usual bounce leached out of it. Then there's a clatter from the fridge and the sound of the TV going on. Tessa doesn't hear anything else because she plummets into sleep, the effort of trying to work out what's going on holding too much sway to anchor her to the world.

When she wakes it's pitch black, down in the very core of the night where even the robins still their voices. Marnie is asleep beside her, snoring. Tessa shivers, pulls the sheet up over her, and Marnie snorfles, turns half over towards Tessa, the bulk of her belly bumping up against Tessa's crooked knee. Inside Marnie's sleep, the baby shifts against the unexpected object, and it's all too easy to imagine that within a matter of months he or she will be with them on the outside.

Tessa pushes up on her elbows and holds still. The baby had definitely stirred. She waits, holding her breath so that she knows what she's feeling. Yep, it's definitely moving. So the baby's all right. Oh, thank God. Perhaps she should wake up Marnie, reassure her, give her some good news to make up for having been so utterly useless last night.

No, she can't do that. Tessa eases back down. To do that would be to have to explain her behaviour last night, and how can she possibly explain when all she knows is that she answered questions on auto-pilot but has no real memory of what she said? She stretches out her fingers, her toes, holding her breath against the return of the tingling.

Nothing.

Dawn has been and gone by the time Marnie stretches into wakefulness. Tessa, awake for hours at this point, places a cup of coffee beside the bed.

238

'It might be decaf,' Marnie has said before, 'but it makes me feel like waking up all the same.'

'I felt the baby in the night.' Tessa's voice pitches forward, a peace offering.

'What? Yeah.' Marnie shrugs.

'The baby's all right, then?'

'Yeah, everything was fine by the time I came to bed.' Marnie's all prickles and Tessa steps away from the bed. 'I could hardly have gone to sleep without knowing the baby was all right.'

Marnie swings her legs out of the bed, her toes searching for the turquoise moccasins. She's level with Tessa now, the scent of her filling the gap between them. Tessa should kiss her, but she can't bear to, doesn't dare to after last night. Marnie pauses and Tessa knows the same thoughts are occurring to her, to this woman she loves. Marnie's a hugger, a kisser, full of easy, demonstrative affection. Marnie will kiss her and then Tessa can kiss her back, and they'll be past it, this strange awkwardness.

Marnie shifts forward and Tessa's body reacts, like it always does. But Marnie was simply reaching for her dressing gown, and Tessa sits back down abruptly.

'This is our baby, Tess. Ours – yours and mine. Not mine alone. You don't get to just check out.'

'I know that. I do.' Her behaviour had been unforgiveable. But she can't promise it won't happen again. Her temples throb. The attacks are getting worse. There's no way to stop them, and no way to help Marnie. She shrugs, palms up, unable to find the words – any words

239

– and Marnie shakes her head, her eyes dull, her usual bounce entirely absent, and leaves the room.

'Tessa?' The voice is full of concern. Marnie must have had a change of heart in the bathroom, realised there's no way Tessa would be behaving like that without cause. Marnie's the first person – the only person – to have known most of her. Marnie will recognise her.

'Tessa?'

She must have dropped off again, mid-step. But of course she's tired; she's been awake half the night, her hand lightly against Marnie's stomach to check the baby was still moving.

'Tessa? We're home now.' There's a hand on her shoulder and she reaches for it, lips curving into a smile. But the hand is smaller than Marnie's, the touch firmer, and Tessa swims back up from sleep, mind whirring.

It's Jo, full of hopeful concern. Tessa frowns, blinks herself all the way up. Jo needs to bugger off again, then she can get back inside the dream, do things differently this time.

But she wouldn't. She'd never have spoken up. All those reasons remain the same. She pushes up out of the car and walks over to the front door. Her legs are functioning fine and in some ways she's disappointed. She's back in the world she doesn't want to inhabit; a world without Marnie in it. But she's got to try.

Chapter Twenty-Eight

Tessa dunks the amber horseshoe in the bucket, steam sizzling into the cold spring air. She takes it over to the horse and burns the shoe level on the hoof, then lifts it back off with the carrying pritchel and walks it back to the anvil. When things are going well, like today, there's a rhythm, a synchronicity to this that puts her in mind of Bamps and the old colliery choir he used to sing with; all those men's voices hitting the beat exactly on time and blending to lift the melody in glorious harmony. The smoke hangs around the horse's hooves like her very own morning mist, and the horse – a young Welsh cob she's been working with for a couple of years now – snickers and ducks his head towards the rope, as if hoping to find straw there too.

For the first time in months, Tessa's back to thinking with her hands. The nail holes clean out easily enough with the back pritchel, then it's just a matter of dunking the shoe in the bucket before taking it back over to the horse. The adjustments are minimal, and it's the work of a minute to get the shoe back on.

These are six-week shoes; by rights they should have been off a while ago, but Geoff at the riding centre didn't mind the delay, was probably grateful for it with the lack of winter custom. The daffodils are out now, though, and the hawthorn edging Geoff's driveway is in full blossom. Soon the tourists will be out here to rent ponies by the hour as if they were mountain bikes, then squeal when the cobs take off down the Forest paths and it's a bit bumpy. It's good, steady business, and Geoff had sounded relieved when she'd called to say she was back. He didn't mind her coming on a Sunday, either, and she trusted herself now to hold steady.

Tessa rings off the nails, takes the foot forward and clenches on in all the remembered places to hold the hoof between her thighs.

A quick rasp and she's done. One shoe down, three to go. Tessa stands up, her hands in the small of her back, relishing the ache. The sun's straggling through and the air's full of horse and spring and hope.

There's a clatter and a gushing sound off behind her. Tessa smiles, her hands dropping from her back, and twists round. 'Found us all right, then?'

'Yeah – right up until that last bit. Sorry about the bucket! Did I disturb the horse?' Jo rights the pail and tiptoes round, as if in a bull ring.

Sometimes Tessa can see why people round here thought Jo might be better suited to a city.

'No, you're all right.' Tessa bends back down. The cob's lame on his back hoof so she'll need to be a bit more careful there. She picks up the clencher, starts easing out the size fives holding the shoe in place.

Jo leans against the barn wall in the slant of the sun. 'Thanks for letting me come along. I've never seen a farrier in action before.'

Tessa can't look up, but she nods. 'You're all right. Nice to have the company.'

Another voice pipes up, smaller and shriller.

'And I love horses, even more than Auntie Jo does, and Daddy's busy, so Auntie Jo said she'd bring me too. Daddy's finished my room; now he's doing Rosie's. And me an' Rosie have to *share* and it's making my new room all messy again.'

Tessa's hands jolt and she misses the nail with the clencher, nearly nips the frog. The horse snorts, tosses its head. Tessa holds as still as she can.

'Chlo, you ratbag!' The laughter in Jo's voice is matched by a softer, higher-pitched giggle. 'Your room got done first and Rosie put up with you without a fuss. Least you can do is have her on your floor now.' The pitch of Jo's voice changes. 'Hope you don't mind me bringing up this ragamuffin? Rosie's at football and Kirsty – Liam's wife – is working, and Chloe loves horses, don't you, poppet?'

Tessa pulls out the last nail and lets go of the hoof. The horse snuffles on the leading rein.

Tessa finally looks up. Jo's accompanied by a small, messy-haired girl in an oversized blue fleece and a pair of welly boots, who beams up at Tessa as if just waiting to say hello.

'Hello! Auntie Jo says I saw you before, but I don't remember.'

She has a child's unrestrainedness, even her hair flinging around.

'It's very nice to see you again – Chloe, is it?'

Chloe nods. 'Can I stroke him?'

The horse has settled back down, waiting patiently for Tessa to get on with the shoeing. 'Aye, he should be OK.' Tessa can't remember the last time she interacted with a child and she has to hold steady, really steady, against everything that comes with it. It's easier now she knows what's going on.

Jo's wandered away from them, is peering into the van.

'What've you got in there – an oven?'

'An oven!' Chloe's hand drops from the horse's nose and she skips over.

Tessa bends back to the hoof. The wall and the sole haven't grown too much, even with the extra wait. She pauses, snips in hand, and looks where Jo's looking.

'A forge.'

'What, like the one in the hut at the back of the garden?'

'Aye. But gas, obviously.' Tessa grins. 'Nobody wants to be driving around with a coal forge in the back.'

'I can't imagine all that many people want to be driving round with a gas forge in the back, either!

What's in here?' Jo's peering at the drawers below the forge.

'Shoes. Have a look if you like.' Tessa comes up beside Jo, grabs the shoe from the forge with the pritchel and hisses it into the bucket of water beside the anvil. Jo starts, and Tessa smiles.

Jo rolls her eyes. 'I know, I know.'

'No, it's not that. It's only . . .'

'What?'

'Well . . . Remind me of Marnie, you do. When you do that sort of a thing, see. Must be you brainy types, always curious.'

'Curiosity's healthy!' It obviously isn't the first time someone's pointed this out. 'Did Marnie come out much with you? Was she a farrier too?'

Tessa snorts at the idea of Marnie hammering away at a shoe. 'No! She worked – works – in Bristol. Management consultant. She didn't come out here much; wasn't all that exciting for her.' Marnie found it all a bit grubby, both literally and figuratively. Not that she would ever have said that out loud.

'I know what you mean. Nobody thought taking over a butcher's shop was exciting.' There's a catch in Jo's voice as if she, too, isn't finding it all that exciting in reality. Tessa keeps her head down. Nobody wants to be stared at when they're figuring out the truth.

'My friends here have always known me and the shop, so there's nothing new there. And the London ones just thought it was a bit weird.'

It's true, thinking about it, that nobody had been down

to stay, and Jo only ever seemed to be on the phone to Liam or her parents. Tessa's heart tugs a bit and she puts down the hammer to be safe, but it passes. The medication actually works.

'Do you miss them, your London friends?'

'Do you know what, not really. I mean, a few of them. I didn't have all that many there, to be honest with you – too busy working.

'I'll tell you what I am going to do, though.' Jo's voice has bent down to a whisper, mindful of Chloe, who's at the horse's head, chatting away to it. The whisper still carries the force of the anvil, though, and Tessa smiles. 'I know it's not the same thing in the slightest, but I'm going to try and talk to Liam again.'

This seems to require an answer. 'Good for you.'

'We'll see. It's no good like this; it's driving me nuts. And I miss him, you know?' Jo shakes herself like a dog leaving the stream, then peers into the shoe drawers. 'Anyway, enough of that. Speaking of people and communication – and don't answer this if you don't want to – but do you ever hear from Marnie now? Or would you not expect to?'

This shoe meets the hoof with a satisfying scorch and Chloe stops twirling beside the loose boxes and comes over to watch. Tessa, carrying the shoe back over to the anvil shrouded in smoke, smiles at her again. 'Careful, now. This bit's hot.' Then to Jo: 'No.'

Jo waves the smoke away and stands behind Chloe, peering over the top of her head, hands on Chloe's shoulders in easy intimacy.

'God, doesn't that hurt the horse, to burn it on like that? At least in the shop the animals are dead before we start on them! Sorry, Chlo. But it's true!'

Tessa shakes her head. 'They can't feel it. Look – he didn't startle at all.'

She moves on to the back hooves, working in silence for a while now. Jo sits down, her back against the horsebox door, and Chloe runs from a bale of hay back to the horse, offering it out on a flat hand. It's companionable.

'Marnie, though . . . Have you been in touch since the sleep clinic?' Jo's persistent all right.

'No.' This shoe looks like it might need a few more nails than the last one. Tessa lines them up in her apron.

'You could, though, couldn't you?'

'I could.'

'But?'

'But nothing's changed, not really.' The tingling's threatening and it's more dangerous now because she's mid-shoeing. She takes a few deep breaths and feels it soften away. The medicine binds her to steadiness.

'You can't say that!' Jo's up again, stepping round the back of the cob as if he might detonate. The cob snorts, ruffles his tail. 'You're so much better, even since I've known you.'

Tessa buffs the hoof, steps out away from it, and leads the cob back into the stable. This next one's a cob too, bit older, one of the most docile horses Tessa's met. The horse nuzzles her, looking for grub, no doubt, and that carefree feeling of earlier is back.

'You're right. The medicines do seem to be making a difference. A big difference, actually. Thank you.'

'God, I wasn't fishing for thanks.'

'No, I know that. Look, the thing with Marnie . . . There were things said and done that there's no coming back from.' She glances at Chloe.

'You can always come back from things.' Jo takes a deep breath. 'Look. You don't necessarily want my advice on this; my various attempts at romance have been a disaster. But it seems like the drugs are working. And when you talk about Marnie you seem happy. So maybe it's worth another go? You never know.'

It's too big a question to answer, but the ember sparks. Tessa places the shoe in the forge and it glows, renewing itself in molten form. Jo's got a point, though there's more to it than she realises. If she wants to make a difference with Marnie, there's only really a limited period to do it in, or it'll just feel too late. And that time is already running out.

Whenever Tessa allows herself to consider that she'd been the one to suggest that they could have a kid together, she all but loses sight of who she is. But she did things differently when Marnie was around. *She* was different.

No – not different. It was more like she'd always been a bit of old pottery, the sort of thing you unearth when you're digging the garden. Nothing remarkable. And then Marnie came along and her light was as bright as the stars in a cloudless sky, and it brought out her own sparkle, polished her up a bit, so that Tessa did and said things that she would never have thought herself capable of . . .

'A baby?'

It hung there, which was something, at least. It didn't crash, rip a hole in the conversation.

Marnie was smiling, but the smile was hard to read through the noise in Tessa's own body. Her head pounded and her bones almost crackled from holding so tight together. There was no going back now.

'Well, just maybe, like.'

Marnie had been scrolling through Netflix, rejoicing as usual in all the options without actually choosing anything. She just liked to know all of life was available to her. Now she put down the remote and cuddled right up on the sofa, her bare feet tucking under Tessa's thighs. Tessa shifted slightly so that her arm was around Marnie. It was always astonishing that this was allowed.

Marnie looked up at her. 'When we first met, it never seemed to be something you'd necessarily set up your life for? I mean, you were living all alone in that cottage and . . . well . . . Family life didn't necessarily strike me as something you were factoring in.'

Tessa leaned back slightly, and the cushions hissed behind her. She couldn't say this to Marnie, didn't have the words. If she did, they'd probably bring on one of her turns. Family had never seemed to be an option. Other people had families; she'd been around Ern's lot long enough, seen the way they joked with each other,

249

fought with each other, all always there for Sunday roast and down the rugby club on a Saturday afternoon. But Tessa wasn't raised like that.

Her family wasn't porous; wasn't soft and messy, bleeding into each other's lives so that you could hardly tell where one person ended and the next began. Her family was upright, each of them in their own slots, no overlap of affection, or really of interest, and Tessa carried that with her outside the house. It had kept her quite separate through playground games – that and the terror of having one of the ragdoll episodes, and she'd watched without understanding how nobody else seemed to have the walls around them that made her incapable of joining in.

But then she'd met Marnie, or rather Marnie had literally arrived on the scene, given her no choice, and the walls around Tessa were melted open by a warmth that'd put the heat at the core of the forge to shame.

Marnie's family was a posh version of Ern's. They met for brunch rather than going down the club, drove cars rather than vans to work, but the internal momentum, the thing that made them all so clearly part of the gang, that was the same. Marnie's family watched out for each other exactly the same as Ern's did. And they accepted Tessa into it, because that's what families do. They have enough to go round.

Tessa could do the basics, she could keep herself fed and watered, but it had always seemed clear that loving anyone else was dangerous and always got taken away. Bethan had shown her that. Mam had shown her that.

Tessa didn't possess the right internal settings to be part of a happy family.

But these past couple of years, Marnie had burned through these assumptions. Marnie was an endless flame. Now Tessa got it. She saw how a family works. She wanted to be part of a family with Marnie.

And a baby.

It wasn't something she'd come to lightly. But at the same time, it was like the idea had been there all along, just waiting to be released.

Marnie pulled her feet from under Tessa's legs, sat cross-legged on the sofa beside her. This was Marnie in earnest mode, back upright, eyes wide, her body perfectly symmetrical in a wide-legged jumpsuit. 'I suppose we should have talked about this earlier but I hadn't ever really expected it to come up. I'm full-on with my career and, honestly, hadn't really ever thought about kids, at least not once I met you. I know you're not that much older than me, but it might be enough to make the difference in terms of fertility—'

Tessa cut her off. 'No, I know that. I couldn't be the one to carry the baby. Not just being over forty; it's my job, too. I'd only need one horse to kick out, and it'd all be over.' If she was going to have this conversation, she had to be honest. 'And then there's the fainting stuff, though that's calmed down a bit.' It hadn't calmed down, to be honest, so much as she'd got good again at avoiding situations where it might happen. But it amounted to the same thing and there was no need to panic Marnie.

251

'So what you're saying is, you want to have a baby, but you want me to go through the IVF and all the hormonal shit that comes with that, and then give up my career while the baby's tiny?' Marnie's tone was neutral, but that just sharpened the words. Tessa had to stay steady.

'It wouldn't need to be IVF, necessarily.'

Marnie laughed shortly. 'If we're going to do this – and that's an if – then I don't want to mess around with turkey basters and mail-order sperm. No sense doing it without involving the experts.'

This was Marnie through and through.

'The expense, though.' Even if Tessa were to start saving now, they'd be waiting a good couple of years. Unless they sold the cottage. But that's her safety net, for when things stuff up with Marnie. Tessa's head throbbed and she put up a hand to rub her temples. She was the one that wanted this baby. She couldn't have it all. If she wanted the baby, she'd have to sell up. She'd have to trust she wouldn't need a safety net.

Marnie put her hand over Tessa's, warm and firm, and Tessa's heartbeat slowed. 'The NHS might still cover me. And if not, I have some savings. This isn't a financial decision; it's an emotional one. That's the really important thing here.'

Marnie said this sort of thing occasionally, an opinion only accessible to someone who'd never had to worry about where the next pay cheque was coming from. It grated every time and Marnie would be mortified if she realised.

'I know. We don't have to have a baby. I just thought we'd make a good family, you, me and a nipper.' She couldn't look at Marnie. It came out as a whisper. 'A real family.'

Now was the time to say it, if it was ever going to be said. 'It feels like . . . it's just that . . . look. Bethan didn't ever get a chance to be a kid, not really. It was my fault, that was. And I can't do anything about that. I know that.' Tessa's nails were filthy, needed a trim and a scrub. 'But I can give a different kid a chance at a real family. Make amends.' She clenched her fists and the filthy nails disappeared like dirty laundry.

Marnie uncurled one of the fists, clasped the hand in both of hers. 'God, Tessa. You know that wasn't actually your fault? Look at me.' Her lashes were wet. 'How could I not want to have a kid with you? If that's what it means to you, then we'll do it. We'll find a way to make it happen.'

Chapter Twenty-Nine

KIRSTY'S OUT THE BACK WHEN they get there, just home and hanging out the washing, her coat on over her work clothes. The lines on her face lift into a smile when Chloe rushes up, and she bends down to chat.

'Did you have fun, love? See lots of horses?'

'It was sooooo good! Auntie Jo's friend has an oven in her van, and we got to see her cooking the horses' shoes.'

'Wow – that does sound brilliant.'

Kirsty straightens up, her arm still on Chloe's shoulders, and levels the smile at Jo now. 'Thanks for taking her; sounds like she loved it. Got time for a cuppa?'

'That'd be fab. I'll give you a hand getting these out first.'

'You're all right. They'll keep.' Kirsty puts a couple of pegs back into the peg bag and makes her way over shiny grass to the back door. 'Li's upstairs – should be nearly finished with our Rosie's room. I'll call him now.'

Jo should go up and see Liam, really, but he'll only snip at her, greet her with that plastered-over façade he seems to use with her at the moment.

'Oh, don't worry, let him get on. You must be ready for the house to be back to normal.'

Kirsty glances at her, turns away to the cupboard. 'Coffee, right? How d'you take it?'

Jo pulls out one of the wooden chairs and squeezes behind the table. 'Just white, ta.'

Kirsty turns and leans against the counter. She's pulled her ponytail to the front and twists it round one finger. 'How's it all going, now you've been back a bit?'

'Yeah, it's all right.' Jo rests her elbows on the table, her head on her hands. Kirsty's sincerity is a sponge, ready to absorb any truth. 'You know, I was raised a butcher's daughter, and I knew what I was getting myself into.'

'But?'

'But . . . oh, I dunno. Maybe I wasn't born to do it even if I was raised in it, you know? I suppose it's hard to tell how I'm getting on, and I'm not used to that. In court, you win or you don't – for the most part.'

'But you're still enjoying it?'

'Bits of it. I still get goosebumps thinking about how I'm carrying on from Dad and Grandad. That's never going to get old. But I'd forgotten – or maybe I'd just never appreciated it as a kid – how this job is a weird combination of really, really boring and really, really gruesome.'

Kirsty laughs. It's so good to actually be able to talk honestly about this.

'Don't get me wrong. Meeting the customers is great, but the ones with time to chat are generally the ones with less to spend, which is hardly a good business model. Ron seems to have made it his personal mission to point out how clueless I am at all times. I mean, fair enough, but it gets a bit much, day in, day out. And I suppose that maybe what I thought about when I was away and missing the shop was really my parents, you know? Being in the shop without them is weird. Empty.'

This business with Tessa had made things clearer, too. The sheer relief that had come from figuring out Tessa's medical condition had brought into stark relief just how much better Jo is at working with her brain than her hands.

'Have you heard from them, your mum and dad?'

'A bit, yeah.' Jo wraps her hands round the mug, the heat almost scalding her palms. 'Lots at the beginning, wanting to check I hadn't destroyed the business or myself, I suppose. Not so much recently. It's good, right? I've been sending them the accounts every month and haven't heard a sausage.'

'They must be busy figuring out what to do now they're in their new house, mustn't they? Liam said your dad's talking about joining a darts team down there.'

Liam's been talking to her parents? Well, it shouldn't be such a surprise.

Kirsty takes a huge slurp of her tea. 'It's bound to be a bit funny, being back. Give it time.'

'The thing is . . .' God, can she say it out loud? 'I haven't mentioned this to anyone else. Not even to Liam. But I'm starting to wonder whether I'm properly cut out for this.'

'For what?'

'For the shop. I mean, I really want to be back here, and that hasn't changed. But I wonder whether I'll ever get so that the actual work doesn't slightly freak me out.'

Kirsty smiles. 'You've always been like that, though. I remember coming to call for you with Li once, and there you were, putting mince into containers with your fingertips, like it was puppies' brains.'

'Fair enough. I just thought it'd be different now. I dunno – that I'd have grown out of it. Or maybe that being in charge would mean I just had to get on with it.'

'And now you think . . . ?'

Jo hunches forward in her chair, cradling her mug. 'I don't know what I think, to be honest. What if I am better suited to the law after all? Or something else? There must be some way of earning a living down here that doesn't involve feeling sick every day. But I don't know what it is yet. And even if I did, imagine having to have that conversation with my mum and dad.'

'You've got the nicest parents in the world! Anyone can tell Brenda and Jim anything – crikey, even Liam tells them stuff and you know what he's like.'

'No, I know that.' The sickness is back, just thinking about it. 'But I talked them out of their old buyer, really persuaded them hard that they should let me try it instead, laid it on thick about me coming back to my birthright. They'd had another buyer all set up and I talked them into letting me take the shop on instead. I can't go back to them now and tell them I got it wrong – again.'

'Oh, Jo.' Kirsty's tone is warm. 'It's a lot. I'll put the kettle on again, shall I?'

It's odd being the person needing the help rather than the one dispensing it. To be sitting here with Kirsty, who's got way too much on already, and doubtless has her own friends with their own problems that she listens to so carefully. Jo settles back in her chair. Kirsty's lovely, but it's Liam she misses. Liam, and her parents. All the reasons for being home. She might not be able to fix this, but she can try and fix some of it.

Chapter Thirty

MARNIE LOOKED LIKE SHE'D FLOAT away if there was a big draught. She looked spectacular. As ever. Tessa reached for her hand, squeezed it quickly, then dropped it again.

Marnie winked. 'I think we're OK. They're probably used to women being affectionate in a fertility clinic.'

Tessa looked at Marnie again, draped against the hard plastic chair as if it were the most comfortable place she'd ever sat, her floaty dress draped in turn over the very hint of her, and marvels that she ever ended up with someone so easy and relaxed. Even the process of conceiving had been straightforward, as if it were perfectly reasonable to expect your dreams to come true. The IVF had worked first time, though Tessa hadn't let herself believe it until they got to hear the heartbeat whisking furiously away a few weeks later. Now it's stored inside her, a noise to replay as she works, her sheer good fortune humming as she remembers that moment.

'Ms Turner?' Marnie nudged Tessa but she was up on her feet already. This was it, then. They were here for their scan, Marnie desperate to find out the sex of their baby, to have her suspicions of a girl confirmed, Tessa certain they were having a boy and keen on the surprise. It was all beside the point; it was probably too early on to find out such things. She clenched and unclenched her fist, longing for a tool to calm herself. This time, when Marnie reached out her hand, Tessa took it, held on for all it was worth.

'Well, everything seems to be in order.'

Relief blew out of Tessa in a long breath better suited to a horse, and Marnie beamed. The doctor smiled at them over the tech, who handed Marnie a wodge of crinkly green paper and a print-out of the scan. Tessa craned her neck to see it again, the whirl of black and white that held their baby. Proof that they were a family now.

'Two arms, two legs, everything else in good working order as far as we can tell here. I'll leave you to sort yourselves out, then book another appointment on your way through reception. Everything's looking great, though.'

They made the next appointment for the soonest date the receptionist would allow and stepped back out into bright sunshine. Marnie blinked, put up one hand to shield her eyes. Tessa stopped. She always stopped; it was Marnie who could never stand still. Today Tessa understood that a bit more. Happiness was fizzy pop in her limbs.

Tessa stumbled, rushed out a hand and stabilised herself against Marnie. Smart, kind Marnie, who's carrying their smart, kind, healthy child.

Marnie stepped closer, looked hard at Tessa.

'You all right there?' Her voice was soft.

'Yeah, yeah, I'm great. Honest. I can't believe it, that's all.' She choked on the words a little, her jaw slack.

Marnie squeezed her hand. 'You are allowed good things, you know, babe.'

If Marnie kept this up, Tessa was going to cry. Tessa never cried, had never been allowed. She squeezed back, wordless.

Marnie's own eyes were moist, a teardrop balanced right on her lashes. She hugged Tessa and the tear transferred across, hot and wet on Tessa's cheek.

'What are we like?' Marnie was half-laughing, half-crying. 'Come on, let's get out of here.'

They walked down the steps into the glare of the day. People walked past, their own lives just the same as they were ten minutes ago. But not theirs, not anymore. The enormity of it coursed through Tessa and she shivered violently.

Marnie stopped beside her, held her firmly by the shoulders. 'This is the start of our family. *Ours*. If I wasn't "with child", I'd be finding the nearest bar and having a massive drink to celebrate.'

You didn't grow up in a family like Tessa's with a

celebration habit ('What about your birthday?' Marnie had asked once, incredulous), but Marnie's influence was slowly, slowly rubbing off.

'You're right. We should do something.'

'I know! At the very least take a picture of me with the scan, then I'll take one of you. Only fair that we take our pictures today too, since the baby's had one done. We can put them up in her bedroom.'

'Or his.'

'Yeah, yeah, all right. Or his.'

'We could take one of us together, you know.'

'We could, but who wants the first photo you see of your parents to be a selfie, for God's sake? We're going to raise this baby to have higher standards than that.'

'Fair enough.' Tessa laughed, shooed Marnie back up the steps.

Marnie's beam was as wide as the Severn and Tessa's forehead cleared, all worries erased. For now, at least.

They swapped places and Tessa peered awkwardly into the sun. It seemed important that the photo contain the essence of everything Tessa would want to say to him when he's finally here (they hadn't found out yet, so they could each preserve their own conviction for a while). *Hello, baby. I'm your mother. One of them, anyway. I'm the quiet, pessimistic one. Listen to your other mummy once you're out.*

Marnie laughed. She was leaning precariously backwards on the steps. 'You look like you're composing some kind of funeral eulogy up there! This is the picture she's going to look at every night and every morning, not the one we're pulling out to scare her into eating her broccoli. Cheer up a bit!'

Tessa laughed too and Marnie whooped. 'That's more like it!' She pressed the button. 'Now we're in business. Happy nursery guaranteed.'

Chapter Thirty-One

IT'S ANOTHER FOUR DAYS UNTIL Liam can be persuaded to come out for a walk, and even then Jo needs to make an excuse to Mo and Ron and leave the shop early to fit in with the one time Liam can manage.

They park at the bottom of the hill and head right into the woods, Ennis bounding on ahead. The visitors' centre shut hours ago and the only other car in the clearing is a battered old Ford Focus, which could belong equally to another dog walker or to a bunch of teenagers drawn, as they themselves so often were, to find their own entertainment in the trees.

Jo waves at the wooden signpost pointing out the bathrooms, the play area, the Gruffalo Trail. 'When did it all get so dolled up?' There's even a gift shop, as if a forest's a place you go for – what? – acorn-shaped mugs? Pine-cone key rings?

'Been like this for years now, it has.' Liam's focused on heading for the trail. 'I can't be too long, got to get the girls sorted and Kirsty's on lates today.'

'Where are they now, then, the kids?'

'They've gone over to Lauren's for tea.' Liam's up ahead of her, his words gusting down the path. 'Amy and Taylor's mum. Went to school the other side of the Forest; you wouldn't know her.'

They leave the new buildings behind, turn off the path away from the Gruffalo Trail and disappear into the undergrowth. The trees are as thick as walls either side, providing a green tunnel and no choice about where to go.

Liam toes a stone up the path and it clatters against an exposed root as they move side by side up the trail. The manicured organisation imposed on the forest by the tourist board recedes as they make their way to the top of the hill. Primal belonging frissons through Jo and lends courage.

'Li. Have I hacked you off in some way?'

Liam kicks the stone on ahead and it catches on the moss of the path, kinks back towards them.

'What d'you mean?'

Everything is packed tight, needs to fight through.

'I dunno, really. This is going to sound childish, or silly, but you don't seem that glad I'm home. I'm sure it's me, not you; probably just the overall weirdness of being back.' Jo kicks at the bracken that's starting to green on the edge of the path.

The leaves rustle beside them, speaking where Liam

doesn't. The path narrows, the tourist trails long behind them, and Jo falls in carefully behind Liam, Ennis crashing through bracken up ahead. There's no room for lawyering up here, no training that will get her through this.

'The thing is . . .' Liam begins.

Jo's breath won't come. She focuses hard on the scuff of Liam's heels on the path, the pat-pat-pat of his soles. He's facing forward, away from her, still going at a fair lick up the trail.

'It's . . . look. I wasn't going to say anything, but you asked.'

Jo's feet are tender in her boots, her muscles jellified by uncertainty. 'What?'

He pauses, kicks at that damn stone. The harder, the truer the truth is, the longer it takes Liam to dig down for it. The band around Jo tightens again.

'You weren't supposed to come home, all right?'

It's as violent and unexpected as if he'd aimed the stone straight at her stomach.

'What do you mean?'

'It was different when you lived away and came back to visit.' Neither of them is smiling. The expression in Liam's eyes bears such weight that Jo drops the gaze first.

'I know,' she mumbles to his boots. One of his feet is turned slightly outwards, the way Liam always pauses. 'I should have come back more.'

'No, it's not that. It's more . . . whenever you were back for a weekend, for Christmas – even when you were still at university and came back longer, for the summers and that – it was different, weren't it? You always went off again, back to your actual life.'

'But this is my actual life!'

'It's not, though, is it? Hasn't been for a long time, not really.' Liam lets go of the branch he's holding and it pings a bit against her palms, his own palms held upright in supplication. 'It's great you're back, honest it is. But it's not right.'

This was supposed to be a quick chat to find out that, who knows, one of the kids was jealous of her coming back and knowing Liam so well or something. It was going to be fixable, something easy to move on from. Not this.

Jo sits down abruptly on the verge. 'I don't fit here anymore – is that what you mean?' It's only what she already knows, but hearing it from someone else – from Liam, of all people – closes any last remaining space. Jo knuckles her eyes with her fists.

'It's not that. Not quite.' Liam sits down beside her, their knees knocking together. 'You and me, right, we could always do it, couldn't we? School and that.'

'You could do it better than me.'

'Not always.'

'*Yes* always.' This is old ground and it becomes a bit easier to breathe.

'And you remember when we were finishing GSCEs?'

Jo's smile, twisted. 'How can I forget it?'

*   *   *

267

Jo had been rereading *The Secret History* in the window-sill, tilting her book towards the dusk because it was too comfortable to get up and switch on the light. There were only the German exams left to go, in a week's time.

Gary was out. Mum was ironing and Dad was out the back, watering the greenhouse.

There was a knock on the kitchen window and Mum glanced up.

'Liam, love! You all right?'

Jo looked over at the clock on the DVD player. Half nine. Not late, but a peculiar sort of time for Liam to come round. By the time she'd found her bookmark and made it to the kitchen door, she smelled the real reason for Mum's question.

'Li! You're shitfaced!'

'Jo – *language*.'

Liam swayed. It wasn't even like he was trying to hide it. His face looked blurred too, but by more than booze. 'I've come to tell you I'm not doing it. Not doing A levels. Not doing no more school.'

'What are you talking about, you nutcase?' Liam and Jo had picked their options yonks ago.

'I can't. Mum says I've had enough – enough of that bleeding education. Time to get out and start earning a decent bloody living.' Liam steadied himself on the back of a kitchen chair. Even pissed, his impression of Debbie on a bad day was spot on. But Liam. Liam never spoke badly of his mum, never did anything but protect her.

'That's fucking ridiculous!'

This time Mum didn't even raise an eyebrow.

Dad came through, wiping his hands on a towel that had given up on its original colour years ago.

'Evening, Liam, mate.' Dad loved Liam, said he had more sense than either of his own kids.

'Hello, Jim.' Liam straightened up, booze or no booze. 'I jus' came to tell Jo and yourselves that I'm leaving school after exams. Mum says.'

Mum and Dad exchanged a glance.

'Her mind made up, is it, like?'

'Oh, come on, Dad! Debbie doesn't know her own mind half the time. Sorry, Li, but you know it's true. We have to talk her out of it.'

Another of those looks. Jo remembered all the times her parents had tried before, when Liam was younger. Sometimes it had worked, if Debbie had been in a good patch.

Liam got there first. 'Don't worry, Jim. It'd only make things worse, to be honest.' He was getting smaller as they watched, his life shrinking in front of them.

'She definitely means it? What if you did more hours, worked while you did your A levels? Would that be enough? Dad – there'd be extra stuff for Liam to do in the shop, wouldn't there?'

It was impossible that Liam wouldn't be coming back to school, wasn't going to get his A levels and then go off to London with her. *It's not about you.* But deep in Jo's gut it was, a tiny bit.

Liam took the coffee Mum handed him and buried his face deep in the steam of the mug.

'I need to find a trade and start being useful, that's what Mum says. More stupid exams won't get me anywhere and it's about time I paid my way.'

Liam had been working as a Saturday boy at the shop since he was legally old enough. But he didn't chuck away the money on fancy things; he'd had one pair of scuffed trainers that he used for footie and school together, until Mum found him an 'old pair of Gary's'. When they fished, he used one of Dad's old rods, like Jo and Gary. All the Saturday money went on food and bills.

Jo slammed her book down on the table. Mum sighed and picked up one of Dad's work shirts, shaking out the creases before laying it on the ironing board. 'It's a real shame, Liam, that's what it is. But if your mum's decided, then we'll do what we can to find you a decent job, of course. There's not much going in the shop permanently, not with Ron and Mo there, but—'

'Oh no, Brenda!' Liam's horror seeped through his haze. 'I didn't come here to scam for a job!'

They all knew that, though.

Dad persuaded Liam that he couldn't walk all the way back home tonight, that now he was here he may as well stay, it wasn't the work of a minute to unfold the sofa bed.

That night, Jo could hear the murmuring between Mum and Dad – murmuring that had trailed lots of Liam's visits, a vapour of concern about a child who was their son in all but name.

Afterwards, they talked to people, sounded out who might be looking for someone. When he found his first apprenticeship, Mum and Dad bought him a sturdy pair of work boots to celebrate. And then later, once he started proper work, about the same time Jo was starting pupillage, they helped him out with the van. It wasn't what anyone had expected when they were doing GCSEs, but sometimes things didn't turn out the way you planned.

Liam turns and looks at her. 'Yeah, there was that, but what happened after?'

'You got the job with Jerry.' From here you can't see a road at all, only the rounded waves of green treetops swaying and darkening against the day, a seascape far inland.

Liam rolls his hand, moving her along. 'Yeah. And what happened to you?'

'I did my A levels, went on to uni.' A levels without Liam had been odd, his absence shadowing every day at college. He still came round to theirs for tea, even once he'd started work, but not every day. More often than not he'd go back, check on his mum, as if being the steady wage-earner had officially tipped the always-shaky balance between carer and dependant. Occasionally he'd stay and figure out a bit of homework with Jo, but she couldn't ask too often because it felt like rubbing it in.

Liam rakes his hand through his hair and it sticks upright. 'That's it. Right stubborn bugger you were, an' all, when it came to persuading you to properly leave.'

He sits forward and there's a frightening urgency in his stance all of a sudden, his muscles tensed against telling this truth that's going to hurt him.

'But that's it, ent it? Can't you see that? You were gone.' That hand through the hair again. A smile that nearly breaks her heart. 'I was so proud of you, mate.'

Jo pulls her knees up to her chest and wraps her arms tight around them, her wrists bumping against Liam's knee.

'I didn't want to go, though. I mean, I did – I couldn't study the law here, and that seemed the best way to do something useful. But I didn't want to leave.'

'That's what I'm saying, see. You had to go. Even if you needed to be moved out of your own way once or twice. You had to do it. I couldn't, but I could make sure you did.'

'Is this what this is about? That I got to go and you didn't?' Jo clicks through her mental viewfinder, searching her memories for envy. Liam had never once made a fuss about her being away; came up in the van to visit her most terms, softening the edges of her London days with rounded vowels and the sandy smell of damp plaster and trodden-down leaves. But perhaps he was just putting it on, giving her what she needed to get through. God knows he'd got good enough at that with his mum.

The leaves catch an early evening breeze, bend and dip and rustle.

'No. I always knew I wasn't going, really, even before the GCSEs. Not with Mum. I couldn't go anywhere. We were always kidding ourselves that I ever could, to be fair.' He leans forward. 'That's why you had to go, see? Go for both of us, really.'

272

'But we had it all planned out! Since we were tiny. We were off together – strength in numbers and all that.' Jo's light headed, all the certainties of her childhood dissolving.

Liam sighs and it's full of years of suppressed knowledge.

'I was never going. It did me good to think I might be able to, you know? But there was no chance.' His grin is crooked but it's the most honest reaction from him since Jo got back. 'I was never going to score a goal like Michael Owen did against Argentina, neither.'

'Going to uni wasn't a pipe dream, though, Li. You really could have done it. You know that.'

'No. No. I really couldn't have. The exams and that, they'd've been all right. But not the rest of it. That's where you and me's different, Butler. You needed to go. You always needed to go. All that world out there and you'd've been nuts not to give it a try.'

'I hated it at first. Not the studying, the law – that made sense. But the rest of it . . .' It had been a hard slap: the grime of London, the greyness of it all, the taste of it on her tongue, the flat, fast words slapped out with urban economy, no meandering down conversational by-roads. Her course had been a welcome relief, the only place where she was sure footed, maintaining the same pace as those around her. But London was full of people who were there for their own purpose, didn't slow down or care. Everything was so expensive and pointless. Liam needs to know it wasn't one great big party – but he does know that.

'This is it, though, see? You settled in, made that the life you were supposed to be having. And now it feels . . .'

'Now it feels what?' Her voice is sharp, and ravens startle out of the oaks above them, cawing.

'Don't take this wrong, OK? You coming back – it's not right.'

'But . . .' Jo's world kaleidoscopes. She presses against the nearest tree trunk, the bark rough and alive beneath her palm. Liam holds his hand up and she stuffs shaking hands into her jeans pockets.

'It was weird, you not being here, but it meant there was a wider world out there, you know? Knowing you were part of it was great. How many kids in our year group went to uni – four, five? It wasn't a thing people did, was it? But you did. And I was happy here. A bit of fishing with Jim and a few pints with the boys – that did me. And then me and Kirst had the kids. I didn't need to go anywhere else, never did.'

This simply isn't true. He's changing the past, rewriting history to fit the present. 'You did, though! You've always wanted to get out there too.'

'No, mate, I honestly haven't. I'm not daft. My mum – even when I was little I could see how that would pan out. She did her best, and I got lucky with your mum and dad, and then half the town looking out for Mum because Jim and Brenda put the word out. You don't repay that by buggering off once you're old enough, leaving people to it.'

There's an unspoken space between them and no knowing what the hell's in it.

'Even without the stuff with Mum, I don't know if I'd've left here, not really. Look at me now. I'm still working for Jerry, all these years on. Kirsty, the girls, the dog – it's all steady. I don't need things to change. But that's why it mattered all the more that you went – do you see? You doing so well, landing that big job – it proved kids like us could do stuff like that, that we were just as good as kids from anywhere else. You're not supposed to be back; you're supposed to be the one that went off to see what was round the next corner.'

Liam shrugs, helpless and tender. 'You being home . . . it's like you're saying there's nothing worth looking at round the corner after all. It shrinks things. I'm having trouble getting my head round it, but I shouldn't have taken it out on you, though – that ent fair.'

'Li – God, no. I'm the one that's sorry. I didn't think. I really didn't mean to make things tricky. I've been too focused on the shop. It's just all a bit crap, you know? London not working out and now here being impossible, too.'

'Hey, now.' Liam's got her by the shoulders as if he's dealing with Chloe in one of her strops. He smells of damp and dirt, of sweat and, somewhere underneath it all, of the Lynx deodorant she'd bought him for a laugh one Christmas when they were sixteen and he decided to adopt. He smells of home. 'You've still got all that training; none of it was wasted. You'll think of some-thing.'

'But Mum and Dad – and their retirement – I can't just leave the shop now.'

'Course you can. There'll be a way. Come on, now. I didn't mean nothing by it. I'm not so good as you at saying this stuff, that's all. Course you belong here. Course you do.'

'Look . . . I . . .' But there's nothing to say. Nothing at all. Even if there was, she doesn't know what it is yet.

Liam glances at his watch, a quick glimpse he doesn't know she's seen.

'You go on – you've got to get the girls. I need to untie this lace, retie it.' It's true, actually, but she's going to have to wait for her fingers to stop shaking.

'You sure?' Then he's halfway down the hill, hand up over his shoulder in a goodbye wave.

Jo sits and works on the knot as Liam disappears from sight.

'*Fuck.*' She insinuates her index finger into a gap that doesn't really fit, and the shoe pops off as the nail, already jagged at one end, rips off down to the quick. She picks up the trainer, considers the lace again. It's buggered, frankly. She pulls on the tongue, widening the gap as much as possible, then forces in her toes, wincing as they squish. Where her toes go, the rest of her foot will follow. If only the rest of life was so straightforward.

Chapter Thirty-Two

S HE'S ONLY GOT ONE SHOT at getting this right, so Tessa's taking the train to Bristol rather than driving, mirroring the very start of her time with Marnie in case there's something lucky about the train. For the first time ever, luck seems possible. Jo's optimism is infectious, finally. Life's come out of black and white, into colour, and there's no sense in wasting any more of it without Marnie. She's not dying. Every day this knocks her for six, makes her almost laugh with the sheer hugeness of it. She's alive, alive alive alive. Jo was right about finding a diagnosis, and that's released Tessa from an early death. What's more, it means she won't be landing Marnie as her carer, will be able to look after the baby – their baby – without fear of endangering it. It's not going to be straightforward; Tessa's temples throb when she remembers the last time she saw Marnie. But the diagnosis has given her determination, and anger at all the time she's lost, all the love she's lost. There's no way she's losing more.

Tessa hasn't got the train into Temple Meads since that very first time she came to visit.

They'd met up a few times by then, finding pubs that Marnie called 'halfway', and Tessa privately thought of as 'somewhere nobody will recognise me'. The last couple of times, after meals where nerves were interspersed with conversation more intense and personal than Tessa had ever known, they'd left Tessa's van in the pub car park and driven further down the lanes until, sure nobody could see them, they'd stopped in a layby and proceeded to get to know each other further.

Last week Marnie had texted: *Come and stay. I'll cook supper.*

The ante had been upped.

'The train comes straight into town, doesn't it?' Marnie had said, and Tessa didn't have the nerve to point out that the train from the Forest would be at least two changes and actually went to the station out of town, so she'd have to get on another one to be where Marnie expected her. The van would be the obvious choice, but the kitted-out farrier van didn't belong in a city, and taking it would only emphasise that Tessa didn't belong there either. The bus was half the price, but even in the early days Marnie didn't seem the type to know about buses, or half-price anything, and Tessa couldn't risk too much of the truth for fear it would put Marnie off. Tessa didn't believe in fate or any of that nonsense, but it was hard fact that the odds of the likes of her meeting someone like Marnie again in the Forest were slim to none.

So she'd halved what she spent on food that week – not such a problem since she could barely eat for joyful fretting – and bought a train ticket. When she'd finally got on the train, she'd spent the whole journey standing, too nervous she'd miss her stop and be whacked with a huge fine.

But that was then, though. It's even less possible to save this time, so she's broken her own pledge to herself and held back the tenner from the account this month. It's all to the same end, after all. Jo would have given her the fare – would have offered Tessa a lift, no doubt – but this is something she needs to do on her own.

She hasn't told Jo she's going. She got out of the house before dawn and waited down at the station until it was time for the first train. She can't let her discover what really happened with Marnie. It wouldn't do to have Jo, who's been so good to her, knowing she's wasted all that kindness on someone capable of such deeply shameful behaviour.

Tessa's taken the pills this morning and has brought more with her. Armour and proof. They didn't stop the dreams last night, but on the other hand she'd barely slept, so the dreams hadn't been as intrusive as they might have been. She smiles. Look at her, all optimistic about insomnia. That's Jo's influence rubbing off. It'll be so much better for the baby if she can be positive.

The baby. It floods her and she stumbles into a man hustling past in a navy suit, head down on his phone.

'Oi! Watch where you're going!' He looks Tessa up and down and scowls, shakes himself off as if she's contaminated him, and strides on. He'd thought she was a shambling drunk. Is that how she comes across? She's in her best jeans – the ones Marnie always said made her want to peel them straight back off – has done her best to scrub the grime from her nails, but there's no hiding who she is.

It doesn't take long to get to the flat. Tessa's brought her key. She can't use it, of course, but the feel of it digging into her thigh brings her comfort.

She hesitates, staring at the doorbell, and a memory intrudes. Mam's door, eighteen months before this.

She pulls herself together, wills away the tingling. She presses the doorbell and waits.

Chapter Thirty-Three

THERE'S NO SIGN OF TESSA when Jo gets up for work and her van's not in the driveway. Maybe Tessa's medications have kicked in and she's gone back to work full-time. The sun's out and it's proper sunshine, the beginning of spring, not deceptive winter sunshine, which seduces you with the temptation of warmth and then mocks your lack of coat.

Jo can't face breakfast this morning. She's fucked everything up, worse than she realises; the very fact she didn't understand the effect coming home would have just goes to show how little she actually belongs here. But talking to Liam about the shop has clarified one thing even as it muddled another. She owes it to her parents to let them know she can't keep going. She'll only end up wrecking things, making them worse than when she started. The business will be worth nothing and she'll have destroyed the very legacy she was trying to protect.

But how? Hurting them when they've only ever shown kindness and love is the worst kind of behaviour. They're supposed to be relaxing now, for God's sake.

She'll figure out a way to talk to her parents, sort things out. She'll have to. And then she'll find a way to make it right with Liam.

Ron's nicked the parking space behind the shop again. At least the puddles have cleared up in this dry spell and a little bit of a walk never harmed anyone. It'll help to put it all aside, at least for the time she's at work.

Jo pushes open the back door to the shop and almost bumps into Ron and Mo.

'Hello, love! Still fresh out there in the morning, it is.' It's like they were lying in wait. Mo thrusts a mug at Jo. 'Got you that decaf you like.'

She's the only one with a drink. Ron twitches, his bandaged finger glowing like a beacon, his expression unfamiliar and hard to read.

'Everything OK?'

Ron twitches again, looks at Mo. Mo implores Jo in a silent game of Chinese whispers, but how the hell is she supposed to know what it's about? She really, really needs to get on.

Jo's phone rings and they all jump.

'It's just Mum.'

Ron beams and Jo steps back involuntarily. It's more disturbing than if he'd slapped her.

'You go and have a word with her, love.'

Love?

'Mum? Hang on a minute – I'm just getting out of the shop.'

Ron and Mo stand either side of the doorway, a guard of honour. They're just plain weird today. Jo half-smiles, half-frowns and ducks round the corner.

'That's better. Hello!'

'Morning, love. You spoken to Mo or Ron today?'

'Only to say hello.'

'OK. Right.'

'Why – what's up?'

'Well . . .' A pause. 'It's the shop.'

Oh, God. This is going to be it. It's one thing, hypothetically, to know that something isn't working. It's yet another to face down the parents who put their retirement on the line for you in good faith and tell them you're not interested anymore.

'What about it?' Her hand's slick on the receiver.

'You probably won't remember, but Mo's mam died not that long ago. So they've got a bit of capital.'

'What?'

Mum's voice has gained strength now, a note of determination creeping in like someone pedalling uphill.

'After that first buyer got cold feet, we were a bit worried there for a little while. People aren't coming into town the same way, and most don't want their meat straight from the animal anymore. They want it anonymous and half the price. We talked to you about all this when you looked at buying the shop, didn't we?'

'Yeah, but Mum—'

'Just let me finish, love. So then Mo and Ron came to us before Christmas, said they'd been thinking about their bit of inheritance.'

'*Before* Christmas?'

'I'm sorry, love. We could tell at Christmas that you were finding life a bit of a struggle and we know how attached you are to everything here. Ron and Mo weren't in too much of a hurry, so when you suggested giving the shop a go, it seemed like a good idea, buy you some breathing space. But they need to know what's going on, see. It's not fair to them if this drags on. We thought three months would be a good length of time, but perhaps it's kinder to just get on with things now.'

This should be a relief, but it's not. 'So you were fobbing me off all along?' Jo's voice is thick in her ears.

'Not fobbing you off; giving you a chance to get back on your feet. Your dad and I have been really proud of everything you've done since you got back.'

'Christ! I'm not a little kid to be patted on the back for passing a gymnastics test!' It's one thing to not want to do this, quite another to be told she was only ever playing shop. 'I've been working my guts out here, trying to make a go of things.'

Jo clings to the phone as if it's a detonator. Two kids passing opposite the betting shop stop and jeer, and she flicks them the V-sign. If she's a child, she may as well act like one.

'Not being funny, but how are Ron and Mo going to manage to revive things if you couldn't and I couldn't?'

Another pause.

'That's the thing, see. They're not keeping it on as a shop. I know you've been working really hard – all those new ideas – but the truth is, and you must see this, love, it's not possible these days. Ron and Mo – we'd talked about this – they're going to apply for residential conversion. Make someone a lovely house, this will – good central location, lots of scope to do with it what you will.'

Mum sounds like an estate agent. If it weren't so horrific, it would be funny. Jo's voice, when it comes, is reedy and thin.

'That doesn't make any sense. Why even bother selling it to them if all they're going to do is turn it into a bloody house? Why not do that yourselves?'

'After the first buyer, we were done with the whole thing, tell you the truth. It'll take some time for all the regulations to go through and we wanted to get a move on and come down here. This works out better for everyone.'

No wonder Ron's been an absolute sod: she's been in between him and his nest egg for weeks. And that weird look this morning – that was *pity*. They knew Mum was phoning today; that's what the welcome committee was about.

She's no good at anything; no good at all. Coming home was a disaster. She should have sucked it up and stayed put.

'I'm sorry if it comes as a shock. We did try to talk you out of the shop, but we know how you've always felt about it.'

'Mum! You say that like it's totally peculiar. The shop's been in the family for generations. Of course I wanted to try and save it – somebody had to.'

Mum's voice turns, sharpens. 'Not everyone has the luxury of doing things for tradition, or because they want to, Joanne. Your father's father started that shop – how do you think it makes Dad feel to know he can't keep it going? He's been worn out this past couple of years struggling to keep things afloat; it's only been since we got to the coast that he's finally relaxed.'

'There's nothing I can do to stop this, is there?'

'Don't be like that, love. You'll get used to it, in time.' But there's no conviction in Mum's voice, and no sense in prolonging this conversation.

Jo says goodbye, hangs up and stuffs the phone in her pocket. 'Fuck!' She kicks the wall as hard as she can and scowls at it. She's ignored all her training, looked at none of the facts. She's given up her flatshare, her career, and there's nothing here.

She'd trusted her parents, met them adult-to-adult with her plans and her analysis of the business, and instead they'd treated her like a small child wanting a go in Mummy's high heels. And now, when it suits them, they're reversing it all again, leaving her worse off than she'd been at the beginning. No matter that she hadn't wanted to do it, that it's saved her finding the words for an awkward conversation.

The ground's shifted. She doesn't know who she is or where she fits in. There's nowhere left for her to go.

Chapter Thirty-Four

DEEP INSIDE TESSA IS STORED the rhythm of Marnie's walk, as distinctive as her voice, and as she hears the tapping along the wooden floors, it hits her again.

Tessa stares straight ahead. She's learning to let emotion back in, bit by bit, but she can't risk it now. Now is not the time for collapse.

Tessa's heart races but the drugs are working, keeping her emotions level so that she doesn't collapse. Her head, for once, is free of biting pain, no warning tapping at her temple, nothing closing in on her as her vision tunnels down. Bitterly, stupidly, Tessa longs for once to feel it all, wishes with all her being that emotion didn't fell her, that she could be normal.

'Tessa!'

Tessa jerks her head forward, whiplashed by holding her emotions at bay.

Marnie is there in the hallway, in the old tracksuit bottoms she used to refuse to answer the door in, a definite bump showing now.

'What are you doing here?' Her face is carefully, deliberately blank, stripped of its warmth.

Tessa, focused hard on the bump, blinks.

'Can I come in?' Her voice is barely a whisper.

Marnie looks impassively at her for a long moment, and Tessa, held hostage by everything she wants to say but can't, finds she's holding her breath.

Eventually Marnie turns back into the flat. Her hair's longer than Tessa's ever seen it, and messier, too. Marnie was always so put together, even in bed first thing on a Saturday morning: white linen pyjamas and a face that somehow never got creased from the pillow or bits of sleep stuck in the corners of her eyes.

The door's still ajar so Tessa follows her down the corridor into the kitchen. It would be the easiest thing in the world to close the distance between them. If she does, Marnie will lose it and it's vital that doesn't happen. Marnie's shuttered up and Tessa's on the outside, unable to find a way in.

Marnie picks an avocado from a bowl and starts peeling it with the little knife she's always kept there for this, her hip jutted out to counterbalance the weight of her bump.

The silence spreads, blackens, a tar spill obliterating everything around it. Tessa breathes in and out, trying to leave as much of it outside her as she can. She was a fool to wish for emotion a moment ago. Emotion is her enemy, always will be.

'So.' Marnie turns round and there's so much menace in her movement that it's hard not to shy away from it. 'What exactly have you come back for, Tessa? I remember every word of that last conversation we had and there was no coming back from that, so what the hell are you doing here now?'

Tessa puts out a hand to stop Marnie. She's not going to be able to stay upright for much longer. But the memory of her last day here bears down on her and there's no getting out from under it.

Tessa was in the kitchen, more or less where Marnie is now. There was no avocado, though, only her backpack. The van was already packed with most of her kit. Tessa sat, her back against the fridge, its vibrations steadying her. She should have gone earlier, but that would have been unfair. Even Mam had stayed for goodbye.

'Tess? What're you doing on the floor?'

She was too deep in thought, had missed Marnie coming home. Tessa stood up and Marnie clattered to an abrupt stop, pulled into the tendrils of Tessa's silence. She'd have to do it now before another collapse came on. They were coming up to twenty, thirty times a day and Tessa was scared stupid. More than that, she knows she could not – would not – leave Marnie to look after a newborn infant and a partner who was sliding not-so-gently into what looked like something that could end up in paralysis and total dependency.

She should have talked more to Marnie about this. You didn't need a fancy education to know that. More than once she'd opened her mouth to start the conversation, but the words were stoppered before they came out. She'd wrecked too many lives by talking to do it again.

It wasn't true that there were words for every situation. How did you tell the person you loved more than anything in the world that you were abandoning them? But it was the only way.

The truth was, life may have been better with Marnie in it – no question – but physically, being with Marnie had made things worse. It hadn't happened much at work yet, but at home Tessa had been collapsing more often, drifting further and further into whatever fate this was that the doctors said wasn't happening. She'd made light of it with Marnie, especially after the doctors cleared her, but she knows, deep down, that something isn't right.

She couldn't drag Marnie down there with her.

She'd killed Bethan.

She'd driven away Mam.

If she loved Marnie – and she did, oh how she did, more than she could even feel without dropping to the ground – then she had to do the only decent thing and let Marnie be.

Tessa took Marnie's hand. It was firm, the nails perfect ovals of saffron yellow today. The world would be falling in and Marnie's nails would be immaculate. It was a superpower.

'Marnie. I love you.'

Marnie stared, silent, and the growing anxiety in her eyes nearly felled Tessa there and then.

'You saved me. Honest, you did.' Tessa closed her eyes and the cold of the cottage, her life before Marnie, fronded out and tangled her in memory, threatening to submerge her.

'These past few years – I've never been happier.' It was costing Tessa every word she had.

'But?' Marnie's hand trembled in Tessa's grip and Tessa clung more tightly. She had to get there in one go or she'd never get through it.

'I can't, Marnie. I can't stay. It's not fair to you. I'm going to wreck your life if I stay.'

She hadn't known it herself, not really, until three days ago.

'I dropped flour the other day.'

She'd been in the kitchen, putting the shopping away, when outside the window someone yelled, the words indistinct but the fury sharp as glass. Tessa, speared by the shock, ragdolled straight down, her head rebounding against the black and white tiles. The bag of flour bashed against the worktop on its way down, disintegrated on impact. Tessa was coated in it, her nostrils tickling, unable to move or to scratch the itching.

A moment later she was free and she pushed up from her hands and knees. Mounds of flour molehilled the stark geometry of the tiles and Tessa's head started to throb as she realised the answer to a question she hadn't dared voice, even to herself.

Back in the kitchen now, one hand pulling her maternity top taut over her bump, Marnie stared.

'I dropped it, and it went everywhere. Everywhere. I had . . . well, I fell down again, and I didn't have no time to stop it, see? And I thought, what if I'd been carrying the baby? What if I'd been right here, between the cupboard and the island, with the baby? What would have happened to it when I went down?' She shivered, edging towards it but not daring to actually give it full expression. The flour was obliterated. If a newborn infant had slipped through her fingers, its head hitting the end of the counter with even half the force the bag of flour had . . .

'Is this about your fainting things, the funny turns? We can get it checked out again. I'll get Arianne to recommend a doctor. A better one.'

'There's no point. We've tried all that. It's just going to keep getting worse. At best I'll be no help at all, and at worst the baby . . .' The image flashed again. A tiny, vulnerable life, dropped to the floor. The crack of its head as it connected. Blood flowing across those black and white tiles as carelessly as a kite in the breeze.

She had to stay. She'd asked Marnie to have their baby. She'd put it all out there, risked every last part of her closed-in life, received the impossible in return. Marnie's joyful, unfettered love. The promise of a new family, one she would create herself.

She couldn't stay. She wasn't built to be around people, that was the beginning and end of it. She was a danger to anyone she loved. The kind thing to do – the *only* thing to do – was to leave.

It would break her to leave.

But it would break them if she stayed.

She bent down for her stuff.

Marnie tipped her head, uncomprehending, and

noticed the bags. A tiny cry came from her and her hand tightened on her belly.

'You can't.' She stepped closer, her free hand imploring, her voice working its way up the scale of panic. 'Tess, don't. You can't. We'll fix it. You're not dangerous. You're not. I love you. I *love you*.'

Marnie's face contorted, grief and fear twisting. Tessa's head pounded from the pain in Marnie's gaze.

'I have to. At least for a little bit. Until I know I can be safe around you.'

'You don't. Tessa! You can't leave me!' Marnie was sobbing now, tears dripping onto the red of her top, her hands clutching for Tessa. Tessa, desperate, was crying too, disentangling herself.

'If I stay, I'll wreck all our lives. Yours. The baby's. I can't do that to you. Not to the two people I love.'

This love for Marnie was the hugest, deepest thing Tessa had ever known. She'd do anything to protect Marnie, even this. She couldn't let down anyone else she loved.

She clasped Marnie's hands to each other in prayer, a prayer for both of them, for all three of them, and let go, picking up her bag.

'I'm sorry. So sorry. Maybe once I've figured out what the problem is, I'll come back.' It was an empty promise, believed by neither of them. But it was all she had to give.

Marnie's staring at her again. Tessa sits down quickly and Marnie sighs.

'Still not listening to me properly? Fucking hell, Tessa.

What did you come back for if you're not going to listen?'

'No – no. I'm sorry. For all of it. I can explain.' The tingling starts and she daren't stand up; everything is too close to the surface. 'That's what I came here for, to explain.'

'You just don't get it, do you?' Marnie's voice hangs heavy, tears looming like cloud cover. Tessa longs to go to her, but she's forfeited that right. Marnie trusted her. She loved her, truly loved her, the only uncomplicated love Tessa had ever known, and Tessa trod all over it. She has to explain – she must explain.

'It's an illness. No. Not an illness. A condition.'

Marnie slices into the avocado with such weariness that the knife barely makes it through. 'What, so even though you refused to go back to the doctor when I asked you, you've randomly made it there after all these years? And not only that, but the doctor's miraculously sorted all those fainting spells? Come off it, Tessa. Give me more credit than that.' She turns slowly, stares long at Tessa. 'Do you want to know what I think it is, really? What made you decide to leave? It was that trip to see your mum. God knows what went through your head afterwards, but honestly? Whatever it was, it gave you no right to start sleepwalking through conversations. Too tired to talk to your *pregnant girlfriend*.'

Her laugh is all bitter exhaustion and the tingling builds.

'Do yourself a favour, Tessa; next time you decide to use an excuse, don't pick one that's so pathetic you needn't have bothered. Fainting fits, for God's sake.'

'It is real, you've got to believe me. It's called narcolepsy. The collapses. I've got pills now. I can help look
after the baby. And you. I'm sorry I wasn't here.' It's
barely a whisper.

'Do you have any idea what it's been like for me since
you left? Of course you bloody don't, because *you
weren't here*.' Marnie's laugh is arrowed bitterness.

Tessa can see it all, everything she missed, and it tears
at her. 'I left because I had to. Because I was afraid I'd
hurt you. Hurt the baby, eventually. I was keeping you
both safe.'

'Safe! Fine way to show it.'

'It's the truth! I couldn't trust myself before. But now
I can. There's medication.' Marnie has to believe her.

'Do you know what really hurts? You didn't even try
to involve me, not really. You may have medication now,
but where was the trust? Why couldn't you say, Marnie,
help me, I'm scared, maybe I need another doctor. We'd
have worked at it together – did that never occur to you?
We'd've got there, eventually. But you just buggered off
without even trying to get treatment. And then you went
and figured it out without me, and expect me to just forget
the last few months? You left me. Left us. For fuck's sake,
Tess!' Marnie's crying now. She angles her head away.

'You know I can't say these things like you can.'

'Oh, don't be so self-indulgent! Of course you could,
if you really wanted to!'

Marnie paces up and down the kitchen, one hand on
her bump. This is Tessa's baby in there, hers and
Marnie's. She should be there to make it laugh, to know

295

the sound of its cry when it's tired, hungry, bored, what to do when it wakes in the night. She should know the weight of their child asleep on her shoulder, the brightness of its eyes when it spots her in the morning. The baby needs them both. Marnie has to see that.

'How've you been?'

Marnie looks at her, incredulous, and the floor wobbles.

'Like you care.'

'I do. I do. Look, this is what I'm trying to tell you, see? I left because I cared, not because I didn't. About you, and about the baby. I want to help. I was wrong, I see that now. I don't get to give up. I'm its parent too.'

Too far.

'Get out. OUT!' Marnie stands tall, her free arm pointing. Her hand's trembling and her nails are jagged. 'You. Have. No. Right. None at all.' Her eyes are bright and her hand around the baby is clenched tight, a warning fist and a protection. 'You walked out on us – on me. He's not even born, and he's nothing to do with you, do you hear me?'

He? The baby's a boy? The boy she'd imagined all along? Tessa is momentarily blindsided, the baby as vivid to her as if he were there now, nestled on Marnie's hip. Determination surges anew.

'But I'm back now.' Tessa reaches towards Marnie, this woman who has shown her that she was capable of love. Now she must show her just how much she loves her.

'What are you doing? Get out! Get out now!' She

marches towards Tessa and Tessa is backed all the way up the hall. 'I don't want to see you here ever again. You made your choice already. You don't get to swan in now and make another one just because you feel like it.'

The door slams and angry footsteps recede. Tessa's on the outside and all that's left is absence.

Chapter Thirty-Five

THERE'S NO WAY SHE CAN go back into the shop, not now. The Butler family tradition gone. Ron and Mo knowing all along, waiting for her to have her go like she's some little kid, before they get back to the business of shutting it all down. Feeling so sorry for her this morning that they brought her her special coffee. Jo's been so naïve. The shame is scalding; her cheeks burning. Ron, laughing behind her back, feeling sorry for the poor little clever girl who couldn't hack the city and isn't cut out for a real job back home either. If she told them she'd been thinking about leaving anyway, who would believe her now?

There's a light touch on her shoulder. If Ron's come to pontificate, she'll swing for him.

'Butler? Aren't you supposed to be inside selling made-up Forest recipes to the gentrifiers? Or a pound of mince to Phyllis, anyway?'

Liam. Oh God.

'Thought you'd be at work.'

He swings his legs over the wall and sits down beside her, saluting to the betting-shop kids, who stare at him as if he's lost his mind and run off, laughing. Jo wipes her face on her sleeve with the arm furthest from him.

Liam nudges her. 'How many times have we sat on this wall over the years?'

Jo stretches out her legs. 'God, I dunno. Dozens? Hundreds, probably.' She holds herself still, legs stuck in front of her like she's died sitting up and they've forgotten to lie her flat before rigor mortis set in. That happened to a call-out Gary went to once, an old man that the neighbours realised they hadn't seen for a couple of days. 'Had to break his bones, poor old sod, to get him onto the stretcher,' Gary had said.

She shudders.

'Cold?'

'No. I dunno. Tired.' It's too soon to tell Liam about the shop, to cope with either his kindness or his I-told-you-sos. She stares at her feet and Liam does too.

'What's with the fancy footwear?'

Jo focuses. She's still got on the plastic outer-shoes for the cold storage room. She forces lightness into her tone.

'Oh, you know. Trying out new fashions to go with the hipster recipes.'

'Glam.'

'Yeah.'

Liam's in his overalls, his hair full of plaster dust.

'You been at work already?'

299

'Yeah. Picking up the girls from school today, so I got an early start.' Liam sighs and Jo sighs with him, as unconsciously as yawning.

'What does your day hold?' It's like they're at the hairdressers. Stupid question, anyway. He's working, then home with his wife and kids, obviously. Idiot.

'Not much. Got a big job for a builder up on the new estate on the bypass. Football for Rosie, you know.'

'Yeah.'

When they were kids there'd been a fad for those blocks made up of individual metal pins that you could press objects into to make a 3D silhouette. Someone always ended up mashing their face onto the grid, pushing through a grotesque outline of their nose, their pouting lips (your lips always seemed to need to be pouting if you were going to get involved with that thing). It's like that now, the air so charged with silence that Jo's pushing the barest outline of herself through, nothing that would make any sense at all to the naked eye.

'Jo, we . . .' There's a tone to Liam's voice that hasn't ever been there before.

'I know.' Her toes curl and the stupid plastic foot coverings rustle. 'Look, Li. I'm sorry, OK? I really am.' Jo's voice wobbles. 'I didn't mean to make things worse for you.'

Liam shifts on the wall, moves a tiny bit away. 'I know that.' It's impossible to tell anything from his tone.

'I wasn't thinking. I . . .' She turns and looks at him. He needs to get this. 'You know I'd never, ever do

300

anything to hurt you, right?' The shame of it curdles and her toes curl again reflexively.

'Oh, aye – I know.' Liam's face is all screwed up. He'll be finding this excruciating; he's had trouble with personal conversations at one in the morning under the shield of booze and the dark, never mind outside the shop in broad daylight.

Jo's shaky inside at her own colossal self-centredness. 'I was so excited about getting back that I didn't think.'

'You, not thinking? That's got to be a first.' But the humour's only a veneer; things aren't going back to normal this quickly.

They sit for a while longer. Nobody says anything, but gradually the silence softens.

Jo stands up. 'I'd better be getting off. Eric and Ernie in there'll be wondering what's happened to me.' She shrugs, palms upwards in a move that's part Beyoncé, part Oliver Twist.

'Aye, me too. That newbuild ent going to plaster itself. Are you around later? Fancy coming round for your tea?'

'No. I mean, you've got football. Look, Li. I'll see you soon, OK? Let's go for a drink, yeah? With everyone, I mean.' Jesus.

Jo slips back in through the back door and waits. The glass is frosted and hard to see through, but she can make out Liam's shadow, the familiar loping. She leans up against the wall and counts to ten until he's gone, then eases the door back open and legs it to the car. Her heart bangs as if she's sprinting uphill and her hands tremble as she fumbles with the ignition and crashes the car into gear.

She indicates to get out onto the main road. 'Come *on*.' She'll go home, get her proper coat and get into the woods for a bit. It'll be all right out there, easier to think. Back in the core of things.

Chapter Thirty-Six

TESSA DOESN'T REMEMBER THE DRIVE home from the station, let alone the train ride, but it doesn't matter now. She's wasted the chance, bottled it right when she needed to finally say something that might mean something. The superpowers these narcolepsy pills give her, this sense that she's untouchable now, hadn't equipped her with the one superpower she needed: the ability to talk to people. If she'd only been able to put into words the feelings that tumbled in her like the washing, all muddled and murky.

Jo had made it sound so straightforward, her version of Tessa approaching Marnie again sparkling with filaments of light. But Jo used words the way Tessa used the pritchel, the clenchers: to shape and bend things, to create something out of nothing and to get someone seeing it the way you saw it. Words don't do that for everyone. Not when you've spent a lifetime avoiding them.

She slams the van into the driveway, peeling off the road still in third gear and standing on the brakes to avoid Jo's car.

But Jo's car isn't in the drive.

For a split second, Tessa's hands won't obey her brain, won't relinquish the wheel. She sits, counts her heartbeats, stares at the clock on the dashboard. She's only been gone a few hours. Long enough to shutter down hope, to cause more pain to the two people in the world she'd want to protect when the aim had been exactly the opposite. Things were never going to fix themselves in one trip to Bristol. Of course they weren't. But after today, Marnie will never let her in again. She's blown it.

Marnie. Their baby, the one they should have together. Her baby. Her chance, finally, at a family. Seeing Marnie again was a knife into a wound, the longing unstaunchable now.

Eventually she can move again. She fumbles for her key.

Jo's door – the parlour door – is shut. Tessa should have trusted her instincts, should never have listened to Jo. That bloody woman, coming here thinking everyone should talk, and everyone should listen, and if we all simply communicated a bit better everything would be peachy. Talk doesn't work like that.

Tessa slams the front door shut and continues down the corridor. Her pointless smart boots clack against the wood of the hall, the opposite of Marnie's socked padding as she took away Tessa's hope. Tessa kicks the wall, kicks it with so much anger that she collapses.

Narcolepsy in action. Knowing what to call it doesn't help, not right now. Falling doesn't hurt; nothing hurts. She waits for her muscles to work again, staring at Jo's useless bloody books lined along the bookshelves. She always trusts the wrong people. It's like Mam says, she's useless. It's all her fault. Remorse hits hard.

That's enough. Just like that she's floppy again, nothing to do but ponder the bookshelves. At her core is regret; it's hollow and rotten and it stinks, and right at its centre is her mother, reminding her that she should have been the one who died.

The episode doesn't last so long this time. Sensation comes back and Tessa staggers to her knees, pushes herself up on the wall. What was it Jo had said when she moved in? That she'd identified herself by her books? Tessa lifts her hand, sweeps it along the bookshelf. Four books clatter to the floor like acorns rattling off oaks.

Tessa lifts her hand again, takes it to the next part of the shelf. There's a rhythm to it that's not unlike rasping a hoof and by the time she's at the kitchen door, every single book is off the shelves and the corridor is lumpy with books and pages like churned-up turf after a hard winter. They've landed on top of each other, splayed and undignified, wisdom and insight reduced to a jumble of angles and obstacles. For a second she's powerful, almost gleeful.

But then it's gone again and she's back with the despair. Her family. Her baby. She'd left to protect him, because a mother must do whatever it takes to protect her child, even if it means leaving. Marnie didn't understand and now she has no hope.

This isn't like the other pains of her life, the brain-fizzing and muscle-melting; not like the kicks and bruises from the horses or the bumps and grazes from endless collapsing. Every emotion she's never allowed herself to feel had been tucked away, fermenting. Seeing Marnie, the baby so imminent, has unblocked things.

Tessa propels from her seat, active with longing. She staggers around the perimeter of the kitchen. The white-wash is rough and cool, soothing, and her breath regulates as the consultant told her it would. She'll make it up the stairs. All she has to do is to stay away from the feeling for a minute. Once she's got upstairs, she can let go.

She puts one foot in front of the other, steady, steady, pacing towards what might have been. Her head is clear – no pressing-in, no throbbing temples – and her stomach is dancing. The heaviness is replaced by light, the fury dissolved.

If she can't be with her family she can at least pretend.

Tessa reaches for the door handle of her room. The rocking chair and the cot are in a corner, huddled together under an old tarp like sheep in snow. She'd found them the week she moved back to the Forest, when she'd still been able to work properly. She was exhausted all the time, working as hard as she could so that she'd come home unable to think. Leaving Marnie and the baby was the right thing to do. The only thing. But the need to be part of the family they were building had been a phantom limb, still needing attention.

Now she yanks the sheets onto the floor and stares at the baby gear in her bedroom. The cot. The rocking chair.

She'd seen them in a skip on the way home from a job, just after she'd moved back here. She'd checked around, heart banging against her ribs, then climbed up and rescued them, the weight of it tickling her shoulders. It's furniture that holds other people's stories, people who valued these stories so little that they abandoned them. But other people's stories can only be an improvement on her own. So instead she'd concentrated on cleaning the cot and the chair, removing all trace of the people who had gone before, sanding and staining and painting, choosing new cushion fabric for the rocking chair so that they speak of a new family, not of anything left behind.

Her breath comes loud and cold into the stillness of the room. The yellow paint of the cot is catching the light through the window, cocooning the room as if the sun itself was warming them. The furniture's simple, unfussy. After the rage downstairs, Tessa's exhausted. She folds into the rocking chair and stays as still as she can, trying to concentrate on the spring breeze dancing in through the open window, the gentle motion of the chair as it bears her weight and gives her what she needs from it.

As the air frosts around her and the light starts to swallow itself as effectively as the dimmer switch, Tessa blinks hard, plays a scale on the hard wood of the chair's arms, and readies herself. She can't think any longer; all she can do is feel. The cottage closes in on her and she twists, pulls herself in tight, anything to avoid the avalanche of feelings that are coming to get her right now, but it's no good.

Staying inside is making it worse. She'll head out, trust the trees for once. The trees will restore the mess that talking to people has made. They'll help her make a plan. Perhaps there's another way.

As if it's heard her, as if it's nudging her outside, downstairs, the front door opens.

Chapter Thirty-Seven

J O'S BARELY GOT THE DOOR open, all her energy on what the hell she's going to do next, when Tessa wrenches it from her.

'You interfering little besom. How dare you!'

It's like being consumed by a flame thrower. 'What? What are you talking about? What's happened?'

Tessa blocks the doorway. She's unfamiliar in smart clothes and shivering emotion.

'Go and see her, you said. Everything will be fine, you said. That's all you ever bloody do, isn't it, say things? Would it kill you to shut up and listen to people properly for once in your life?'

Jo hasn't got time for this crap, not now.

'Look, I'm just here for my big coat.' It's just over there on the coat stand. There are books all over the floor but they can wait. She needs the soothing infinity of the trees, to go and stomp and kick things and scream into the leaves. She needs proof that this part of home, at least, is immutable.

But Tessa blocks her way so that they're chest-to-chest in the doorway now.

'Tessa!' Jo edges along the side of the corridor.

'I should never have let you in in the first place.' Tessa's words flare out into the cool of the hallway. Not a witch after all. A dragon.

'Seriously? You want to do this now? It's not a good time, OK? My life's just been pulled from under me and—'

'*Your* life? What about my life?' Tessa's shouting now and Jo yells back, hands chopping the distance between them.

'I couldn't give a monkey's about your life right now, truth be told!' Jo hooks her coat off the rack and moves towards the door. She just needs to get out. Tessa stands as rigid as if she herself were made out of cast iron, watches her go with those glittering eyes.

Jo huddles into her coat, her hands trembling, fumbles the key in the car ignition. Whatever's going on with Tessa, she can't take it now. She needs to get out, try and clear her head. Hopefully by the time she gets back Tessa will have calmed down again. Or not. But she's had enough. She's done with helping.

Chapter Thirty-Eight

WHEN LIAM SLOWS THE VAN at the crossroads at the top of the hill, it sputters out. He bangs his fists against the steering wheel and the horn blasts into the trees.

He pulls the lever for the bonnet and gets out to have a look, but there's no point. The van's knackered. He straightens up, runs his fingers through his hair. God only knows what they'll do about a new one.

Liam drops the bonnet shut again, drops the van into neutral and drifts it backwards into the verge out of the way, grabbing the torch from the glovebox. He's got an hour before Rosie needs picking up from football and Chloe from her play date.

Tessa's cottage looks as dark inside as it's getting out, but Brenda's – Jo's – car and Tessa's van are in the driveway. He stealths up closer, up on the balls of both feet so that the gravel doesn't crunch. Some things you learn in childhood can never been unlearned. One way or another, Liam has always been unsure of his welcome at other people's houses.

Except at the Butlers. That's why he needs to sort this now. Something was up with Jo earlier, and if it's about what they talked about last night, he'd better sort it, even though he'd very much rather not have to talk about things. He'd thought they'd got to the bottom of it, but she wasn't right when he left. Liam's gut shrivels with his own unknowing.

He taps the door knocker. The sound clangs through the old cottage but there's no returning noise of footsteps. Won't be if it's that Tessa, mind; she sneaks around as quiet as anything. 'Handy as you like with the horses, that is,' old Ern had told him once.

He rings again, tiptoes to the windowsill and cups his hands against Jo's window.

There's a heap of discarded clothes on the bed and the usual two, three books on the pillow, but there's definitely no Jo here.

He tries the door again but nobody's going to answer if they haven't already. Those old door knockers were made to be heard all the way into the garden.

That's a point. Liam walks down the side of the house, pushing past the shrubs. The chill's left the air this week; it'd be just like Jo to be out on that old stone seat at the back of the house in the dregs of the daylight, with a cup of coffee and a book.

Jo's not out the back, though, nor nearby; there's no discarded coffee mug, no book lying waiting on the bench. No Tessa either. Since he's here, he may as well check they're not in the kitchen. Liam's reverting to his old muscle memories, casing a joint before breaking in, the way his mum taught him, if only by example. His face flushes and he steps hurriedly away from the window. If Jo were here she'd've noticed the movement, read into it the confirmation of the things he's never dared actually give words to. But even Jo doesn't know the full extent of what home was like for him. There are some things you never tell.

There was one Christmas – he must have been about eight – when his mum insisted on getting a present for Jo's parents. In retrospect it was the beginning of the end of a good spell, though Liam hadn't yet reached the age of being able to identify that kind of thing. When she could, she cared about him, cared about bringing him up right. So when he'd got home that day she'd done jazz hands, a little twirl, and shown him a kettle – some expensive make, from memory – and a toaster, insisted that he take them round for the Butlers next time he went.

Liam was proud for once. His mum acknowledging this other family rather than sneering, like she usually did when he came back from Jo's and ventured any news of what they'd done that afternoon.

The kettle and the toaster were in massive boxes, and he was terrified he'd drop them, dent them and cop it from Mum. So he waited until the next time Jo's mum dropped him off and asked her to hang on a minute. Mum was inside watching telly and roused herself to watch, proud, as he staggered back through the front room with the first of the boxes.

'Helps to know the security guard at Wilkinson's.'

'What?' Liam said.

She'd beamed, pleased with herself, and the sofa had wobbled. 'You don't think I paid for them, do you? We ent got that sort of money.'

She levered herself into a half-sitting position. 'Don't you go telling that Jo, mind.'

Liam's pride in the gifts curdled on the spot. He put the boxes down, went and stood by the gate, shoulders hunched, and muttered over to the car, so quietly that Jo's mum had to lean across and open the window.

'Sorry. I can't find it.'

Jo scowled. 'You said you had a present for us.'

'Jo! Don't be rude.' Her mum smiled at him. 'Don't worry, Liam. Happens to all of us.'

The next day he'd avoided Jo at home-time, let himself in and found a packet of crisps that did for tea. After the weekend, when the bruise of shame had faded, he went back to Jo's again. Her mum and dad were as friendly as ever. That made it worse.

Liam trudges back round to the front of the house, memory shrouding him. After that, sometimes when he came home with Jo, Brenda would say matter-of-factly, 'The camp bed's made up, Liam,' and he'd know Mum was having one of her turns. They'd talked to him once about the prospect of moving, going to a new family, but Mum had her good stretches too, whole weeks sometimes where there would be food, and she'd be up and dressed when he got home. The older he got, the easier it was to read the signs, and by then he only needed to stay home when he wanted.

He lifts the door knocker and lets it fall heavily. His phone has no signal, as usual. Jo wasn't at the shop; he'd called back in at closing time, but Ron and Mo had shaken their heads, denied all knowledge, as if she didn't exist. Right cagey, old Ron Cooper was, come to think of it. Barely wanted to pass the time of day, and clammed right up at the first mention of Jo.

Nothing for it but to try the forge. Tessa might know where to find Jo. He shakes his head again then strides over the old drystone wall at the bottom, not bothering with the old gate that leads to the forge. The closer he gets, the more tentative his footsteps become.

He swore he'd never come back.

That was different. Tessa will understand why he's back out here.

Will she, though?

But there's no finding Tessa – or Jo – down here today after all. The bolt's shot through the forge door and the padlock speaks of absence.

Where the hell can Jo be? Liam stops to think, one foot up on the drystone wall. She's not at the shop. She's not in her car, as the car's here.

She's got to be inside. He isn't looking hard enough.

Trickling fear shifts him round to the front of the house, all thoughts of keeping quiet gone. This isn't like Jo. He puts his palms flat against the front door and pummels.

315

The door opens on him with a start and he half-falls inside.

'Butler! Where the hell have you been? I've been trying to get in for gone ten minutes now!'

Liam's heart rate hasn't copped on to the fact that Jo's safe, standing in front of him. He's panting, half-shouting as if she's one of the kids and has run out into the road. She's standing there looking at him as if he's the mad one.

'I've been looking all over for you!'

'What? You've been out here a while?' She's dazed, completely elsewhere.

'Yes! What the hell have you been up to?'

'Did you see Tessa?'

'What? No.' Something's definitely off. It's not just vagueness; she looks like he does after a day's work, covered in dust, smears on her cheeks and her hands.

Liam cranes over Jo's shoulder. There's something on the floor behind her.

'Did the bookshelf fall down?' He hadn't banged on the door that hard, surely.

Jo barely glances behind her. 'No . . . that's . . . something else.' She shakes herself like Ennis, and the woman he knows comes back into focus. 'Have you got a sec? Come and see.'

She holds out her hand with complete trust, like Chloe does, and he takes it, like he always has. Her hand's soft, and freezing as usual, and he sags with the familiarity of it.

'This way.' She treads on up the stairs. 'I was out for a bit, and when I got back Tessa was gone. But look . . .'

316

She's holding open the door to Tessa's room.

'Whatcha doing? We can't go in there.'

'No, Li. You have to see this.' Jo pulls again on his hand and he follows her. Of course he does.

'Crikey-oh.' It's half a nursery. A rocking chair with a Peter Rabbit cushion in it, and a bright yellow cot. Furniture that seems to belong to a different house. Furniture for a baby.

Jo rubs her eyes hard. 'She's not here, Li. There's this, and she's not here. And I think it's all my fault. We've got to find her.'

Chapter Thirty-Nine

Tessa's never come this far into the forest on foot, never dared before, but all bets are off now. Fury and hopelessness roar at her through hell's teeth and she snatches zig-zagging breaths along bridleways and biking trails. Soon there's no paving anywhere in sight, just an upward climb between trees that tower and sway as if nothing had happened. As if her whole life hadn't been put back in sight then whisked away just as suddenly.

She diverts off a Forestry Commission track, her breath hard and fast in her ears. The camber shifts and she stumbles down the shallows of the verge and pushes on up through the ferns, her jeans soon soaked to the knee. The light's starting to tire and the trees silhouette into each other like paper dolls.

Tessa pants her way on up a never-ending hill, past tufts of grass and clumps of fern, images whirling and swirling as she climbs. She's alone again, the only sounds the call of the birds, the whistle of the wind through the branches.

The climb's in the tops of Tessa's legs now, burning, her throat hoarse with effort, boots scoring her shins. It's good to feel things and she climbs harder, faster, twigs rolling and crackling underfoot until the branches of the spruce below form a bobbing green carpet. She's at the top of a cliff, what looks to be an old quarry scattered below.

The path flattens out and Tessa stares at the village off in the distance, patchworked through the trees, so far below as to be in a different time. The path fringes off as the trees recede. She edges right to the lip of the quarry, feet slick on dew-damp grass, daring herself to look down. Below her is only the puzzle of the cliff edge, the bowl of the quarry an amphitheatre, oaks standing in silent sentry beside it. Tessa reaches back, clings with fingernails to the bark of the nearest tree.

Soft twilight pushes through, mellows everything to rich swathes of yellow, the same colour as the nursery furniture she's kept hidden for months, even from herself. There's nothing left for her here. No path forward that holds any happiness.

Her grip loosens on the tree branch swaddling the edge of the quarry and she falls forward. Down, down, down she goes, bouncing into branches and crashing back off them, her pace seemingly unslowed by obstacles. Eventually she's out of sight. The leaves sway, marking her absence. All is still.

Part Four

Finishing

Chapter Forty

IT MUST BE LUNCHTIME, JO thinks dully as Liam comes through the door. He's scrubbed to within an inch of his life, no glimmer of plaster dust. He'll have changed in the loos when he got here, taken his dirty work clothes back out to the van. It's a tiny, huge gesture and Jo's throat closes to see him.

'You should be at work.'

Liam scrapes a blue-backed plastic chair up beside Jo and passes her a cup with a mis-fitting lid. 'I brought you a cup of tea. Any change?'

Jo takes the cup from him. 'Ta. Not really. Just waiting still.'

It's been three days since the air ambulance came and got Tessa out, brought her up to the hospital in Gloucester. It's the only time in her life that Jo's been grateful for her brother and his medical training. He patiently translates the grainy photos of the monitors she sends across to him whenever she can get enough signal. The first time, he'd phoned her within a minute.

'Nobody's talked to you about these?'

'Not really. We know she's broken some ribs, fractured her pelvis, broken a leg. No damage to the brain, they don't think, but we won't know until she's properly awake. Don't know what internal damage there is. They say she's been lucky, Ga. How is this lucky?' She hadn't meant it to come out like a wail. It was hearing Gary's voice, even this strained version of it.

'Is there someone there with you?'

'Yeah, Liam's here when he can be.' She'd pulled a face at Liam, the 'Gary's on one again' face from when they were teenagers, but Liam's face was soft as he watched her half of the conversation, and she'd had to blink away, concentrate on what Gary was saying: 'It's not great . . . Wait and see what they tell you . . . Try not to dwell.' But Gary didn't know it was her fault. Dwelling is penance for interfering.

Now Liam looks through the window where Tessa lies hooked up to untranslatable machines.

'I am at work. Well, I have been. I can't stop long. Kirsty says she's made spag bol for tonight – call in on your way home and she'll keep some for you. Don't matter what time it is.'

Liam reaches into his jeans pocket, pulls out a key on a fluffy unicorn key ring.

'That reminds me. Take this and you won't be worrying about keeping us up.' His smile is crooked. 'Our Chlo chose the key ring.'

'Thanks. For the tea and the key. And, you know . . .'
Liam's spent every lunch break this week driving forty
miles to Gloucester and back to keep her company.

Jo digs her nails into the clammy plastic of the cup
and stares gritty-eyed at Tessa, moving with the monitors.
The doctors say it's just as well they found Tessa when
they did – one of those medical-drama phrases that
sounds ridiculous in real life.

If only they'd started looking properly straight away.
Jo tried her best to explain the whole thing to Liam,
how Jo had meddled when she shouldn't have, sent Tessa
to go and see Marnie when there was no hope and no
need, the row when Tessa came back, and her storming
off. Liam had calmed her down, said there wasn't any
way harm would have come to Tessa.

In the end, though, she convinced him. They went
out into the woods, searched around the cottage in
circles that got progressively bigger as the sun grew
dimmer.

Nothing.

When Jo almost lost her voice from shouting and they
really did lose all the sun to the night, they gave up.
They had no proof that Tessa was out here and no way
of finding her in the dark if she was.

Liam went home to Kirsty and the kids, and Jo sat
and stared, unable to think of tidying the books, unable
to think past the cot and what it could mean.

Dawn arrived but Tessa didn't.

Jo phoned Liam. 'We have to do something now. She's
been outside all night. Anything could have happened.

She's got this thing – a medical condition.' No time to go into it all fully.

'You don't know she's outside.'

'Where else would she be?'

'Have you tried her customers?'

'The ones I know about. Nobody's seen her. I think I should call the police.'

'They won't care. They'll say she's old enough and there's no proof she's in any danger.'

But the police took it far more seriously than Liam had expected, especially once Jo mentioned Tessa's history of collapses, the recent narcolepsy diagnosis. They searched all day while Jo paced, confined to the cottage, waiting, increasingly desperately for Tessa to come back, its walls closing in again as the day shut down around her, her mind scuttling through rabbit holes of disaster, each possibility worse than the last.

Eventually the door knocker clanged through the cottage, the wrought iron heavy with intent. Jo jumped, her limbs heavy and sore.

It wasn't the police. It was Liam, his face twisted, hands on knees as he caught his breath.

'They've found her.' Her voice clanged in her ears.

Liam nodded, bent over still. 'You'd better come quick.'

Guilt seamed through rising panic. She grabbed her parka, stuffed her feet into boots.

'Is it bad?'

But Liam didn't hear, or refused to answer. She pulled

the door shut behind her, stepped down onto the path, shivered.

Tessa had gone off the cliff at one of the old quarries, miles from the cottage. She'd landed on a grassy bank about halfway down and a climber setting up in the quarry had mistaken her at first for a tent left by someone else, and gone over to investigate.

She hasn't regained consciousness for any length of time yet, so all the questions remain unanswered.

Jo doesn't need them all answered; she knows. She nearly killed Tessa with her stupid need to help people. Now, if only Tessa will pull through, she needs to help properly. Try and make it all right again.

Chapter Forty-One

THERE'S NO WAY THIS IS their best idea, but the moment Tessa came round and was lucid, Jo begged him to at least look into it. So here they are, a week from the accident, and Liam's palms are sweating in front of the forge.

He tries to jimmy the lock again and it senses his reluctance to do this, refuses to give. It's warm out here today, the green stalks of the daffs still visible around the edges of the forge, as if once upon a time the building had been a scene of domestic bliss rather than a place for sweat and metal.

He leans his head against the forge door, gathers his breath and his nerve. Now Tessa's going to live, things are retreating to normal like a house of cards being slowly packed away. There's talk of moving her from Gloucester down to the Dilke Hospital, so that she can recuperate, and after that she'll be back in the cottage.

Things just need to click back into place with him and Jo, too. Properly back into place. Though they're better now than they were.

The day they found Tessa, they hared up to the hospital behind the ambulance, their silence packed with speculation. The roads were clear and the ambulance easy to follow, but it was going to be tricky parking when they got there. Liam couldn't stay put in the Emergency Bay and he wasn't sure how many pound coins he'd got in the glovebox if they needed to park. Cost a fortune, those places did. He glanced at the clock. Rosie would be almost done with football by now, Courtney's mum dropping her back at theirs.

He texted Kirsty when they found Tessa and she'd sent back one word: *Go*. She'll have sorted everything at home, found someone to cover her shift, got the kids' tea. Liam's throat tightened. They were like the little figures in those ornamental weather houses, him and Kirst. You'd struggle to see them in the same place at the same time, but you needed both of them for the balance, for anything to work at all. The two of them had been bumping along for years now but he hadn't ever stopped to consider how they made it work – who had time for that in a marriage? Until Butler came back, and moved in with the farrier. He'd never told Kirst about any of the old stuff – the stealing and that – though he was pretty certain she'd figured out some of it. Kirsty got on so well with his mum; it would feel almost like a betrayal to mention anything that might get in the way of that. And some things were better just buried than giving them light they didn't deserve.

'Liam – about the other night.'

Jo's hands were tight in her lap, her eyes still trained on the road in front of them. They're coming into the outskirts of Gloucester now, not far until the hospital. Economy and urgency drives the words out.

'I shouldn't have said nothing. It's great having you back, honest.' Liam stitched down the gears as the ambulance slowed for traffic lights, flicked the indicator on. They'd talked about this once already, hadn't they?

'I just want us back like we were.' There was a quickening to Jo's voice. 'And the shop – I need to talk to you about the shop. I need my mate back.'

It didn't take a second to reach out and place his hand over her clasped ones. 'Me too.'

It's only been a week since then and they're both trying too hard, tell the truth. Things are still off-kilter, like one of them's been living in a foreign country and keeps throwing words into conversation that don't make any sense to the other. Jo told him about the shop, bits of it, at least, as they'd sat there watching Tessa. She couldn't look at him, her hands twisting in her lap, and he wanted to reach out, pull her over for a hug. But they weren't back there yet.

The shop decision didn't come as such a huge shock to him, if he was honest. Jo hasn't been around here for years, not properly; she's missed the steady drop-off of regulars coming in. However many new people came around who might fancy the idea of a local butcher, from what Jim said when they got out fishing, they didn't do enough actual buying to make up the difference. Once Aldi moved in, that was that, really – writing on the wall. Jim and Brenda could have handled it better, maybe, been straight with Jo from the outset, but it makes sense when you knew them. There isn't another couple like Jo's parents for trying to help someone out when they could, and that goes double for their own kids. Crikey-oh, he'd do the same for his Rosie and Chlo in a heartbeat. Give it time, Jo will see their actions were the result of an excess of love. It's the better problem to have.

Butler will be OK, even if it doesn't feel like that right now. However much she tries to forget it, she's still got that law degree. She'll find another job, once she's worked things out.

Right now she can't think of anything but Tessa, can't see this isn't necessarily her problem to solve. Liam huffs wryly. She's her parents' daughter all right. She phoned him last night.

'What's she going to do when she gets out of the Dilke?'

'What's that now?' He was mixing plaster for the downstairs hallway, straining to hear her over the radio and the paddle drill, Ennis barking in the background as one of the kids played some mad ball game with him. Rosie, no doubt.

'Tessa. When she's out of hospital. She hasn't been

earning anything since she's been in there, and she won't be able to earn anything when she gets out, not to begin with, at least. I've been thinking . . . I think there might be a way we can get Tessa some money to come out to; something that'll keep things afloat for her.'

'What, one of them fundraising pages? We can try it, but I don't know how many people would really know her.'

'No, not so much that. I was thinking about all those amazing things she's made.'

'We can't break into her forge and sell what we find in there!'

'No. I know that. But we could know what she's got, have a quiet word about it in a couple of craft shops? At least there'd be a plan for when she gets out, if she wanted it.'

The morality of breaking and entering seems flimsy at best, even if it is to try and see how they can help. But Kirsty agreed it made sense to at least see whether the ornaments and that made by Tessa – 'look for bottle holders made from horseshoes, tiny butter knifes,' Jo had instructed – would be saleable, keep her safe for a bit.

There's no way he could explain his real reluctance to go back into the forge to either of them, let alone both. Better to let them ascribe it to squeamishness.

Finally the lock gives and Liam tenses. Iron filaments and scorched charcoal waft to greet him. Tessa might never forgive them. But it's the best they can do for now.

Chapter Forty-Two

I T'S BEEN FOUR DAYS SINCE Tessa was transferred to the Forest cottage hospital, a fortnight since the accident. Her injuries are nasty but no longer life-threatening, though recovery is going to take a while.

Jo stares at her phone, wondering whether she should phone Ron and Mo, see how they're getting on.

The strangest thing had happened two days ago. Ron had shown up at the hospital, almost deferent. 'I heard you were here most of the time, didn't want to bother you at . . . her house.'

He'd wanted advice. *Advice*. 'We know it should be possible to convert the shop for residential use. The Black Horse on the Coleford Road did it, and now it's a house. But we're not sure how to go about it, not the technical stuff.'

Ron answered the obvious question before she got there. 'Your mum and dad was going to ask you when you were still up in London, said it was handy having a lawyer in the family when it came to this stuff. But then you got the idea to come back here.'

It was hard to want to help Ron, but her parents? That was different. Jo's throat closed at this proof of their pride in her, realised what it must have cost them to swallow down their plans so that she could come back and achieve some distance from the life threatening to overtake her.

'Of course I'll look into it,' she promised Ron.

To be honest, it's a relief to think about this, to do something practical. Property law has stuck in her brain since her university days, it turns out, and the localised parts of it are a matter of research. Fortunately the hospital has half-decent Wi-Fi, unlike the rest of the area (nobody should tell the Forest's teenagers this; they'll be abseiling off cliffs without the brakes on just to get admitted). A few searches and phone calls later and she's able to let Ron and her parents know what they should be doing. It's a funny way of dealing with the family legacy, but oddly enough it feels right. There's the occasional childish knife-plunge to the gut when she wishes she'd got in first that day Mum phoned, explained that she wasn't cut out for the work, but that'll pass. She's doing her best by the shop, even if the best isn't what she originally thought it was. If she gets her way, the Butler name and the façade will stay, part of the appeal that can be sold to these metropolitan incomers looking for something 'quirky'.

It's there again, that satisfaction that came when she

ferreted out Tessa's diagnosis. Is this what she's good at? Digging through rabbit holes with a shovel made of persistence to get to the bit that helps people she cares about?

She's due another month's worth of what barristers call 'age debt', the back-paid money from the cases she worked on a life ago in London. Maybe there's leverage in this new idea. It's always seemed too obvious to make money from, the urge to ask questions, to fret a problem to the very end, but perhaps there's something there, some way to stay in the Forest but actually use the thing she's good at. She's still living at Tessa's cottage for now. It's tricky to know if this is entirely appropriate but there's no real room for her at Liam and Kirsty's, and this way there's rent money coming in for Tessa, someone keeping an eye on the place. If she keeps saying it, she might eventually believe it.

Kayleigh, the nurse who lives next door to Liam and Kirsty, comes gently to the side of the bed, looks down at Tessa.

'She's fine; she'll be sleeping a lot now. Why don't you go home, get some kip yourself?'

Jo hadn't meant to conduct a bedside vigil. She'd assumed that eventually someone would arrive who knew Tessa better, at which point the chair beside the bed was all theirs.

But that hadn't happened. Tessa seems to have existed firmly in the world of acquaintances rather than that of friends. All the time she was in Gloucester, only Jo visited, Liam coming up to keep her company when he could. It was as if nobody else missed Tessa at all.

Once the tension of the first few days had worn off, Jo thought about going back to the cottage, looking for details of the ex-girlfriend. Tessa needs someone who loves her more – knows her more.

But – that last row with Tessa, in the cottage. Jo shivers, remembering. If she hadn't interfered in the first place, then she and Tessa would never have had the argument that sent Tessa over the cliff. Meddling further might make her feel better because she's actually doing something, but what good will it actually do Tessa? None at all. The conflict twists and frays, Jo's head cloudier and more muddled the longer she contemplates it.

Once Tessa was moved more locally again, the idea of nobody visiting pierced Jo. How could it be that this quiet, thoughtful woman has nobody at all who would miss her if she didn't show up for a week? And how could it be that this community that basically built Jo, that she's spent half her life trying to get back to, has gaps in it big enough for someone to fall through? Sick at what this exposed on both sides, Jo got hold of Geoff, the owner of the riding centre she'd visited with Chloe, and he contacted the rest. Susan from the livery yard has been in a couple of times; as have Ern's sons, who Jo's known for years, and who've said they'll deal with Tessa's farrier clients until – if – she's ready to come back. The vet came. Jo caught her eyeing Tessa up with a professional eye and started to giggle, had to excuse herself. Tessa was lucky it wasn't the vet who'd found her in the quarry; she'd've been put down. Liam and

Kirsty pop in most days; Matt, on his way up to his shifts. Poppy came, alerted by Mo on a Wednesday post-farmer's market trip to the shop. 'Thought you might need a bit of company yourself,' she'd said, plonking down beside Jo and handing over a huge bar of chocolate. Poppy's a keeper, it turns out.

But no family has come for Tessa. No friends from that time in Bristol. Jo's the only person who seems to know about Marnie, who might have an idea of why Tessa ended up on that clifftop. She can't leave her alone.

Jo starts to explain all this to the nurse, but fatigue mashes her words into garble. Kayleigh sits Jo back down in the visitor's chair, hands her her coat.

'So you haven't been in touch with this Marnie?'

'No.' Jo searches Kayleigh's face for clues. 'Should I, d'you think? It's just . . . I already screwed Tessa over once. It seems wrong to go behind her back on personal stuff while she can't even know about it.'

Kayleigh looks at Tessa, haloed by monitors. 'Tessa'd gone over to Bristol, is that right?'

'Yes. To meet up with Marnie. At least, I think so. But it couldn't have gone well – you should have seen her that day.' Jo shivers again. 'I should have known then. I'm such a self-centered idiot.'

Kayleigh puts her hand on Jo's arm. 'There's no point in blaming yourself. What I'm wondering now is whether it'd help Tessa if we could find this Marnie.'

'But surely it'll have the opposite effect?' Was Kayleigh not listening to anything Jo had just said? 'I don't know exactly what went on, but they clearly hadn't parted as new best friends.' She can't tell Kayleigh about the cot. It would feel like an invasion of privacy.

'No, I see that, but it would probably help her to recover faster if she had a loved one around, a reason to be here. Not that you're not . . .'

Jo waves away Kayleigh's stricken expression. 'So you think I should try and get in touch?'

'I'm just saying it couldn't hurt. This girlfriend will know what went on between them, and if she's not interested or she thinks it'll do more harm than good, she'll stay away, won't she?'

'I hadn't thought about it like that. Cheers.'

Kayleigh hands Jo her coat. 'You need to get some kip, then it'll all feel a lot easier. You can't keep her going all on your own, you know.'

Kirsty's probably put her up to this conversation. Jo's so pathetically grateful for this evidence of community webbed all around her, so muscle-achingly knackered, that she leaves, the noise of the birds almost an assault after the ordered beeping of monitors.

But back at the cottage there's no sleep to be had. She concertinas under a cold, heavy duvet and tracks the grandfather clock making its trip around the dial, the owl slicing the black with its call. Somewhere between the two o'clock and three o'clock chimes she gives up, scuffs into her slippers and out into the hallway.

Jo creeps along the corridor and up the stairs, avoiding the censure of the clock. Liam came back with Kirsty while she was still up at Gloucester and straightened everything out. The books are all back on the bookshelves

338

and Tessa's room is tidy, but they've left the door ajar, like you would if a baby was asleep alone up there. As the moonlight catches the rods of the cot, bedding hunched in it, Jo shivers. There's so much she still doesn't know. And it might be that this is entirely the wrong thing to be doing, but talking to Kayleigh has at least made it worth a try. If Tessa goes mad at her again it'll be fair enough. Jo's already basically squatting in her house and rifling through her stuff; it's not like Tessa will be short of ammo.

She fumbles for the light in this room. It's a dimmer switch. A memory filters in from when Liam's Rosie was first born, Jo teasing him about the dimmer switch he'd installed in what was to become Rosie's bedroom.

'What, she's going to need mood lighting?'

Liam had rolled his eyes. 'Believe me, if she's crying in the dead of night, the last thing you want to do is bang the light on full blast. You'd yell if I barged into your room and turned it into an interrogation suite. It's no different for her. Babies are tiny humans, y'know.'

Jo didn't know, though, not really. But Tessa, like Liam, had been thinking about an actual person when she came back to live here. This isn't a showroom for a baby; this is a room for a baby – for a tiny human – to live in. With its mother.

Jo comes all the way into the room and slumps down into the chair. It rocks, tilting her further in. She's never properly been in Tessa's room before, only that time she found the rocking chair and cot, when events overtook them. It's even more of a violation than asking Liam to have a look in the forge.

Tessa's better off in the hospital if this is what she comes home to. The bedroom is desolate, somehow contriving to be stuffy and clinical all at once. The lightbulb is dim and the room is bathed in gloom, despite the moonlight gilding the leaves on the apple tree outside.

There are no pictures on the walls, but three darker patches in the paint. There's a painted kitchen chair beside the old wood-framed bed, an old-fashioned alarm clock on it in a way that's very much not an Instagram trend. The rocking chair and the cot seem not so much placed as stuffed in here, hollow dreams that still take up space. They clash in this room, both chair and cot gleaming with newish paint and hope. Jo trembles, worry and uncertainty arpeggioing up her spine. If she had only understood better – only understood at all – this might not have happened, or at least not like this.

Up against the wall there's a tall chest of drawers, black garments yawning out. There are photos on the chest of drawers – three of them. They're grouped together, the only familiar face in the wrought-iron frame at the back. It's Tessa all right, but Tessa looking free, unlocked. Jo eases the picture out past the others. Tessa's smiling, and while she hardly looks carefree, she looks as carefree as probably Tessa ever gets. It's in her eyes, crinkled with a joke she's sharing.

Jo picks up the other two pictures and sinks back into the chair, its comfort enveloping her and the photos clanking together. This top one must be Marnie. It's easy to see why Tessa was so smitten; even the photo is awash with Marnie's utter happiness, the joy – you never see that sort of easy joy in people. Marnie's not even doing anything dramatic in the photo. She's standing outside a pretty clinical-looking door, one hand up and out of sight as if she was waving something at whoever was taking the photo. Her eyes are crinkled too, as if this is a woman who lives her life beaming. She's got a mass of curly brown hair and she's wearing what looks like some kind of vintage jacket over a T-shirt, but not in a studied, see-how-hip-I-am way, more as if she simply couldn't help but look like that.

Marnie is that woman. The one that makes everything better for people around her, the one with that mad charisma that nobody else can quite qualify but is undeniable. Losing Marnie would devastate anyone.

Jo shuffles the photo frames in her lap and peers at the last one, a replica of a photo taken years ago. It's in colour, but faded so that everything has that yellowy tinge you couldn't really call sepia. There are two young girls in Welsh national costumes, their arms around each other, bellies sticking out in that way that little kids always seem to have in photos. The bigger one must be Tessa, one hand on the tall hat the other one's wearing. The little one, her hair bright orange against the black of the hat, must be only, what, two or three, and there's definite mischief in her grin. She's standing with her weight on her back foot as if she's preparing to make a quick getaway.

Jo puts the photo back on the chest, slides her hand into the top drawer as if it's a mousetrap, her insides shrink-wrapped with inappropriateness. Her eyes ache from crying and lack of sleep, her throat's sore from all the explaining she's had to do to various people over the last couple of weeks, and this feels like an act of vandalism. But if the nurse thinks it will help, she has to put that aside. It's not about how she feels. None of this would have happened if she had just kept her opinions to herself, quite frankly. It's about getting Tessa to respond, about helping her to heal.

Everything in the drawer is muddled up together but it seems to be just a jumble of underwear. The second and third drawers contain black tops, T-shirts and jumpers, four of each, smelling of Tessa. They're upsetting to look at, faded and unravelling at the edges. Jo shakes herself, steels herself for the final drawer. It slides open smoothly, betraying the series of bank statements almost too quickly.

They must be to do with the business after all. Jo glances briefly and tosses them back into the chest of drawers, where they fan out onto the thin ply.

She looks again.

Seen like this, there's a pattern to them, the words and numbers uniform on either side of the paper. There's what seems to be a one-off starter payment, then it's a tenner a month for the following couple of months.

Perhaps if she took this into the bank? Lindsey was at school with her, and quite friendly with Matt; maybe she'd be able to shed some light on it if Jo could get Tessa's permission.

The bank statement's in Tessa's name, but there's a weird addition: 'c/o Ms M.J. Turner'.

Jo sits down on the bed. Tessa's recently out of a relationship. But this is a joint bank account, set up once she was back here. Or no. Not even a joint bank account. And the payments are recent. An explanation glimmers.

The grandfather clock strikes loud into the night and Jo jumps. 'Christ!' She will never, ever get used to the damn clock.

Jo picks up the bank statement again and pads downstairs. Her laptop's underneath the chair in her room and it hurts to bend down after all these days of not sleeping. She rubs her eyes and wills the Internet into action, holding her breath until the screen lights up with its request for her curiosity.

'M.J. Turner, Bristol' throws up five links. Jo shimmies up the bed until she's propped up against the headboard. The first one's a chartered accountant. Plausible, but the wrong gender.

The second one's a sculptor based the other side of Bristol. Her stuff's gorgeous – big metallic artworks threaded through trees. Jo sits up. A sculptor. She might work with wrought iron.

The third one's a flight instructor, and much as she'd like to keep him in the running, it's the fourth link, complete with corporate bio and picture, that yields the answer. It's the woman from the photo in Tessa's bedroom. The same beam. The same easy confidence.

Ms Marnie Turner, partner.

A management consultant. Bingo.

The firm's website conveniently has click-throughs to emails for all its partners.

Jo pauses, takes a steadying breath. She's walking blind into this and it goes against all her training to not know what the situation holds. There's absolutely no knowing how Marnie will take this news, and she might go deservedly ballistic.

It's going to come across better if Jo seems to be a professional, too; it's the only armour she has. Jo logs onto her chambers email account, ignoring the message pile-up, and pastes in Marnie's address. She'll tell the truth, as best she knows it. No – she'll stick to the facts. No need to mention the baby stuff; if Tessa wants to do that herself, that's her business. If this doesn't work, at least she can say she gave it her best shot.

Chapter Forty-Three

THEY'RE NOT HAUNTINGS ANY MORE. They're joyous.

She didn't know about the happy parts. They'd been buried.

But.

Daffodils. The first winter they'd moved to the Forest. Daffodils out round the falling-down building they turned into the forge. Dancing and bobbing, bringing movement into their still, silent house.

Susan's old cob, shaking his head against flies on a soft summer's day.

Marnie's face when they'd got that first positive pregnancy test.

Bethan discovering the stocking in her cot, that first year she'd known about Father Christmas. 'He been! He been!'

The first shoe she'd done all on her own. Ern clapping her on the shoulder, delight ringing out in his guffaw. 'Put me out of a job, you will, girl!'

The oak she'd drawn when she was sixteen. The change in Mrs Primrose's expression when she'd given the homework back.

The weight of a foreleg in her lap, warm flesh yielding to her as the horse recognises her, trusts her.

Dad, the first spring after they'd moved to the Forest, out in the garden on a Saturday afternoon. Foot on the shovel, B & H in the one hand, the rise and fall of the football on the radio in the background. 'We'll make this garden a beaut, you'll see, bach.'

The crunch of her boots underfoot in Geoff's yard on a clear, frosted day.

Marnie, when Tessa had lugged up that sunflower coat stand. Her face, opening up like one of the sunflowers itself before she stepped forward two paces, took Tessa's own face in her hands and changed her life.

If she's going to feel anything, she has to let these in too.

Chapter Forty-Four

THE MONITORS BLEEP AND JO jumps, the tea scalding her wrist and spilling down her jeans. It prickles her skin not unwelcomely and seeps across the grain of her jeans. Tessa doesn't stir. The painkillers keep her out of it for much of the day, but it's nothing to worry about, the nurses say. She's making the progress you'd expect.

It's been a fortnight since Jo emailed Marnie. Tessa's other visitors are tapering off, back to their lives, calling in less often. It's natural. But there hasn't been any response from Marnie, and Jo's going to need to re-enter the world properly herself soon.

She'd had a really good chat last night with Poppy, who had persuaded her out to the pub. Not the Star – it would be wrong, somehow, to be there with Poppy – but the King's Head, further up the high street.

'So, what are you going to do?' Poppy didn't believe in preambles, Jo was learning.

'Well, hypothetically I could just renew my licence and go back into the law. I've only been gone three months so it shouldn't be too complicated.' Jo's voice flattened out. 'But . . . I dunno. I get dizzy if I go backwards. If this whole shop thing's taught me anything, it's that.'

'Could you open another shop, learn from this one?'

'God, no. The whole point of that shop was the family connection.'

They were at a table in the far corner. Poppy leaned back in her chair, balancing it against the wall, gin in hand. 'So what comes next?'

'Well, I want to stay here, or as near to here as I can afford.'

'If you end up having to leave the cottage before you've sorted out somewhere to live, we've got two spare rooms. You'd be welcome with us.'

'God – really?' Maybe it was the stress of the whole situation, but Jo was almost tearful with relief.

'Of course! It'd be good to have a local around, show us what's what. What are you thinking you might want to do, job-wise?'

'Well, growing up here, it didn't ever feel like I had a useful skill. Everyone else could do things, *make* things, and I really envied them that. I only had to look at a chair for it to break, and the things I was good at were all cerebral and of no practical use. It's why it made sense for me to leave, really – go somewhere where I might be a bit less useless.

'But it turns out the things I thought were of no use might be helpful, too. I was taking it for granted, this urge to figure things out, ask all the questions. I assumed everyone felt like this, but it turns out that's just me. I don't know exactly how yet, and maybe it's another case of me being hopelessly naïve, but I wonder if there's a way to combine my legal training with the fact that I grew up here and people know me a bit, and use that to help more people. Help them properly, I mean; not suing for cold pizza, or making rubbish sausages.

'There are so many people here who only don't slip through the net because someone else is looking out for them, and it's pretty haphazard. I want to build a better net. Something that won't feel off-putting, for people who would be intimidated by a real lawyer. A partnership with the Citizens' Advice Bureau, maybe? I haven't looked into it in any real way yet, so I don't know how feasible it is . . .'

'It sounds fantastic, Jo. I can help you with the feasibility plans, if you like.'

'You've already done enough by getting me thinking about it seriously!'

'Yeah, but come on. This stuff is my specialty. Let me help you figure it out.'

'Are you sure?' Jo was lighter just for thinking about it.

But first she needs to make sure Tessa's being looked after, practise what she wants to preach. Perhaps she should email Marnie again? Even if she doesn't want anything to do with Tessa, Marnie would surely know who else to contact. Jo doesn't need this woman she's never met to like her. She just needs to know Tessa will be cared for.

'Here.'

Kayleigh's on the other side of the bed with rubber gloves, changing Tessa's water jug.

'What? Oh, cheers.' Jo comes back into herself and accepts the wodge of paper towels Kayleigh's offering. She scrubs, the towels disintegrating to brownish nubs, but most of the liquid's already made it to her skin.

'I'll go and see if I can find you a cloth. Those tissues are rubbish for that kind of job.' Kayleigh picks up the tray with the old water jug and backs out of the room.

Jo picks up the cardboard cup that had contained the tea and stares into it. Maybe her future's concealed within its depths, showing where she'll be living, what she'll be doing in a year's time.

But there's only one brown drop, chasing itself round the grooved velodrome of the inside of the cup. Not a tea leaf in sight.

Still, she's got a plan now, or at least the makings of one. A proper one, this time. A way to belong again.

Chapter Forty-Five

THE BEEPING HURTS TESSA'S EARS. She's told the nurse so, and the nurse was kind but firm. The beeps stay.

Underneath them, though, there are other sounds, which cocoon her. The soft soles of the nurses, their murmurs as they take her temperature, sort the bedding, change the water. Jo's voice, greeting her every day, sounding less tinny, more confident, since Tessa can sometimes stay awake long enough to chat.

Tessa hasn't been able to ask her about that last day at the cottage. They haven't talked much about anything, but that seems OK. Mostly Tessa sleeps, and when she wakes, perhaps people are there and perhaps they aren't. Liam came one night, let in by the nurse with the quiet hands, and tried to say something about the forge, how he would never have gone near it again except that Jo insisted it would be all right this time, that in fact Jo was right, the things they've had in the craft shop are selling faster than anyone expected. She hadn't understood, not fully, but there was a weight of emotion in Liam's voice that showed what it must have cost him. She's gradually learning to identify the shape and heft of other people's feelings, not just her own. The toll it always takes to be in the world, whoever you are.

She'd smiled at Liam, told him she was sure he was doing the right thing, and then she'd drifted off again.

It's peaceful, this state of nothingness. There's a crack of sky that shows whether it's day or night, there are tubes and wires, and sometimes there's pain so searing from her gammy leg that it knocks Tessa away again. But it comes in waves, or sometimes as spears, and then it recedes, and she's beginning to recognise how bad it's going to be. It's becoming more familiar, less scary; and the less scary it becomes, the less it knocks her out.

Perhaps one day the pain will have found someone else and she'll have space for thinking, but right now she drifts in the gaps, and occasionally she talks, but more often, as usual, she listens.

There's a whoosh of draught from the door opening, and clickety shoes stop beside Tessa's bed. The waft of Marnie's perfume drifts up. Tessa should open her eyes, but they hurt from the beeping, and Marnie will understand.

Tessa opens her eyes.

Marnie.

Her face is drawn, fear shadowing it, her hair scraped

back so tightly it's almost straight. And she's heavily pregnant.

'Marnie?' It's a whisper, an apology, a question. Marnie's eyes are dry and huge, full of her own questions, explanations. They're hopeful, and concerned.

Marnie's here.

Tessa closes her eyes and sinks back into the bed. Marnie murmurs something. The emotion overwhelms, the beeps recede. For now, this is enough.

Acknowledgements

Thank you to Carys Bray for our multiple discussions about this novel, for reading more drafts than anyone should ever have to endure, and for a comment which resulted in the title. Above all, thank you for a friendship which is more valuable than any of this.

Enormous thanks are due to my agent, Juliet Pickering, for her editorial brilliance and constant support, guidance and friendship. Thanks too to all at Blake Friedmann, especially Hattie Grunewald and Kate Burke.

Thank you to Eli Dryden, under whose expert counsel this novel first took shape, and to Margaret Stead and Katie Lumsden for further insightful editorial input. Thanks to the rest of the brilliant team at Bonnier: Kate, Steve, James, Nico, Stuart, Vincent, Sahina, Clare, Francesca, Ellen, Sophie and everyone else; also to my copyeditor Natalie Braine and proofreader Laetitia Grant.

I was lucky to receive feedback from a number of

brilliant early readers. Huge thanks to Sarah Adams, Dave Franklin, Lucas Franklin, Henry Nicholls, Cara Powell and Craig Taylor, all of whom went above and beyond in providing careful and often very specific advice.

Several people were kind enough to share the specifics of their jobs and/or lives as I researched this novel, and their expertise, honesty and incredible generosity is enormously appreciated. Thank you to Jason Brown, Kate Harper, Antonida Kocharova, Henry Nicholls (again), Leander Reeves, Tara Vindis, Claire Wright, and the team at Warners Butchers. Particular thanks to Mel Pullen, without whose extraordinary trust, friendship, and openness this book would never have been written. Any errors that remain are mine.

Henry Nicholls's book, *Sleepyhead*, is a fascinating exploration of narcolepsy, cataplexy and much more, and highly recommended.

I'm grateful to Professor John Cook for his gracious permission to use the Dennis Potter epigraph from an interview he conducted, and to Don Congdon Associates and Universal Music Publishing, for similar permissions.

I didn't write a bookshop into this fictional small town because there are so many brilliant independent bookshops already out there. Thanks in particular to Matt Taylor at Chepstow Books, Zool Verjee and the incredible team at Blackwell's in Oxford, Cliff Shephard of Totnes Books, and booksellers in small (and larger!) towns everywhere.

Thank you to the indefatigable Roger Deeks, Jason Griffiths and Cheryl Mayo of Reading the Forest for friendship, advice, help with research and all that you do to support the literary heritage of our beloved Forest of Dean.

Thank you to Michelle Franey (and Freddie!) for the time and space to write.

Without Carys Bray, Stephanie Butland and Shelley Harris, writing (and life) would be a LOT harder and a lot duller. Ditto to Francesca Main and Alison Hennessey, in all the ways. Huge thanks also to the glorious staff and students of OICP at Oxford Brookes University and to the Short Stories Aloud gang.

Every time I sit down to write, Jenn Ashworth's voice is in my head, and I'll always be glad of it.

For decades of unconditional friendship and support: thank you, Caroline Baker, Ilona Blue, Lynette and Neil Harper, Melanie Martin, Alex Morgan, Rob Nichols and Andy Richards.

Thirty years ago, a conversation with Alan Shirley tipped the course of my life in a specific direction. More recently, another discussion with him helped to crystallise some of the central themes of the novel. Thanks, Al, for those chats and all the ones in between.

Saving the best for last: thank you to Dave Franklin for entering into endless discussions about made-up people, for understanding, and for the unwavering support which allows any writing at all to get done. Jonah and Lucas: you are both fab, and you make me want to try my very, very best. Thank you.

Reading Group Questions

1. *How to Belong* has a strong sense of place. In what ways does the Forest of Dean influence the story?

2. Did you identify more with Tessa or with Jo? Whose story is at the forefront for you?

3. Do you think Tessa and Jo ever truly become friends? How do you read the relationship between these two very different people?

4. In what ways do you think Tessa and Jo's desire to belong are similar, and in what ways are they different?

5. What do you think of *How to Belong*'s portrait of modern rural life? To what extent do you think Jo has romanticised the place she is from while living elsewhere?

6. Jo is a butcher, Tessa a farrier; both are women working in very traditionally male spheres. How does the book explore gender?

7. How has the position of women changed in modern rural society, and how do you think the book examines this?

8. Liam tells Jo that he never wanted to leave the Forest, that he was content because she got to. Do you think this is really true?

9. Jo is in many ways trying to get back to her past, while Tessa is haunted by hers. How is the theme of memory explored in this book?

10. Tessa's medical condition is triggered by extreme emotion. How does emotional repression and the inability to let herself feel affect Tessa's behaviour and those around her?

11. Why do you think Jo chooses to come back to the Forest of Dean?

12. The author leaves the ending fairly open. What future do you see for Marnie and Tessa, and for Jo?

13. Do you think a sense of belonging is more linked to a place or to its people?

14. Why do you think the author has chosen the epigraphs at the front of the book?